The
Rune Snatcher
and the
Primal Heart

dpInk: DonnaInk Publications

U.S.A.

The
Rune Snatcher
and the
Primal Heart

by

jeramiah think

illustrated by

chris turtle

dpInk: Donnalnk Publications, L.L.C.
Through former sole proprietorship, "The Book Nook / Donnalnk Publications."
129 Daisy Hill Road, Carthage, North Carolina 28327-7733
Visit our website at www.donnaink.com

Cover Design and Illustrations: Chris Turtle.
Editorial Team: Author and dpInk: Donnalnk Publications, L.L.C.
Layout and Design: ZenCon an Art of Zen Consultancy.
First Paperback Edition: August 2014. First Electronic Edition: January 2015.

Library of Congress Cataloging in Publication Data

Jeramiah Think, 2014 -
    The Rune Snatcher and the Primal Heart / Think, Jeramiah. - 1st ed.
                                        ISBN: 978-1-939425-01-0 (print aka)
            274 p.cm.

[1. Literature - Fiction, 2. Fantasy - Fiction, 3. Young Adult - Fiction, 4. Coming of Age - Fiction, 5. Thriller – Fiction, 6. Dramatic – Fiction, 7. United States – Fiction, 8. Korean – Fiction, 9) New Adult - Fiction.]
            I. Title. II. Title: The Rune Snatcher and the Primal Heart
                        Dewey Classification: 813

                                                    2013936106

            10 9 8 7 6 5 4 3 2 1

Printed in the United States of America

contents

Contents

acknowledgement

special thanks to.

my father. the man i look up to the most

my mother. a survivor. and a legend to the family

my sister. the newly wed.

adam tyler   pasha beresnev. always inspiring friends.

hoffmann kim. the man who started it all.

and chris turtle. who volunteered to the cause.

dedication

i dedicate this to my family, they have waited so long

The Rune Snatcher

and the

Primal Heart

epigraph

passion is fierce as fire.

wisdom is vast as water.

expressions is true as wind.

and belief is stout as earth.

chapter zero ~~~~~~~~~
Hollow's Colloquy

" ... "

Silence. It wasn't peace. A creeping blackout. But that hardly mattered to him. He could sleep for eternity in here.

" ... "

A wordless lullaby. What grim, lamentable, and blasphemed dimension . . . The same went for him; out from filth, came filth. Well, not all were so stained, but he was. He despised that. It angered him. It saddened him. It worried him. How could someone emerge so pure from centuries of imprisonment?

" ... "

"Looky here, looky there, I can see you anywhere!"

He grinned.

"Status?"

"In place and ready, sir . . . just as you instructed."

That was a relief.

"Thank you, all of you."

"Sniff, sniff, sniff . . . I saw—sniff—I saw—sniff . . . It was all—sniff—brokeeeeeeennnnnnn!"

She began moaning her heart out.

"Argh, shut your mourning trap! That's the hundredths time I've heard that!"

"Calm down, Ire," he soothed. "And you too, Woe, enough with the tears. It will be alright."

Moaning stopped.

"Sniff . . . Okay . . ."

"That's a good girl," he said. "Where's Grudge?" he asked quietly.

"He says he'll search a little longer, sir. You know how he is."

No comment to that. Yes, that was exactly how he was.

"Then let him be . . ."

"What is he like? Will we meet him soon?"

He laughed. "No, Bane, not quite yet," he said kindly. "What of the rest of the preparations?"

"As you ordered, sir." There was a pause. "I'm still not convinced, sir. Not entirely . . ."

He knew where this was headed. They had discussed this many times before, but the answer wasn't going to change. It couldn't change.

"I wouldn't have it any other way," he breathed. "He will understand." He closed his eyes. "Rest, all of you, until the time is ripe. There will be movement, soon."

"Yes, sir."

"Oooooooh, yes! Yes, yes, yes! Yes, yes, yes, yes, yes, yes, yes!"

"Aaarrrggghhh! Quiet, you crazy dimwit!"

"D-don't—sniff—f-f-fiiiiiiiiiiggggggggggghhhhhhhhhhhhttttttttttt!"

chapter one ~~~~~~~~~

A Child's Grief

Simon finished the last piece of the puzzle. He rubbed his eyes and observed his finished product. It was a fine piece of work. It matched the cover picture perfectly. He had worked on it for nearly a week. It was a good way to kill time, and it also helped him to take his minds off of . . . *things.*

"Uuuuuuhhhhh . . ."

A dragging, guttural grumble came from outside. Simon knew too well what that was. He got up and glanced outside his window. A zombie-like man was traipsing the front door of his apartment complex, obviously showing signs of creepy deformities. It had a compass for a head, and the giant needle was able to indicate in a spherical range rather than a restricted circular motion. The body was muscular and broad, easily weighing over three hundred pounds. Skin tone was sickly grey, as if the layer was too thick for any kind of light to penetrate it. One arm was coiled with a link of chains, shackles barely skimming the ground as they clinked menacingly.

Simon instinctively shut the window, closed his eyes, plugged his ears, bashed his head against his desk, and waited. And waited. And still waited. Waited until the clinks of chains and the guttural grumble diminished. Go away, he thought, go away.

He chanced to remove his hands. There was no sound. Peeking passed the glass, he saw no one outside. He checked the end of the blocks and the dim street. Not a glimpse of movement. The anxiety piled in the bottom of his chest seemed to dispel into thin air as Simon regurgitated a sigh of relief. At least it passed. He spotted his shaken face and observed.

Simon Dreamwalker had curious amber eyes and short bister hair. Even from the front, his forehead was almost perfectly round and smooth. He had a normal, plump face that any other twelve years old would. A dot was placed beneath the edge of his left eye. It was shaped as a single teardrop, thus it looked like he was crying.

There was a complex of his. Not externally. It was a mental disorder. He saw things others couldn't see. Things others wouldn't see. Things others *shouldn't* see. The compass monster he saw below was not the only thing abnormal in his life. Many more that he would rather not explain appeared at night. Beasts the size of sedans often lurked behind street lamps. Two legged, four legged, six legged, and even more. Fanged, clawed, horned, spiked, scaled, furred, tailed, hooved, finned, winged, shelled, gilled, webbed, and tantalized. Crawlers that scuttled the dirt, prowlers that stalked like predators, trotters that pranced like horses, and just like tonight, monsters that ambulated aimlessly; he had seen countless images that had no resemblance to reality.

He wasn't afraid of them. No, he had too much experience for that. He feared *himself*. It just happened more and more regularly, which was an obvious sign his condition was getting worse. *Dramatically* worse, especially over these past few months. He hated the hospital, thus he never got an official diagnosis. But he knew he would go crazy. There was a reason he knew. It all started years ago, when he still had his mother.

Simon's mother was a one of a kind beauty; a rare flower, people said. But her mental stability was always at question. People often found her vibe to be very unsettling. She expressed no emotional discharge; maybe a thin smile, but nothing else. No joy, disgust, grief, fear, dread, hate, desire, etcetera. *Nothing*. That gave people the creeps. When she *was* amused, she allowed a few thoughtful seconds, always commented, "I see . . ." and then reverted back to her usual self.

But it was at age four that Simon took notice of the severity of her condition. His mother had a spontaneous habit of tucking him closer to her whenever they were walking in the streets. She did not explain why. "Watch your step, Simon." That was all he got, which Simon eventually admitted she was seeing things that weren't exactly there.

And then he reached age five, and that's when things started to get terrifying. Simon began to see things, too; blurry at first, like a ghostly product that failed to take physical form. In weeks, details became more concrete; every line and wrinkle became crystal clear. The compass man tonight was probably the first hallucination he saw. It scared him to his wits. He never held his mother tighter before. Watching his son shiver with eyes big as quarters, Simon's mother showed no worry or concern to his instability, which was shocking now that he recalled. She merely patted him as if he was some puppy.

"Don't worry," she said. "They won't know. Not yet. Just don't tell anyone."

But Simon wasn't really good at hiding his emotions. He was only five. He was too true to his fears, unlike his mother. One day, he saw a snake of brilliant silver scales with a pointed arrow-head, a frightening size of an anaconda. It materialized abruptly, just like any other fantasy, and started coiling around his feet. Simon couldn't hold it together. He scream-ed and stumbled backwards in the middle of downtown, the whole townspeople bearing witness to his derangement. Of course, nobody saw the snake except him. He curled up next to his mother, who watched Simon with placid eyes. Her reaction was the same: *pat, pat, pat.*

"I told you not to tell anyone, dear."

The whole lot who heard her took the situation the wrong way. First came child abuse. He later read the reports himself, but the sprain and bruises he inflicted upon himself when he fell that day were cruelly used against the case. And then, medical attention was issued. That really scar-ed him. There were guesses that he and his mother would permanently part ways if tests turned out positive. He begged for her not to go, cried the whole day. But her reply was, "Remember, don't tell anyone. It will only make matters worse for you." That was the best remark she could bring up to sooth her crying child. Even a lollipop for a distraction could've been better. That day, Simon's heart broke like glass.

Test results came, scanned positive. It was a new type brain disorder. He still had the papers stuffed somewhere under his bed, something men-tioning disorderly brain function, on top of unknown cause of anhedonia. It was a hard reality for a five year old boy to take in. The conversations that went back and forth summarized the effects that would take place: that she would go crazy soon. Doctors approached Simon as well, postu-lating there was a high chance it was a hereditary ailment. But whatever questions and tests they conducted, Simon lied just like his mother told him to, and he was spared.

Hospital visits became more frequent, all the way to Seattle. She didn't bring Simon. She just said she was leaving for *work. Work.* A terrible ex-cuse. Ms. Bluebell became his caretaker when Simon was left alone. Simon never shared his condition to Ms. Bluebell, even when he spent nights curled in a ball, gritting his teeth to persevere endless nightmares.

Two years passed. Simon's mother's syndromes grew extensively more visible. She was speaking to walls, lamps, cars, and thin air. She often went missing for hours, eventually found in the mountain woods or the outskirts of the town, talking herself away.

Simon woke one morning. There was a note by his bed in his mother's handwriting.

Simon,

I'm afraid my time is up. All the trouble you went through because of me, I'm sorry. Maybe if you had a father it would've been less painful. After the hearing, I knew this moment would come sooner than expected.

Long time ago, your father also mentioned I was unnatural. I know now what he meant, not to mention my malady.

Value every minute and second, and my last words to you: you're worth much as people think of you.

Eternally love, my dear Simon.

She did not return. That day was her appointed check-in to the hospital in Seattle, but no records showed. Mr. Sunglow, the forest conservation worker who lived in a cabin outside of town, testified he witnessed Simon's mother at the edge of Diablo Lake, her dress dirtied and ripped. It was a five mile walk from the town; it was beyond imagination how she managed to travel through the forest. The night was also engulfed in a relentless storm, a chance in a million that she was even spotted in the midst of bleakness.

Mr. Sunglow described in detail, how he anxiously approached her, attempting reasoning and persuasion, watching her bend backwards and slipping into the cloud of hissing foam. Investigating for a body was impractical; anything or anyone was bound to have traveled for miles. The case was concluded that her medical conditions took a drastic turn, most likely losing the sense of fear as well as developing hallucinations.

Mr. Sunglow was a rueful, self-blaming man. He begged Simon for forgiveness, repeatedly moaning how he should've acted rather than trying to verbally resolve the incident. But it was not a matter of blame for Simon. It was the loss that struck him, like every bodily sensor was deprived from him. The ability to smile was the one that remained forgotten. He never got it back, the feeling of joy. Well, with his worsening symptoms, his hope was already dwindling.

He crept into his capacious bed and cocooned himself under fluffy protection. The pillow morphed as he patted it to the ideal shape and size. He dug into it and stared at the ceiling. It was already three in the morning. Sleep was required. But as always, a hollow absence haunted him.

When he looked back, Simon had to wonder which course would've been less painful; living in constant fear knowing one day her life would not coexist with his, or being unaware until it hit him like a freight train. Maybe if he was older he'd know, but as of now he was just a twelve year old boy. Ms. Bluebell, his legal guardian now, advised him not to cling to those thoughts. But how could he move on? He never had a father, so his mother was all he had. That was why he preferred to remain in the old, dingy apartment rather than move in with Ms. Bluebell. Reality was still too cruel to accept, and people never understood.

Simon drifted away in his blackness, and then into a present of a woman. His mother took him in. Together, they walked away, to the far distance of dreamy fantasies. But this was just another dream, another yearning deception he would have to wake.

chapter two ~~~~~~~~~
The Whisper

Simon . . .

Again, her voice. He just crossed the valley that he always met on the way to school. That dream was still echoing in his head. He paced himself up the slope as the sunray split through the woods. The morning air was fresh as a glass of water, and the chirping wilderness snapped him to life. Apart from the morning dew that made him slip, it was perfect.

Minutes after he passed the water, Simon crawled up on a rock and faced the sunlight. Nocville was rooted on an upward slope, embarked on the mountainside of Washington Cascades. The foot of the mountain was mostly green with herds of cattle and sheep, and at the far distance there was a faint glimpse of Diablo Lake. His stomach churned at the sight. He withdrew his eyes back to Nocville.

Simon spotted the early wave of students, heading past the residential blocks, and into Nocville School that towered over the entire village. The school wasn't exactly luxurious; just spacious and very old fashioned. A brick fence enclosed the grounds. The third level was not being used, and the air conditioning system was poorly maintained. He was absolutely grateful the heating system was still functioning properly, or they would not only be cooking during the summer, but freezing in the winter.

Just beyond the outskirts was where he stood and observed. Nocville was a small town. He could map it easily. He dropped to his bottom and rested as he pleased. The back entrance to the school was open, and his attention shifted. A band of kids appeared from the right corner of the school building. They cackled like wild hyenas. Without the care in the world, they pranced away as one of them chucked a pack of milk against a car. A few stories above them, a little girl peeped out the window and yelled in distaste.

The school bell rang. The mischiefs returned to the school building. The girl from above also vanished. He sighed. The gang made him weary. But school was school. He jumped down the rock and descended.

"Metaphor is a figure of speech; an indication through comparison. The subject can be compared with practically anything, and even with phrases with no resemblance to the subject. Sentences such as *she is an early bird* symbolizes a person waking in an early hour; in other words, she is a brisk person. The seed of the sentence must be delivered, or else metaphors could be interpreted incorrectly. Beware of that, class."

The bell indicating the end of the hour struck, and Mrs. White clapped her hand to draw attention.

"Assignment: hand in ten metaphorical sentences by tomorrow. For those who don't, you will be dealing with twenty. That will do."

Students quickly packed their belongings as they muttered their complaints. Simon squirmed through the bustling crowd and reached his locker. With a paining sigh, he unlocked the door and shoved his book in the top shelf.

Let's see . . . next class was . . . ?

The door swung shut with a loud *BANG*, catching his arm. Simon took a step back as a group of students closed in on him. He bit his lips. It was the familiar gang from the morning, and even worse, old acquaintances. A boy stooped before him. He was taller and bulkier. There was a mean sneer drawn on his face, and he had hungry, beady eyes. His flat nose puffed as if breathing smoke, and freckles were dotted across his cheekbone.

The boy addressed thickly, "*Dream Boy*."

That was Simon.

"Hi, Marcus," said Simon weakly.

Marcus Graywater hissed with pleasure as he towered over.

"You have money, right?"

Simon shook his head. He was tired of that stupid question. There was no luxury of spare money for him.

Marcus was like the head bully of his year, and the rest of the underclassmen. There was an unpleasant memory between him and Simon, and that made it a mutual dislike.

Marcus's father was a terrible drunk, and his habitual misbehaviors one day got to Simon's mother. They were taking a walk around town when Mr. Graywater teetered before them. The stench of intoxication left no room for fresh air. Simon couldn't help but cough, and that probably set an alarm. Mr. Graywater belched a gurgled laugh and began to slur some twisted logic to him. When Simon hid behind his mother from fright, Mr. Graywater converted into a furious rant. His heavy arm entangled around Simon's mother. The drunkard's leg hit Simon, and he fell like a twig.

Simon always wondered if his mother was completely emotionless. Well, she was diagnosed with anhedonia a year later, so maybe so. But there was a particular expression, a mask that she would put on when Simon dared to test her patience. He only ever saw it once when he was four, and that was enough to teach him his place.

The moment Simon looked up, every fiber in his body stiffened. Her face, already lacking expressions, turned absolutely stolid. She looked unreal. Her gaze shifted to Mr. Graywater, barely glimpsing from the corner of her eyes. A few words slipped through her lips, but only audible to Mr. Graywater. Simon never saw someone turn so white in his life, like he had just walked out of a flour mill. What secret did she share? Wiping the cold sweat off his forehead, the drunkard dithered off in mute shock.

From then on, Marcus started to hate on Simon, and after his mother's death, the foul attitude only became worse. Ms. Bluebell had told Marcus to cease the bullying, but the Graywaters as a whole never let anyone boss them around, not even from the Ashbloods. Thus, Simon didn't make a big deal about it.

There was one thing, however, that Simon got out of it: he was light on the feet. The gang opposed a constant threat to him, therefore Simon evolved. He became faster, and yet faster than faster. But he didn't like sports, like track or cross country. He was foxy, lean and light to overcome rough terrains and mountain paths. He was pretty confident he could even outrun hounds if he was put up to the challenge.

But, this was school, and he was already caged in a tight circle. Not many bright ideas struck him right now.

"You know I don't have any."

Marcus snorted and said, "Should I take your pants off again?"

There was a whooping laughter from behind. A little kid with greasy hair popped out. His front teeth were extremely large, and he had a large dot on the tip of his nose. His ears were big as his hands, and he often made a weird *chip* sound. If there was a tail whipping from behind, it was apparent what kind of animal to imagine.

"Pants off! Go on!" squeaked the little boy.

Snickel Dirtwheat was always the annoying sidekick for Marcus since elementary school. As he was a scrawny, non-physical type, his natural attraction was stronger groups of children who can deliver punches for him. He gained Marcus's trust by often ratting out where Simon was, what he was doing, or if he actually did have any money. He existed as an information database, monitoring all the students, sticking his nose into other people's business, and reporting back to the gang. He was the second most hated student in Simon's year.

Simon, after the gang died out, gave a reply.

"I really don't have money with me."

Marcus and his band cornered him like vultures on a feeding frenzy. Buffets were delivered for brief intimidations.

"I'm ten cents short from buying a pop. I know you have some."

Marcus reached for the pockets.

"Hey!"

Everyone halted. Up ahead, a girl marched straight at the group of mischiefs, her rosewood ponytail snapping the air. She was slightly taller than Simon, and her strides were full with confidence. Simon immediately recognized her in the same morning as well. She was a popular figure in their grade, and thankfully an old friend in the neighborhood.

In a flash, she ripped him away from Marcus and glared reproachfully.

"Stop picking on Simon!" said the girl.

From the corner of his mouth, Simon quietly whispered, "Hi, Rachel."

Her name was Rachel Fairburn, the daughter of Fairburns that lived near downtown. They were nice folks, both doctors, and Simon was always welcome for a free checkup. But Simon had mixed feelings. The Fairburns were the ones who counseled mental examination. It wasn't their fault that Simon's mother was diagnosed, but he knew a small part of his heart still blamed them for *something*. Maybe Rachel knew how he felt, since she always demonstrated the obligation to look after him. When Marcus began to harass Simon, she would become his shield. When Simon left school late, she would always wait and join him. When his mother was no more, she stayed with him the whole day, night, and then the next day, until he finally fell asleep. Whatever happened, she was there, like a tree made of steel.

Simon liked Rachel, despite the permanent resentment. She was nice, responsible, reasonable, reserved, everything you could expect from a hard working student. It was nice to have a friend like her.

"Don't butt in!" hissed Snickel.

Rachel creased her eyes in disgust before snapping back, "Can't you at least wash your hair, Snickel? And Marcus," Rachel directed her eyes back at the ring leader, "Go pick someone your own size already! What has Simon ever done to you?"

"It's none of your business," grunted Marcus.

"You're hurting him!" said Rachel aggravatingly.

Marcus looked away.

"Rachel, its fine," muttered Simon.

"*Rachel Fairburn!*" called a voice.

Everybody looked about, and Mrs. White stalked through the corridor. She looked most displeased. Mrs. White was his English teacher, and also his homeroom teacher since elementary grades. If there was one person not to cross, it was her. She graded her students strictly, mercilessly, and aggressively. She was the icon of fear, the woman without a heart. But Simon never judged her by rumors. She was a good teacher, just a hard one to impress.

When she stopped, nobody spoke.

"What unsightly behaviors! You would do well to keep your voice down, young lady!"

"But Mrs. White——!"

"Not another word! I will be seeing you at homeroom later this afternoon." Mrs. White turned around and added, "And Marcus, you will keep your hands to yourself. If I see any misconduct, you will be answering Mr. Brown. Is that understood?"

Marcus was annoyed, but he quietly answered, "Yes, Mrs. White."

Mrs. White gave a last glance before commenting, "For goodness sake, Snickel, wash your hair!"

Snickel made his usual *chip-chip* sound as he inched back like an irritated rodent. With everything said, Mrs. White walked back into the crowd, emitting her aura to the bystanders. Marcus scowled before parting.

"Let's go."

With Snickel scuttling from behind, the gang left. Simon spotted Marcus shooting angry words at Snickel. Most of the students were now absent from the hall, and the clock was already ticking closer to the next hour.

"Thanks," said Simon, pulling out his notebooks. A hand slapped him on the shoulder, and he yelped. "What was that for?"

Rachel glowered at him as if to melt his face off.

"Why don't you stand up for yourself once in a while," she snapped, poking him hard in the chest. "You've got to stand up for yourself!"

He shrugged. It was easier said than done. He was smaller than Marcus, fairly skinny, and not very popular. There was also the shared grudge. It was unlikely Marcus would cease to bother him just because he said so.

"Sorry I got you into trouble," he mumbled.

Rachel rolled her eyes.

"The worst that can happen to me is a few warnings. Just don't get kicked about like that this year."

" . . . Alright."

The bell rang, and Rachel stalked off.

He slipped away from the dispersing crowd and set out through the back gate. Rachel had asked to wait for her to reschedule her classes, but Simon felt like being alone for the day. He decided to apologize to her tomorrow.

Simon approached the rocks. Like an idle fox, he sprung and wormed his way up the rough terrain. He saw the monstrous boulder blocking his path, and also the tree growing next to it. A detour to the —

"Excuse me."

Simon turned. A girl with sharp brows stood behind him. Hair was short; a peculiar shade of ivory which skimmed across her eyes and ears. She looked at ease, almost bored. But then her sight was composed, as if she was on a race.

"Hi, Vel," said Simon.

Velox Windly said nothing and passed him. She was the quiet type, so Simon took no offense. When she neared the tree, she sprinted, kicked off the trunk, and caught a higher branch that was at least ten feet high. She nimbly ascended another ten feet, jumped across to the boulder, and then vanished out of sight. It was very impressive. She was the only one in school Simon thought was more agile than him. They sometimes met, like today, on their way back home, but greetings and dialogues were rarely shared. Simon just watched her back as she went ahead most of the times.

Whatever, Simon continued up (taking a detour around the boulder). The dream last night emerged in his thoughts. That was somewhat annoying. He naturally missed his mother, but today it was really getting to him. Trying to shut off excess thoughts only made it more painful.

Simon . . .

The symptoms were taking effect. Fine, if it was going to be like this, then he will just embed in it.

"Yes, mom."

Simon, dear . . .

He felt hypnotized. The buzzing pleasure in his stomach was multiplying like a cancer. More climbing, more voices, and again more climbing. He could hear her more clearly each step he took.

Dear . . .

"I know, mom. How are you?"

Simon . . .

"I haven't told anyone. It wasn't easy, though . . ."

Simon . . .

"It's been getting worse. I'm seeing things, just like you."

He paced himself into the woods. The valley emerged, the brook, the cascade, and the small pool just below. He treaded the stones.

"You know, mom," muttered Simon. "I kind of wondered . . ." He stalled. "What did *you* see?"

Simon . . .

Simon stopped midway. He searched halfheartedly, and then dropped into despair. What was the point? Disappointment was all that awaited his fruitless efforts. She was gone, forever. The voice was nothing more than a manifestation of his woeful desire.

Here, Simon . . .

But, he couldn't help himself. It was coming from below the cascade. He put his weight on his toes as he stooped. A lone silhouette danced back in the splashing surface. He looked at it dreamily. It looked taller than him.

I'm here, Simon . . .

". . . Mom?"

The pond smoothened like glass. The mirage took form. Hair of black coal; fingers of slender delicacy; eyes of blank coolness; and the tiny smile that was almost artificial. The image that he wished to be actual. He couldn't stand it. Was there a way to make it real? Was it too much to ask the impossible? Her outstretched arm, ready to embrace him, was a gesture he could not resist. He would rather be with her than in eternal torment. All she needed to say was the incantation, and the spell would be complete.

Come, Simon.

And there it was. He keeled forward.

"Sim—!"

Splash!

He could see her. Close, but not in reach. She was drifting downwards. *Deeper*, Simon thought. He floundered to the depths. Why was the water forcing him up? He didn't want that. He struggled with all his might. She was not that far. They were almost at the bottom. They *were* at the bottom. She merged with the rocks. Simon cried *No!* He clawed at the large slab that blocked his way, fury fueling his dimming strength. But to no avail. She was sinking to the underworld, to a place he cannot reach.

But he *can* reach her. Yes, he could. He wrenched the slab before him free and tucked it under his arms, forcing his body to remain submerged. He will stay here until his soul would become one with the water. The reunion would then be possible. Sink with her. Reach the afterlife. Dark. Cold. Mute.

. . . But he was rising.

Splish-splash!

Simon released a torrent of water before inhaling a mighty gulp of air; it felt like fire. Someone was dragging him to shore. No, they were already at the shore. Hissing, the person tugged him upwards. He was too heavy.

"Simon!"

Another pair of hands locked over him. With combined strength, they managed to haul him up to dry land.

"Simon! Simon, wake up!"

A hand slapped him across the cheek. That brought him back to life. Simon finally saw the heavens, clear blue with a couple of white clouds. To the left was Rachel, blanched like chalk.

"Are you okay? Can you hear me?"

She was already checking his pulse. Simon heard a soft grunt. He craned his neck backwards. Vel was just as wet, and furiously breathless. She looked at him, confusion etched in her eyes.

"Simon, let go. Let go of it."

Rachel was tugging his arm. Simon realized he was still clutching onto the slab, hoping it would take him to the abyss, where no one would bother him; *them*. But . . . but . . . reality finally caught up.

Simon ripped himself away from Rachel. He even almost hit Vel, who reacted just in time to avoid. He glowered at them reproachfully, tears eventually flooding his eyes. Both girls looked shocked.

"Simon, what—?"

"WHY!" screamed Simon. Both girls jumped, Rachel speechless, Vel alarmed. "WHY?! SHE WAS THERE! I SAW HER! I WAS WITH HER! WHY COULDN'T YOU JUST LEAVE ME ALONE!!!"

Simon slammed his forehead into the ground and wept, pressing the slab as if it was his dearly lost. The soft breeze delivered his sorrows to the woods above, and the girls watched with troubled hearts.

chapter three ~~~~~~~~

The Metaphor

"Simon, you have to change."

"No."

"Then drink this. It will help."

"I don't need it."

"Let go of that, now. It's not going to help."

"No."

Rachel stayed knelt before him. Vel watched as she dried her hair.

They were in an abandoned barn that was just outside of Nocville. Rachel persistently asked him to come with her to the clinic, but Simon didn't want to go anywhere at all. He wanted isolation, an environment where there was nobody but him. In the end, she managed to bring him here, but not to the clinic. He will not let anyone have the satisfaction of doing any sort of tests on him.

"Simon," said Rachel, almost pleading, "let's just go to my place, hmm? We need to be sure you're not hurt."

"I'm fine," Simon said bluntly.

"You don't know that."

"I'm not going anywhere. Drop it."

Rachel clenched her fists. She sprang up angrily.

"Fine, you don't have to go, but I'm bringing my dad over, and don't even think about arguing. I'm not letting you go home until a doctor says you're okay."

A house of doctors; Simon guessed that was to be expected. She was stubborn as an ox.

Rachel pointed and said, "You stay here, and don't move. If you do, then I'm going to tell on Ms. Bluebell, and I know you don't want that." Rachel turned away and stalked up to Vel. She quietly added, "Look after him for me, okay? I'll be back." Vel gave a short nod. Rachel pointed back

at Simon at the exit and yelled, "I'm warning you! Stay with Vel!" And then she hurried off.

Now passing time became awkward-passing time. Simon remained slouched against the rotting wood post, and Vel stood watching by the broken window. No words to share. Well, what words to share. They hardly had anything in common.

He observed her. Seeing her stand still, he found the full scope. She was indeed nimble bodied, neither big nor skinny. The way she carried herself was effortless. Her ankles were a tad thin, well fitted for sharp turns and endurance. Great sense of balance; she didn't sway even though her weight was mostly on one foot. Was she in sports? She looked perfect for track. Or any kind of sport. She certainly swam like a champ. It was she who pulled him out anyways.

"You said you saw her." Vel spoke. That was a surprise. It was mostly Simon who attempted a conversation. "Was it you're mother?"

Simon stared at the slab cradled in his arms. "I don't feel like talking about it," he said quietly. "Just leave me alone for a minute, okay?"

Vel crossed her arms. "Are you sick?"

Simon mechanically responded, "No."

Vel observed him very thoroughly. She was obviously not convinced with that last answer, but something else caught her attention. Simon browsed himself subtly if anything out of the ordinary was attached to his clothes. He looked up, meeting eyes with Vel. She looked awestruck.

"Your eyes . . ." she slowly explained, "look . . . *dead*."

Dead, thought Simon. Did she mean he looked fatigued? Or was she implying he lacked the will to live a life? Well, it was befitting. Each day was just another countdown until his insanity took the better of him. Not a glimpse of hope for five year was bound to sap the light out of his soul. Today's despondent event just proved how fragile his outlook in life was.

Feeling like an old geezer, Simon let that thought pass, and time went along with it. Where was Rachel now? Probably on her way back? He thought about leaving. He could try, but Simon knew she would just emerge before his home, probably with her parents. Besides, he wasn't entirely sure if he could outrun Vel. She spent more time in the woods then him, and she looked pretty determined to keep him under surveillance. Well, with the rock he was holding, it was really not . . . *Wait a minute* . . .

The slab. Was it a slab? It was acute, almost perfectly rectangular. It had cuts that were clean and straight. Simon let it fall onto his lap. The rock was solid metal, maybe a nature of copper judging by its reddish brown tint. The heftiness finally dawned upon him when he noticed his arms aching quite a bit.

Now he saw a front. It was decorated with some weaving artistry. Metallic wheels were embedded into the cover; they looked promising. In the center there were two sentences written as:

Passion is Fierce, Wisdom is Vast, Expression is True, and Belief is Stout.

Was this a book? Nah, it couldn't be. Not with . . . three or four pages that were made of metal. Simon tried to pry the book open with his hands, but the wheels clicked in position. It was glued shut like a bolted template.

"What are you doing?" Vel asked strangely. Simon held the slab up and showed it to her. She creased her brows, expressing her interest. "What is that?" she asked.

Simon shook his head. He stared at the quotation. It looked like a riddle.

". . . Passion is fierce, wisdom is vast, expression is true, and belief is stout," he read out loud.

"What did you say?" Vel said sharply. She was up straight, eyes alert and sharp, maybe even startled.

"Right here," said Simon, pointing, "Passion is —"

He stopped. The sentences were snaking out of shape, like they had a life of their own. Simon watched in awe as the warping lines refigure themselves. One letter at a time, a single word was presented.

C . . . y . . . b . . . e . . . l . . . e . . .

Cybele

Vel was already kneeling before him. She pushed the slab further down so she could make visual inspection. At the same time, Simon read, "C-Cy-Cybele."

The shock in Vel's eyes was veiled by a shower of luminescence.

Rumble!

Vel went flying backwards, and Simon literally broke through the wooden post and landed in a pile of hay. He was dazed, out of breath, blinded, and aching. In what order was he supposed to take care of himself first? The atmosphere wrung in a low hymn. Great, now he was deaf. He did his best to crawl, clutching his back as he struggled. He planted a foot, and then a knee. Taking three massive breaths he fought against the light and strained his eyes.

In the midst of the blaze, a faint outline of the book was spotted, but that was not all. It was, with all odds against modern physics, floating in the middle of the room. It was not strung with any wires, and nor was it supported by any objects. The wheels cricked into motion. It was . . . like *magic*.

Tick!

The wheels halted. The object, the *book*, flipped ajar, and a scarlet, azure, beryl, and bay bulb shot out like giant fireflies. They hovered. Hovered. *Hovered*. At ease. No. They revolved. Faster. Faster. Superfast. Oh no. This wasn't good. It didn't look good at all.

BOOM!

Simon covered his head. The lights literally blasted the roof into a million pieces, presenting the sky a shower of splinters. They soured straight to the heavens, so fast they became a dot before Simon could even count five. There was a blink, a blast like a jet, and streaks of four lines coursing their own separate directions. The cause of discord was gone, leaving the scene in shambles.

Simon gaped heavenwards. The ruined spectacle was off the scale. How could something so tiny obliterate an entire barn? *What was it* that did this? Was it a hidden nuclear weapon that some mad scientist developed from a secret government lab? Was it aliens that were mysteriously collecting data to annihilate the human population? Or heavenly spirits that god sent to earth to bestow justice and order? Was this all part of a hallucination, a movie that his mind brought about to play tricks on him? Was he finally nearing the insanity stage? Or was he already caught in dementia?

Clunk!

He nearly shriveled with shock. The book landed heavily. But besides that, him, and Vel that was sitting dumbfounded, there were a few more additions to the picture that wasn't there before. In fact, there was *someone*, with a few *things*, and all together, they were as the following: a girl, a cat, a sea turtle, a bird, and a hedgehog.

The girl had lucent hair, the brightest white Simon had ever seen. There was a dark star printed on her forehead. Her lips were pale-pink, and her skin was flawlessly clean. She looked no older than ten, but her clothes were immensely large; it was more like sitting in a crinkled blanket. A mantle, visibly too big for her, sat tilted on her head; any sudden movements, and it was about to slide down.

The cat, crouching by the girl's knee, had fur of dark apricot. There were three stripes running down its spine, and they were an unbelievably profound shade of yellow. Its ears were sharp and large. The tip of its tail puffed, and then converged like a brush.

The turtle: oddly enough, it had very droopy eyes. The shell, the most captivating, was almost like glass. Simon could barely fit both of his feet on top of it. There were no structural patterns; more like lines that weaved in loops.

The bird was the most extraordinary. Compared to its tiny bulk, it had a huge beak, and it hooked inwards. Adding on to the irregular proportions, it had sturdy talons that could easily wrap around Simon's wrist. It was a wonder if it could even fly.

The last animal, the hedgehog, had its own bizarre characteristics as well. Its thorns were not thin; they were angled, sturdy, and spacious, almost like rows of knives. It had big paws, and its claws were also like blades. The claws appeared more threatening than the quills.

Neither Simon nor Vel dared to make a sound. If worse came to worse, Simon was ready to jump (one foot was already locked in place). There was a light flicker, and then the girl's eyes split open. She blinked, twice, thrice. She searched the room. She appeared addled. She sat there like a doll. Her eyes found the metal book. Simon thought to himself, *Uh-oh*, as the girl gradually expressed a sense of distraught.

"Oh, no!" gasped the girl, and the mantle slid down her head and on top of her shoulders.

He would've run, but Vel was charmed into a blank shock; he couldn't leave her like that. Besides, the occurrence that followed was a surprise he did not foresee, and all thoughts of fleeing simmered out of mind.

The cat spoke (in a male tone), "Milady!"

The bird (remarkably) flew and started aviating in circles. In a crisp, restless voice, it shouted, "Oh no! Oh no! They're gone! The Runes! *The Runes!*"

"What happened?" cried the hedgehog. "How did the *Tome* unbind?"

"We . . . must . . . be patient . . . and think . . ." said the turtle in a deep, ultra-relaxed, tranquilizing croak.

The cat's eyes caught sight of Simon, who felt his muscles stiffen like stone. It hissed and pounced. Simon yelped and fell. The cat protracted its claws and threatened the air.

"You!" growled the cat. "What have you done?!"

Simon couldn't speak. What did he do?

"Find . . . peace . . . *Ignis* . . ." mumbled the turtle.

"Peace, *my fur*; don't you see what's happened, *Aqua!*" hissed the cat.

"Emergency! This is an emergency! We need to find them!" the bird shrieked, throwing an explosive fit as it danced beneath the ceiling.

"Shut it, *Ventus!* Or I'll eat you alive," roared the cat.

"Milady, what should we do?" squeaked the hedgehog.

The girl was supporting her head with both hands, her eyes strained as she composed her scattered thoughts. Simon cried as a second slash brushed his nose.

"I'll tell you what we should do! We see it through that this boy meets his punishment, and then we squeeze the truth out of him!" The cat really looked ready to do so. "May my wrath—!"

"Lady Cybele?"

All heads turned to the entrance (or what used to be). Rachel stood behind her father Mr. Desmond Fairburn, a broad man with impressive height. He was supposedly neat and combed, but his windswept hair and breathless appearance signified he had sprinted to the explosion. He had ripped his tie off and was holding it in one hand.

Mr. Fairburn stared from Vel, to the girl, to the animals, and to Simon. Simon threw a pleading glance, hoping the doctor would rescue him from the alien cat that was about to rip his face to shreds. Mr. Fairburn entered the premises, but only a few steps.

"Milady," said Mr. Fairburn, his voice thick and hoarse. "Do you recall who I am?"

The girl, who once looked troubled, showed some relief. She spoke, her voice clear as running water, "Desmond Fairburn. You are the spouse of Remei Fairburn."

"Yes, Milady," replied Mr. Fairburn. He bowed. That was an odd scene.

"How long has it been?" the girl demanded softly.

Mr. Fairburn took out his phone.

". . . Exactly three years."

"*Blast it,*" growled the cat (Simon winced).

"This is an emergency," said the hedgehog. "She perhaps already knows, but inform the Head Scholar of Passion to report back. We will return immediately."

"As your orders, governess *Terram,*" said Mr. Fairburn, bowing again.

The girl gathered her hands. "Come."

The cat, which glared down with searing reproach, hissed at Simon, "Thank your fortunes, boy. I would have cooked you alive for what you have done . . ."

The claws sank, piercing Simon's skin like knife in butter.

"Ignis!"

The cat pounced off and regrouped with its fellow creatures. The girl pulled her hands apart, and Simon saw a flash of light. Traumatized, he automatically threw his arms over his head. This couldn't be happening. It had to be a dream. What was going on? What —?

chapter four ~~~~~~~~~

After The Dream

"—mon . . . Simon . . . SIMON DREAMWALKER?"

He jerked awake. The whole class casted their eyes at him, and he dumbly stared back. A male instructor watched him over a clipboard as he took attendance.

"Are you Simon Dreamwalker?" asked the male teacher.

". . . Yes," croaked Simon.

The teacher observed, and then returned to taking attendance.

Simon rubbed his head. He was sluggish. Waking up in the morning never felt so agitating. He was haunted by a nightmare. What sort, he knew not, but a blinding ray of light was recalled. What came before that? *Was there . . . ?* Simon clutched his temple. His brain ached. He couldn't focus. His fingers took seconds before they even managed to curl.

The attendance was finished. The male teacher dropped the clipboard. "So Rachel Fairburn and Velox Windly is not present . . ." He looked up and spoke, "Hello, class. As you can see, I am not Mrs. White. She is taking a few weeks off due to her sudden change of health. My name is Mr. Green, and I will be substituting for Mrs. White."

"Is she alright?" asked someone.

"She says not to worry. This is the first time she has called in sick, but the staff has high hopes she'll recover.

"Now, beginning class, please pair up with a partner and share your metaphorical sentences. After you've shared, please hand it in."

Chatter aroused as kids pulled out their binders. Simon hardly comprehended the instructions. He was thinking about Mrs. White. Yes, she was a hard worker, and most likely past her fifties. But she looked fine yesterday. Was it something serious?

He began to trace his memories. Mrs. White gave a full lecture, assigned ten metaphorical sentences, and then gave a few warnings to Marcus, Snickel, and Rachel. Ah, yes, Rachel. He was supposed to meet her after school, but Simon left without her. She said something about adjusting her schedule. He then met Vel, who vanished beyond the rocks. He crossed the valley . . .

And . . . I went home . . . He went home. He went home . . . He went home?

Simon creased his eyes. He felt like he was missing a few links. Why was that? He remembered getting back, fatigued, dizzy, and a bit wet. Wet from sweat? He took a shower, ate broth that Ms. Bluebell had cooked for him, and then dropped dead in his bed. And what woke him was dazzling sheet of blank. A dream of —

His head hurt again. Simon grunted. This was the worst headache he had ever had in his life. It was like something inside his temple was flailing to break free. A tremendous throb made him burry his face in his arms. Something was going to come out. Clearly something big. Otherwise his head wouldn't be in suffering such pain. He would rather welcome it. This was too much. His head was going to split in two.

Cybele.

His eyes flew open as an image flashed across. It was the bright light again, but continuing on. There was a girl, hair lucent white, skin clean as silk, and voice clear as water.

The headache died as if he never had one. Simon held his breath. Her name was Cybele. He knew, but didn't know how. She was just Cybele. It was like someone had turned on a switch. But there was more. Yes, something was beckoning him. He needed to go.

"Simon Dreamwalker?"

Simon turned mechanically. He was the center of attention again. No wonder. He was already out of his seat with his bag on his back. Mr. Green peered over his glasses.

"Where do you think you're going?"

Simon stared right back, not even positive of what he was really observing.

". . . To the nursery. I have a really bad headache."

Mr. Green didn't seem pleased. He inquired, "Not skipping out on class, are you?"

Yes.

"No," lied Simon. "It's been getting worse since this morning."

A pause. This wasn't a stare-down, but if it was, Simon emerged triumphant. Mr. Green reached under the desk and retrieved a pad of small
notes. He scribbled a few words before ripping the top note off.

"You'll need a pass, then."

Simon reached the valley. He whipped the sweat off his face. It was
here he needed to be. The truth was within this vicinity. He treaded the
stones until he was in the middle of the stream. He glanced down the cascade.

Simon . . .

The headache. Simon knelt to his knees and rocked back and forth. He
welcomed the splitting pain. *What was it? What am I missing? Show me!*

Ask and you shall receive; another revelation broke through with the
company of blinding pain. He was falling, downwards to the bottom of the
pool. He was racing after a spectral entity, someone he was willing to die
for. Yes, how could he forget? It was his mother; her image dallied in the
midst of the pool.

"More!"

Another skull-cleaving pain threw him into a trance. He was in a barn.
With a flash, the roof was shattered to a thousand pieces. Four, beautifully
radiant colors streaked into the sky and soured in separate ways.

Agony alleviated. Simon panted and got to his feet. Without further
due, he ran into the woods.

The demolished barn was sealed off, and a few policemen were still
on site. Simon stood in the woods a few yards downhill, merged with nature.
He pushed his eyes into their sockets hard. He had another episode, but
vague. Very blurred outlines of four animals nested in the back of his head.
It was like they were painted on soaked paper; disfigured. He remembered one of them attacking him, and it had claws. Why was that? What
happened in the barn?

"Hey!" yelled an alert voice. "You there!"

Shoot!

Simon skedaddled. He heard pursuers. He ducked through a compact cluster of trees, pounced across jagged rocks, met dirt, caught a branch, and swung down a steep slope. He cut to the side that directed to his home. Confused barks of the police officers reached his ears. They had obviously lost sight of him the moment he disappeared through the leaves.

Before they set the hounds on him, Simon descended.

Simon collapsed before his door. It was the most tormenting episode yet, and an appearance of the girl loomed, angelic and flawless. A being of such sublime nature was sure to leave a lasting impression. She was there, with a company of four. Yes, the animals. One with a lot of thorns, one with fins, and one with disproportioned head and feet, and the last one . . . the last one . . .

He was sweating. He sat up on the stairs and stayed hunched. All these flashbacks were making him weak to the bones. Perhaps continuing after a good rest was well deserved. Simon fumbled through his bag and took out his keys. He forgot to turn the knob and face-planted into the wooden surface. When he corrected his mistake, the first thing he searched for through the crack was his beloved bed. It was there, in the corner of his tiny apartment. But there was a problem; it was already occupied by a little girl.

He stared. The purest white hair; the pale lips with a tint of pink; the eyes that glittered even in nightlight; the star displayed in the center of her forehead; everything was as he remembered.

"Oh, so the child came?" asked a female voice.

And there was more. A hedgehog was sitting at the foot of his bed. By the windowsill, a bird with an oversized beak and talons spread its tiny wings. On the desk, a sea turtle with a glossy shell nodded up and down.

"He's here! He's here!" cried the bird.

"Welcome . . . young one . . ." said the turtle.

Simon slammed the door shut. A flash of pain brought forth the memories of the animals. Conversable. Unearthly. Paranormal. How was this possible? Was his senility collapsing to the point of ethereal construction? Yes, it had to be. He was suffering another episode of delusions. Besides, it didn't correspond. One animal was missing. Sea turtle, bird, hedgehog, and . . .

Simon's jaw dropped. There was the cat, orange with yellow stripes running along its spine. It sat opposite to him, pinning him between the corridor and the door. It flicked its brush-like tail.

"No," breathed Simon, backing himself into the blocked threshold. "You're not real. Go away. Leave me alone."

The cat's eyes glinted.

"I knew there was something fishy about you."

His apartment door swung open, and simultaneously the cat tackled Simon. Simon fell straight through the threshold and hit the floor, the cat on top of him, and the girl stood by as she held the door by the handle. The cat drew a claw and pricked his nose. Simon saw a single droplet of red blood swell up his nose. It was then that he finally collected all the pieces together. He left school, fell into the pool, got rescued by Vel, went into the barn, watched Rachel leave, quarreled with Vel, read the ancient looking book, witnessed a massive breakout, found these five mysterious beings, and coward backward as an orange cat leaped to strike, very similar to how he was positioned right now.

Simon performed his strained incantation. He smacked his ears shut, closed his eyes, smashed his head against the floor, and muttered hysterically, "Go away, go away, go away, go away . . . "

"So he remembers?" the hedgehog said in a surprised voice.

"I'm beginning to question that myself," growled the cat. "He *shouldn't* be able to. The boy is definitely hiding something. And he can see us."

Simon wasn't interested in what should and shouldn't be. He persisted in mumbling his heart away.

"What is this imbecile blabbering about?" growled the cat, apparently perplexed.

"He's losing it! But he's so funny!" yelled the bird, which landed on top of Simon's head. Simon violently rang his head until the talons finally lifted and landed elsewhere.

"You're not helping," said the hedgehog. "Well, since he does recall, that saves us some time."

"You . . . must . . . be calm . . . young one . . ." said the turtle.

Calm. That was the direct opposite of his state of mind.

"Go away, go away, go away . . ." The claws sunk into his chest, just like last time. They hurt, like fire crawling beneath his skin. *It's all fake,* Simon thought, *get a grip. Keep it together.* "Go away, go away . . ."

"What stubbornness," said the cat in a malicious voice. "Should I break him?"

"Stupid cat," cried the bird. "Like that would help!" The cat leaped up the bed and slashed the air. The bird escaped by a hair's width. "You'll never catch me, you sneaky cat!"

The cat hissed and raised its hair. "I'm going to have you for dinner, you disproportional bird."

"*Enough*," said the girl, her voice cutting through all noise.

The bird landed on the wardrobe, and the cat took seat on the bed. The sea turtle and hedgehog remained where they were. The girl brought the only chair and seated herself in the center of the room. Simon remained wrinkled against his wardrobe, mumbling like he had severely incontrollable autism.

"Good afternoon. I understand it is confounding, but it will serve you best to acknowledge everything I tell you.

"On the previous day, you were related to a certain event. As a result, I have lost most of my powers. There is no animosity, but this puts you in a very delicate spot. Your memory remains fully intact despite my efforts to obscure them until I revisited you, so naturally we suspect you have foreign secrecy. You can either assist us to familiarize what happened, or admit you have committed criminal deeds. Unfortunately, you do not have the option to ignore the calling. You will be accompanying us back to Eldwoods."

"Go away, go away, go away, go away . . ."

His joints cracked from the strain he put upon himself. Simon brushed all consciousness aside; noise, feel, smell, sight, and even the taste of blood that trickled from his lips he so intently bit down on.

"Words aren't getting through this blockhead," growled the cat impatiently. "We'll have to use force."

"Not so aggressively, Ignis," commented the girl.

A paw, claws retracted, tapped Simon around his cheek. "Get up, boy. Wake, I told you —"

The world began to bend and warp, like a veil of steaming heat was ascending from the floor. Simon furiously incanted, "Go away, go away, go away!" But all it did was add on the fuel. Floorboards cracked and lifted, nails bending like noodles. The window shattered to dust, welcoming a torrent of relentless gusts to disarrange his apartment. Furniture swept off the floor and furiously crashed into one another. The sink literally exploded and water sprayed like a fountain. The chaos gyred and stripped the room asunder, and Simon sat in the midst of his supernatural hysteria.

He was going mad. Nothing was working. The harder he tried, the worse it got. Simon took away his hands from his ears; both hands were kindled in flames, skin on every finger crimpling into severe burns and angry blisters. This was it. The day had finally come. His mother must've experienced the same thing, where everything started to format like a whole new dimension. What else was he going to see? Oh, right, the compass man. It was tearing the front door apart as it barged through. The animals were frantically opposing the onslaught, conducting weird mumbo jumbo. The chaos was incomprehensible. Simon vomited. He ignored the fire expanding up his clothes and bed sheet and cradled himself. He was terrified. There was nothing he could do. He wanted out.

"Go away . . ." Simon moaned feebly. "Go away . . . Leave me alone . . ."

A gentle hand brushed his hair. Simon looked up, tears fogging his eyes. The girl was kneeling before him. Every screech and destruction was muffled as if a pillow had been stuffed against his eardrums, but when the girl spoke, it reached him clear as a chiming bell in a windless afternoon.

"I understand," she soothed. "Rest, now. *Sopor.*"

His eyes drooped. The last thing he saw was the blanket of white hair, and Simon plunged into painless twilight.

chapter five ~~~~~~~~

Second Colloquy

"Sir."
He opened his eyes.
"What is it?"
"We have a problem . . ."
He got up. He didn't like the tone.
"What happened?"

chapter six ~~~~~~~~~~

The Tale of Elds and Hollow

"How suspicious . . ."

"Quite extraordinary how he managed to hide for so long."

"Or was he?"

"What are you implying, Altum?"

"There's a good chance he is not aware of who he is, Frao."

"*Absurd.* I would recommend we *parse* him to the last memory and —"

"Enough, Venator."

"He's a walking monstrosity cloaked in human skin. He can hardly control his own self. He must be contained and observed —"

"I said *enough.*" Something brushed his forehead. "None of you saw his eyes like I did. It was not the eyes of a child. I've never seen despair so deeply engraved. He is a danger to himself. We mustn't discriminate."

End of discussion. A pause.

"He's really . . . just a boy."

"Yes, quite young."

"I understand why the pupils wouldn't know. Not even Frao was in that era."

"Where is the Head Scholar of Passion?"

"I'm afraid she won't be present tonight, Lady Cybele. She is investigating the human world as we speak."

Simon jerked awake. He was staring at the ceiling. The soft texture that covered him indicated that he was in bed.

A man was looking down upon him. He had glasses that were large as his ears. He was a bit twiggy, but there was a solid edge to him. His high nose bridge helped his heavy spectacles stay fixed. Scalp shined, and that oddly suited the man. His wrinkles, expression, and gestures produced a vibe of sincerity. He looked unquestionably trustworthy, like some sort of pastor.

"You are awake."

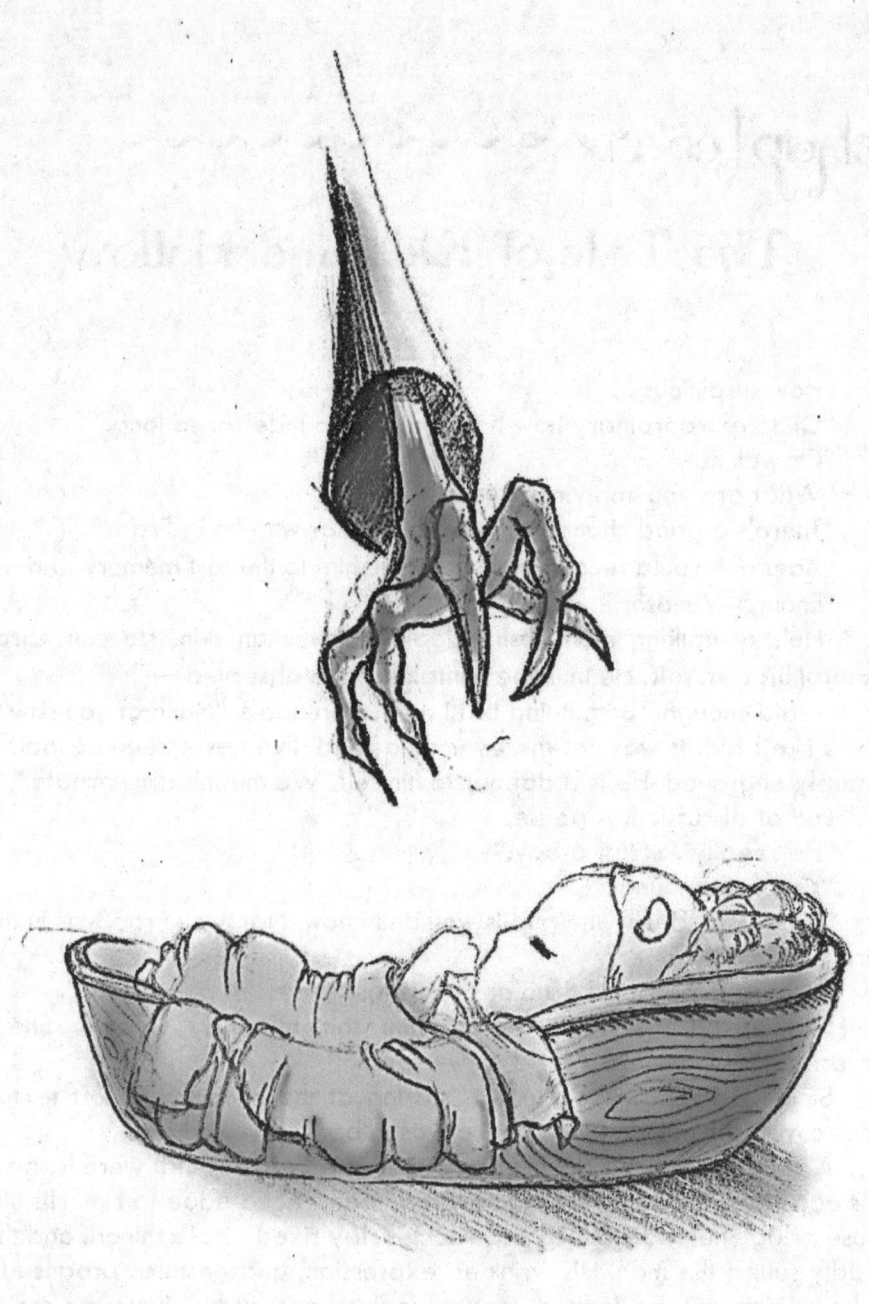

Simon said nothing. He couldn't think of any words. How long was he out? Was he still hallucinating?

"Ah, so he's regained consciousness," said a calm, elderly voice.

The man responsible for the voice stood behind. He looked very old, and he grew a long white beard (although not the whitest he had seen) that nearly brushed his knees. Eyes were oceanic blue, just perfectly tinted to be both paranormal and legitimate. Simon couldn't fathom how old those eyes were. They certainly saw a lot, and knew just as much. He felt so puny when they stared; it was like looking at an ancient artifact, countless years of experience and knowledge shown.

"Are you feeling better?" asked the elder.

Another mute duration. He was awake, but not really feeling a whole lot pleasant.

"Is he really *just* human?"

A third person was by the foot of his bed. He had a cold, quiet, and prickly voice. Simon felt a zap shoot up his spine. He couldn't sense any ill will, but he was definitely becoming a lot more cautious. The man had two, big, round eyes that glared about. He was nearly bald, and what was left of his hair were more like feathers. His fingers were lengthy and twiggy. What was most noticeable was his nose; it was sharp, and it protruded so long, it was like a beak of a macaw.

What a bunch of . . . weird people, thought Simon.

The girl with white hair was sitting by his head. The four conversable animals were present as well. The girl and the animals . . .

Simon instantly pulled himself up, plugged his ears, and closed his eyes. But before he could proceed with his ritual prayer, the glassed man grabbed Simon's shoulders. They were surprisingly powerful, and they easily restrained Simon from banging his head against the bedpost.

"If you would be so kind, *Philosopher*," he said, his voice just as auspicious as his looks, "hear what we have in store. You need rest. If you haven't noticed . . ."

The glassed man tapped on Simon's hand. Simon removed them and stared. There were bandages swathing his hands and arms. They smelled of bitter ginseng, and icy coolness numbed his fingers. "It looked very grave." The glassed man examined the thick layer of bandages. "We were afraid they were burned beyond repair. Most fortunately, the nerves and muscles weren't inflicted. The skin can be easily remedied."

Simon processed what the man was saying.

"My hands . . ."

"And your arms, yes."

"Repair . . . ?"

"That would be the case."

". . . Burned?"

"Very much so. But like I said, they will be good as new."

There was a polite pause to ensure Simon was aware of his condition. Well, he sort of caught on, but the questions that followed were more to himself. He directed his hand to the animals and feebly began his interrogation.

"They're real."

"Yes."

"They can talk."

"Yes."

"She's real, too."

"Lady Cybele, yes."

"You guys are with her."

"Always loyal by her side."

"I'm . . ." He was anxious just by suggesting the postulation. "I'm . . . not . . . mad . . ." He stared straight into the man's eyes, flashing a primitive glare. He necessitated an honest, unembellished answer. "*I'm not mad?*"

The glassed man looked mildly amused, but he smartly brought back his grin and remarked, "I see what you implied, Lady Cybele." He offered a hand. "You may call me *Frao*. I am the Head Scholar of Belief, and quite substantive." Simon shook hands. It was impossible to make out any textural details, but the weight and pressure was convincing. Head Scholar Frao made swift indications and continued. "The man with the white beard would be *Altum*, the Head Scholar of Wisdom (the bearded man bowed). The one standing the furthest away is *Venator*, the Head Scholar of Expression (there was no movement from that end). The young lady standing before us is Lady Cybele. The ones beside her are the Governors whom embody great power and stand superior to all besides Lady Cybele. They are Governor Ignis (he pointed at the cat), Aqua (the turtle), Ventus (the bird), and Terram (the hedgehog)."

Simon carefully surveyed the animals. They haven't spoken since his resuscitation. Simon exchanged a lasting stare. Were they not speaking because they couldn't, or by choice? Or because Simon was imagining them not to?

"You can talk?" demanded Simon.

Terram the hedgehog carefully crawled up to Simon. "Yes, child." It was a *she*, judging by tone, manner, and affectionate, tender amiability. "We're able to converse."

Terram stroked Simon's knee, solacing him like a mother stroking her child to sleep. Simon felt the bladed paws compress the blanket and gently caress him. "How do I know you're not fake?"

Terram crawled up to his lap and settled there. She spoke, "I'm sure whatever we tell you it won't be a reality you can accept so easily. But," she looked up at Simon, "wouldn't you agree everything you see right now is quite tangible?"

Tangible. Yes, everything was extremely solid. Then what was the case? From where did it all begin? When was he hallucinating, and when was he not?

"What happened here," Simon looked at his wrapped hands. "*Exactly?*"

Many faces looked relieved Simon had finally asked a question that sponsored mild acceptance. Terram, showing most enthusiasm in his change of demeanor, curled herself between his legs comfortably and closed her eyes. She began her illustration.

"You were caught up in your own awakening, child. An abrupt usage of immature power often results in a dangerous backlash. Your hands," Terram patted the bandages, "are visible proof. We call it *paroxysm*."

"We took the liberty to restore your room from the damage." Head Scholar Frao side stepped and revealed the apartment. Everything was organized and cleansed the way they should be. The sink was intact, furniture was repaired, floorboards were intact; it was like nothing happened. "But the destruction you conjured demanded great labor to conceal. You must be careful from now on, Philosopher."

Philosopher?

"My name isn't Philosopher," Simon pointed out bluntly. "I'm Simon Dreamwalker."

"Yes," Frao answered kindly. "Yes, we are aware of that, but this is a historical moment for all of us and we would like to uphold formalities. Of course, we will have to take a blood sample and test its validity, but the mark is more than self-explanatory."

Blood sample? Mark? This was not a topic Simon was familiar with.

"What are you talking about?"

Frao's kind smile faded away. He looked troubled whether if he should take this as a joke or not. He cautiously asked, "Why, you are a Philosopher. There is no doubt about it. The commotion, your potential, the mark; it all sums up. Haven't you known all along you were quite different from others?"

Simon couldn't concur. He made a confused crease between the brows said very firmly, "I'm Simon *Dreamwalker*. I was born on January first in Nocville. I'm not a — a *Philosopher*."

Frao no longer bothered to hide his bewilderment. He adjusted his spectacles and searched Simon's face very speculatively. Head Scholar Altum, however, looked untroubled and convinced.

"I had my doubts," he said cheerfully. "We might as well trust him, Frao. He demurs because he doesn't know."

"He . . ." Aqua the turtle spoke in a dreamy slow croak. "He . . . is . . . speaking . . . the . . . truth . . . I . . . I . . . I . . . can . . . sense . . . it . . ."

"There is a way to make sure," said Ignis the cat acutely. He leaped onto Simon and matched eye level. "Give me the word, and I will —"

"No." The order came very humorlessly from the girl, Cybele. Simon was unable to understand how her voice cut through air so clearly. It was like anything and everything were tuned into her. "I forbid anyone to tamper with his thoughts. I felt his anguish. I understand."

Simon felt a hot bubble pop inside his chest and spread like a web. What did she understand? He didn't like people saying they *understood* him. Sure, they could imagine, but they never understood. Wherever he was, home, school, streets, or the wilderness, it was all a means if distraction so he could escape his hell. No one could understand that. Not even Rachel knew.

Frao rubbed his head, appearing slightly stressed. "But he needs informing now. What to tell? Where to begin?"

"Ah, to begin." Altum chuckled merrily. "To begin, we must begin from whence it began. If you would be so kind to recant the tale, old friend."

Altum beamed under his silky mustache, and Aqua nodded. "Yes . . . old . . . friend . . ." His eyes drooped as if he was dozing off. "There . . . was . . . once . . ."

"Ah, my apologies," said Altum, now turning to Terram the hedgehog. "Would you be so kind, Governor Terram?"

Terram nodded. Ventus the bird hopped on top of the bedpost and cried excitedly, "Story time! Story telling!" Ignis the cat looked annoyed and hissed, "Silence, you deranged bird."

Terram closed her eyes again, and the commotion was hushed.

"Child. What you are about to listen to is a very ancient past. A past that coexisted with human history, but remained shrouded."

Simon was all ears. If it was going to help him comprehend the situation, then it was worth the time.

"Go on . . ."

At first, there were the Elds. They were children of nature, the prologue of time. The Primals were the life bearers, at all times nurturing and noble. The Governors, beastly gods with unrivaled pride, bestowed great power to the land they reigned upon. The Philosophers, the ingenious and talented, were the scholars of the ancient periods with unparalleled talent for innovation. Each displaying their celestial competence, the Elds shaped life and land with flourishing vitality.

Then there was Hollow, a world distinctively apart from normality. All time and space was twisted and broken, and creatures and magic of horrendous malignancy existed within. Amongst those cursed ones, there was a mastermind: the Rune Snatcher. He was deception defined; a villain of cunning formidability.

The world of Elds was fruitful and harmonious. Their alliance brought forth the Runes, stemmed of Primals, made by Philosophers, and governed by Governors. The Rune Snatcher, born in chaos and corruption, schemed to overtake the world of Elds and possess the Runes for godly power. That was when The Plight stained the lands.

An invasion of Hollow brought forth an alliance to oppose the darkness. Governors fell one by one, and their lands died along with them. The Philosophers, fighting on the front line, returned with corpses of their brethren. The Primals, few as they were, were kidnapped, tortured, and eventually killed. Many young followers also gave up their lives, and their loss meant great sorrow to the Elds.

For many centuries the war waged on, but hope slowly waned until one moment, through foul arts, the Rune Snatcher managed to thieve the Runes. It was defeat. The Elds needed a champion. One that would change the tide and save the world they labored to ameliorated.

And one emerged. The head of the Philosophers, Milvinus, proposed a secret mission. He and the remaining Philosophers would enter Hollow, find the Rune Snatcher, and retrieve what was once theirs. The ruthless plan was set in action, and for many days and nights the people waited. Waited. In quenched breaths, waited . . .

And their prayers were answered. The Runes returned with the Governors that accompanied the mission. But only them. Not one Philosopher returned from the depth of Hollow. They had all died; a courageous sacrifice for the greater good . . . peace.

But, the creatures and magic which spilled from Hollow lingered in this plane. For the sake of containment and

protection of those who stayed oblivious to the cataclysm,
the Elds established an academy to raise the protectors
of earth. And they were called the wranglers.

The tale ended, and Terram went quiet. Lady Cybele sighed. When all eyes were on her, she spoke, "To honor the lives lost, the Philosophers are remembered as a symbol of courage." She got to her feet and climbed onto the bed. She had the saddest, and warmest, smile. Her fingers on Simon's chin, she said, "And you, Simon Dreamwalker, have the Philosopher's mark."

chapter seven ~~~~~~~~

The Philosopher's Mark

"Excuse me?" said Simon.

"*That*." A sharp voice came from Venator, who unfolded his arms and was now pointing at Simon. "That mark below your left eye."

What mark? What was on his face? It took him a few seconds before he understood that *what* was. The dot. Shaped like a tear drop. Placed half an inch below his left eye. Remarkably prominent and hard to not notice.

Frao kindly explained, "That mark, Philosopher, is proof you are a direct descendent; and Eld. All Philosophers bore that mark exactly where you have it."

Simon made a quick analysis of the conversation. And then he immediately dismissed it. There was obviously a mistake. It was a simple dot, nothing more. "Sorry, but there's nothing special about me."

"You are mistaken," said the girl.

"I'm not," said Simon. "If I was special, I would've . . . would've known by now. That's what you said about the Philosophers, didn't you? They could do . . . magic or something."

"But you *have* exercised magic," said Altum. "You have unlocked the Tome and set free the Runes (although this was quite against our interest). For all my life, I have seen and felt many things, but you, young one, are not ordinary. It took centuries to perfect its spell, but it only took a moment for you to undo it. You are a remarkable individual."

Aqua, who was constantly dozing, pulled himself out of his dreary state once Altum had finished his sentence. He slowly croaked, "Young one . . . you . . . queried . . . if . . . you . . . were . . . mad . . . did you . . . not?"

Simon brought himself to nod.

"For . . . many . . . years . . . you . . . must have . . . seen . . . subjects . . . ordinary . . . folks . . . could not . . ." Aqua inched closer. "That . . . was . . . probably . . . your reason . . . to assume . . . you . . . were . . . mad . . .

But . . . young one . . . I assure . . . you . . . you were . . . never . . . mad . . . to begin . . . with . . . You were . . . and are . . . just . . . among . . . the gifted."

"What you have seen, and felt, are all real, child," said Terram, shifting in his lap. "We can inform you, little by little. You will understand in a matter of time."

Simon couldn't comply. For all these years, he was living in a nightmare, and now some random folks and talking animals were telling him it was not a dream? Hardly a convincing matter. And what of his mother? What was she, then? There was no *dot* on her face. Were they saying she was genuinely insane while he was not? That couldn't be possible.

"This is a moment of joy," said Frao, getting to his feet. "A celebration is demanded. A fest will be prepared for your arrival to Eldwoods. Many will be thrilled to witness the return of the lost linage."

Things were spinning out of hand. Simon said, "Wait —"

Altum addressed, "I have rarely seen you this excited, my friend."

"Steady, Frao," said Lady Cybele, "it is true he's a Philosopher, but the first step is to give him comforting hospitality."

"Yes, Milady, I will arrange a living quarter that befits him."

Simon shouted again angrily, "*Wait!*"

Frao turned to him and bowed.

"Yes, Philosopher? Is there anything you have in mind?"

He was getting fed up. For the first time in his life, he commanded, "I'M NOT PHILOSOPHER! MY NAME IS *SIMON DREAMWALKER!*"

A roaring gust came and went when he let out his frustration, as if it was screaming along with him. There was a heavy silence afterwards, and Simon huffed and puffed. His cheeks were flushed. He had fists clenched in both hands, and his jaw was locked tight. He had never felt so satisfied in a long while. It was like a large lump of molten stress was spewed from his chest, and now the air was fresher than a morning breeze.

He sat up and repeated himself. "My name . . . is Simon Dreamwalker."

Altum nodded and said, "Apologies, young one. We were hasty."

From the corner of his eyes, Simon could see Venator surveying him very pointedly. He looked like he was waiting for Simon to make another outburst, or maybe even lose control so that he could witness the chaos. Simon restrained his inner beast with all his might. He was not some monkey in a circus.

"Mr. Frao?"

"Yes?" Frao looked eagerly at Simon.

"I . . . want to be alone. Please, leave . . ."

There was a short exchange of looks.

"Yes, yes of course," said Frao quickly. "But, there is one proposition you must give answer to us."

It was not in his best interest, but he went along.

"Okay."

"The Runes are . . . well, scattered. In the manner they have been released, there is no telling exactly where they would be lying dormant or what they might cause. With a — person of your stature — it would be a great asset to Eldwoods," Frao bowed sincerely, "Mr. Dreamwalker, it is our plea to recruit you as a wrangler."

Simon could tell just by the looks in everyone's eyes most were highly expectant of him. The only one who was not staring at him was Altum, who was observing his reflection upon the window with amused concentration. What was the old man thinking? Was he just as hopeful as Frao? Or indifferent whatever answer was given? Venator, in all sense, looked leery, appearing awfully more like a vulture with his arms tightly crossed and chin tucked in. The animals (or Governors) were still and observant. Cybele . . . she was acting most polite, giving no pressure as she collected her hands above her lap.

Despite the request, or plea, Simon was already having a hard time recollecting his thoughts. All he wanted was to be alone. An odd sense of misery was weighing him down, and he felt his heart sink all the way past the mattress and into the floor.

"Please leave," said Simon weakly, feeling another wave of fatigue fogging his thoughts. "I don't want to think right now. Just leave me alone."

Of course, that wasn't the answer the party was seeking. But it was Cybele who quickly upheld his opinion.

"If that is your wish, Simon Dreamwalker," she said, getting off her seat. "Rest at ease."

The party got to their feet. Cybele, who was the first to leave, scooped up Aqua and headed to the door. She gave a tiny inclination and walked out of sight. Frao squeezed Simon's shoulder ever slightly before following Altum, who had followed Cybele without delay. Venator, almost gliding to the exit, kept his eyes on Simon as long as he could before vanishing beyond the threshold.

Only the hedgehog, bird, and cat were present. Terram, slowly getting off Simon's lap, patted his foot and said, "Sleep, child. You've had a rough night."

She descended to the floor. Ventus spread his tiny wings and flapped away, making full loop around the house before crying, "Bye, bye!" Ventus, too, left without a trace.

Now it was just Simon and Ignis. The cat was stationary, watching Simon with those brilliantly gold eyes. Being perfectly honest, Simon thought no cat could ever come to be as memorable as this one. Fur was fine as silk, and paws were broad. Maybe the razor sharp claws weren't the most admirable features to be infatuated, but everything else the cat had was admirable.

". . . *What?*" demanded Simon roughly.

Ignis flicked his tail and growled, "Undisciplined as ever. You put your ancestors to shame."

Simon looked away. "I told you I'm not a Philosopher. You guys got the wrong guy."

"Do not deny *facts*, boy. You *awakened*. You've seen the Runes. You have had us — Lady Cybele — come before you. It is about time you exercised reason over emotion."

Ignis hopped off the bed and tread to the door. But before he slunk out of sight, Ignis turned his neck and said, "Lady Cybele has referred to your *despair*. Judging by tonight's discourse, I would dare assume you have no joy in your life right now." Simon stiffened. Even if he wanted to, he couldn't defend himself. Ignis added with a note of finality, "If you have no current bliss, you have the right to chance a different life. *A new life.*"

With that, Ignis the cat slipped away. Simon was once again alone. He looked past the window and into the moon. His body was asking for rest, but he sat there completely awake. Minutes passed, hours went, the moon dropped, and the stars vanished. Sunrise illuminated Nocville, but Simon still sat there, the morning ray warming his body, but not quite reaching his heart.

chapter eight ～～～～～～

Payback

The first week was almost over. There was loads of work to be done. There was a sense of gap inside Simon's head. He felt like there was still a piece of some puzzle he was struggling to remember. He was also having trouble sleeping, and when he did, the conversing animals haunted his dreams like a joke of a nightmare. Flashbacks made his mornings grumpy, and once or twice the explosion of light and shattering barn made him jump awake with a fit of cold sweat.

Today, without exception, that haunting sensation followed him all the way to school. He crossed the brook. His hair abruptly stood on ends. He felt like someone was watching over him for the past week. Many times he looked over his shoulder, but visual confirmation was unsuccessful. He even ran all the way back home the other day, but by dawn the same doubt emerged. Physical wounds were remedied within a couple of days, but Simon suspected, by meeting with those people, some permanent effects were inflicted upon him.

Well, one thankful change was noticeable: he wasn't seeing any fiendish images anymore. Whatever that damage was, it had finally negated the craziness in Simon's life. Maybe he should be thanking those folks, but he did not feel like it just yet. He thought he would have stopped isolating himself from people once he realized he was no longer sick, but it was quite the contrary. He felt nervous that everything proceeded so . . . *normally*. He was not spotting any monsters, not hearing any sounds, and not trembling in fear. But the running hadn't ceased. What was it? Wasn't this what he wanted? If it wasn't, what life had he yearned?

I'm going nuts, thought Simon, rubbing his eyes. *Stop thinking too much.*

Even during homeroom, he was extremely paranoid. Nothing that the class said got through his head.

"Now, we've news Mrs. White is near full recovery," said Mr. Green.

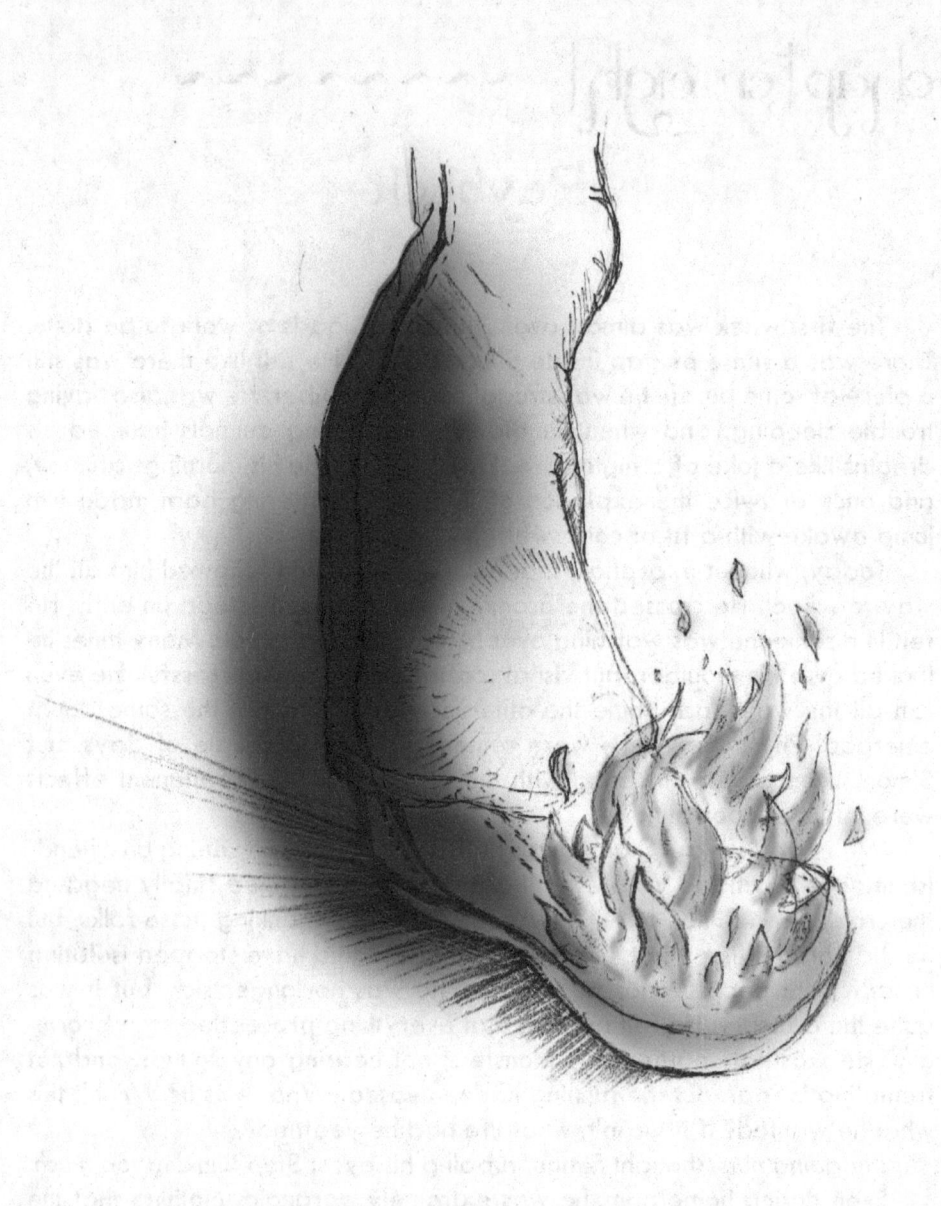

"When will she be back?"

"She will return on Monday and attend to you all. This will be the last time I will substitute for her stead. Make sure you don't stress her too much."

The bell rang, and Mr. Green said, "Have a great weekend."

Simon was absent with the matter. Instead, he mutely went to lunch just like always. As the line proceeded, he picked up a fork; it reminded him of Terram the hedgehog. He filled a cup with water; Aqua the turtle's slow voice came to his ears. A chicken leg was served on his plate; surely Ventus the bird would squawk in disapproval. He saw a kitty-cat watch on some underclassmen, and Ignis the cat came to thought.

Cybele.

Simon shook his head and almost dropped his tray. *Wow*, he thought, *get out of my head already.* He marched into the courtyard. The sun showed like it was the most wonderful day of fall semester. There was a lone tree that was not occupied, and an invisible bird cried through the branches. He approached it.

I need to get my mind straight. I **need** to——!

"Simon," crooned a voice.

Simon's heart sank into his stomach. He turned around, and Marcus was already looming over him. His gang, just as usual, caged him in a circle.

"Look who's here?" barked Marcus, distracting a few students to look around.

"What?" said Simon uncomfortably.

"Nothing much," said Marcus hungrily.

The circle tightened. More eyes were on them now.

"I know you have some in your pocket." Marcus hit Simon on the shoulder. "Cough it up."

Simon didn't bother to resist. He went through his pocket and extracted fifty five cents. Marcus snatched it away like a cougar.

"Thought so," hissed Marcus. "Good thing you weren't stupid like last time."

He relinquished Simon, and the gang finally loosened. They were snickering. Simon kept his peace. It was just a few coins. It didn't matter. He had better things to worry about.

"Too bad *she's* not around."

Simon stiffened. A million different emotions gusted past him, throwing everything in shambles. A knuckle cracked as he squeezed his tray as if to break it in half.

"She was dumb, but she at least got you a few more coins."

His feet shifted before he even heard the last words. Using his legs as leverage for torque, Simon did a complete spin. His shoulder felt like it was going to pop, but he carried on by clouting his fist into the back of Marcus's head. He felt his middle knuckle lit with fiery pain, but that didn't matter since he knew Marcus was going through the same pain just above the ears. Oh boy, how much that one punch meant to Simon. . .

Marcus stumbled a few steps. Simon readied for another assault, but then got tackled by Clark Bristler's, his bulky and stout capacity making it impossible to fend off. When they hit the ground, Simon wriggled out before Clark's arms made a permanent lock over him. James Dimhall used his long limbs to his advantage and launched a kick. Simon jumped back, but it still hit him in the chest. Simon rolled once before managing to hop back to his feet.

"You want a piece?" shouted Marcus, sounding manic.

WHACK!

Simon didn't even see the incoming missile. He felt the fist make contact with his entire cheek, and if that wasn't enough, he was forced off his feet while twisting in the air. The time of aviation must have been short, but to him it felt like a thousand years. Maybe being knocked out would have been a better outcome, but no, the pain reverberated like a crying gong. Simon finally hit the ground with a large grunt.

CLANG!

Marcus now kicked the food tray Simon had abandoned. It struck Simon square in the face. He yelped as coleslaw got into his eyes. Simon lashed at his eyes to undo the goo. A foot pinned him to the ground. Marcus seethed, his gang cheering on top of their lungs. Simon groped the foot above him as his eyes watered in pain.

"I'm not finished with you," chanted Marcus. "You're going to love this!"

Simon felt a rush of fury as agony began to convert into anger. He was not going to forgive Marcus this time. A sudden gale stormed across the courtyard. Screams erupted as trays began to fly out of people's hands, and the abrupt force put Marcus off balance. In the midst of panic, the ground gave an almighty jolt, and every student lost their footing and buckled down to their knees. Marcus, who was already teetering, fell backwards onto his bottom. A faint aroma of burnt leather was detected. Simon heard a yowl and looked up; Marcus was on a fit, kicking in terror as one of his shoes ignited in flames. The fire hydrant just behind him exploded and assaulted Marcus at the buttock with a jet of water.

"EVERYONE!"

Simon took a painful glance with coleslaw still in his eyes. From the far end of the courtyard, Mrs. White was hurriedly striding to the commotion. Simon screwed his eyes and stared at his English teacher. He vaguely remembered her return was to be on Monday.

"STUDENTS, YOU HAVE EXPERIENCED A SMALL EARTHQUAKE!" Mrs. White bellowed in her sharp, charismatic voice. "THE FIRST SHOCK HAS PASSED! DO NOT ENTER THE BUILDING! PROCEED TO THE SOCCER FIELD, MR. GREEN WILL BE THERE! IF A SECOND SHOCK IS FELT, DON'T PANIC! DUCK AND COVER! THIS IS NOT A DRILL! I REPEAT, THIS IS NOT A DRILL!"

Mrs. White certainly had the magical touch with students. The moment her instructions were given, all students hurriedly proceeded to the school field. Marcus snarled as he got out of the puddle, successfully putting out his burning shoes. He looked unpleasantly puzzled, and he glared at Simon through the shower.

"*MARCUS, MOVE IT!*" Mrs. White pointed at the rest of the gang, including the invisible Snickel, and thundered, "THAT GOES FOR ALL OF YOU AS WELL!"

The gang skulked into the crowd of students. As Snickel passed Simon, he kicked an apple at him. Simon raised no complaints. He went down on his bottom, covered in corn, coleslaw, chicken leg, beans, and water. He knew it wasn't an earthquake. He had done it again. There was no mistaking it, now. Cybele's forecast was correct: he was a danger to himself, and to everyone else in that matter. He heard footsteps trudging the wet ground and knew it was Mrs. White.

"Simon —"

"I know," said Simon, getting up. "I'm going, Mrs. White."

But he did not go to the soccer field. Instead, he slipped away from the students and took refuge in a storage room on the third floor. He collected his gym clothes on the way up. He had only worn it once after he washed it, so it was not that bad. He pulled off his dirty clothes and changed attire. Tucking his laundry into his bag, Simon sat on a dusty old chair. The window was slightly open, and he listened to the crowd dispersing and heading home. They sounded excited. He had never envied them so much. They needn't know the truth, while he was miserably facing his conscience. Today was exceptionally dangerous. He imagined students beginning to fly, collide, burn, just like his furniture. What would've happened then? What was Simon to do? He could've killed tens of innocent boys and girls all because he had something different. Or . . . *was* something different.

His left scalp tickled. There it was again, that blasted feeling. Everything came to him like a beacon of light. He blurted out, "What do you want?"

A cat landed outside the window. It slid inside the classroom. Ignis the cat gazed back at him.

"Your intuitions serves you well, boy."

Simon threw down his bag. All his misery began to flow over.

"WHY ARE YOU STALKING ME ALL THE TIME? YOU THOUGHT THIS WAS FUNNY OR SOMETHING?!"

Ignis did not flinch. He just said, "Apologies."

"SORRY DOESN'T CUT IT! WOULD'VE YOU DONE THE SAME IF IT WAS THAT LADY OF YOURS YOU HAD TO SNEAK ON? OR DO YOU THINK IT'S FINE BECAUSE I'M SOME SORT OF FREAK OF NATURE? I DON'T KNOW WHAT KIND OF WORLD YOU GUYS LIVE IN, BUT THAT'S SOME MESSED UP LOGIC YOU HAVE THERE, ALRIGHT? YOU HAVE NO IDEA HOW ANNOYED I WAS ALL THIS TIME!"

Simon turned away and kicked a desk. He didn't care if the cat was going to scratch him. That boiling frustration needed to get out one way or another. He shouldn't have needed to suffer the mental stress. *Nobody* should, by all rights.

Gasps took up seconds, and then minutes. Surprisingly, the cat did not attack him. It hopped across a few desks before sitting. Simon looked back and glared. He wasn't ready to accept any apologies, but the cat looked like it really meant what it said. How amusing; the tables were turned for the moment. Simon sat back down. How many more minutes passed was a mystery. A final announcement warned any people staying in school to desert the building, but Simon ignored the orders. The storage room was the exact place where he preferred to be; secluded and isolated.

The cat stayed. Simon thought it would've left by now. When it continued to stay, he finally grunted, "Was it you this whole time?"

"No," said Ignis the cat. "It was Aqua and Terram in the forest. Ventus has watched you from above."

"So in the courtyard . . . the bird . . . ?"

"Was Ventus, yes," said Ignis calmly.

Simon snorted. Of course, it was.

"You're going to say it was all me back there, aren't you?"

"If you know, I won't press, boy."

Another minute passed.

"You've been watching me?"

"Ever since that night."

Simon buried his face in his hands. ". . . *I'm dangerous, aren't I . . .?*" Simon was surprised by his own bitterness. His voice was not of grief or remorse. It was heavy with acknowledgement, like a man surrendering his pride. He had never heard himself so weak, yet so sure. Even Ignis shut his lids as a sign of sympathy.

"Yes," said Ignis, more softly than the past.

Not a sound disturbed them. Simon remained buried. He was afraid his thoughts would scatter if he removed his hands at the moment.

". . . Can you help me?" Ignis looked up. Simon asked very quietly. "If you can, what will I learn?"

Ignis whipped his tail and said, "It depends on your resolution. Improvements can only be achieved as long as the student is tenacious."

Simon finally put his hands down. The sunray was illuminating every dust particle present. *If the student is tenacious . . .* Well, he was unsure if he *wanted* to, but he certainly felt the *need* to. Was this the answer he was looking for? Would learning to control magic free him of his miserable life? Would it give him strength? It was all so uncertain, but he had nothing left. It was either live like a ticking bomb, or take a wild shot and see where he would land.

"But I can assure you, boy," added Ignis, "an Eld is meant for greatness."

An Eld. Was he an Eld? No, he still wasn't convinced he was that significant. But he wanted to see it, a world where he would fit in. A desirous spark lit in Simon's eyes, and Ignis did not miss that. Ignis got on all fours. Simon looked at him; the cat was apparently hopeful. Simon clenched his fists and squeezed the blood out of them. This was it . . .

"Fine. I'll do it."

Ignis the cat inclined his head.

"We are most grateful."

chapter nine ~~~~~~~~~

The Ghost of the Sky

He was in an empty plain. There were no boundaries or limits. He clapped his hands. A tree grew. It stretched higher and higher, until he couldn't see the top. He clapped again. More trunks crawled heavenwards. Clap, clap, clap. He was in the midst of a forest. Trees were so huge he thought he'd drown under their caring shelter for eternity. His body was oddly light, lighter than leaves or even air. Creatures lurking in the distance shied away as Simon strode ahead. The woods grew thicker and taller, and light correspondingly dimmed by the second. Soon it felt like it was late afternoon. He squinted. A blotch of darkness was waxing. He was getting closer. He realized what it was; a cave. Its shadow was casted by titanic roots. Something blinked in the abyss. He stopped. What was it? He stared right back into the bleakness. Faintly he saw them, a pair of pupils bleached with yellow and puke-green. He felt cold shivers down his spine as he retreated. Something was pressing against his chest. It was heavy. Some sorcery was suffocating him. It was a monster. It was —

"SIIIIIIMMMMMMOOOOOOONNNNNN!"

Simon jerked awake. He was staring at Ventus, who was sitting on his chest quite comfortably. Sweat made his skin frigid and numb. Before he knew it, he was pushing Ventus off of him. Ventus took immediate flight and perched on the bed post.

"He's awake! He's awake!" cried Ventus, her voice ringing like a siren.

Simon started quite angrily, "Don't do that! You scared me!"

Ventus leaned forward and clicked her beak. "What is it? Nightmare? You wet your sheets!"

"I didn't *wet my sheets*," said Simon indignantly. He wiped wet beads off his brows and shuddered. He was a bit cold. "It's just sweat."

"What was the dream?" said Ventus, looking positively excited and eager to know. "Tell me, Simon. Tell meeeeeeee —"

"Stop it," Simon snapped.

"Noooooo . . ." Ventus, now speaking an absolute misery, dropped her head onto the sheets and turned away. She was acting like an infant with dreadful mood swings. How was this erratic creature said to be a beast that ruled over lands with great power and pride? "He won't tell meeeee . . ."

Simon pushed his cover aside and accidentally dragged Ventus off the bed and straight to the wooden floor. He quickly peeked over the mattress to see if there was any damage done, but instead of writhing in pain, Ventus was now walking with her oversized head dragging across the floor. She kept mumbling "Tell me . . . tell me . . . tell me . . ."

"I won't. Stop doing that," said Simon, getting on his foot. "Why are you here?"

Ventus collected herself and started flying crazily. "It's today!"

Simon didn't recall any arrangements. "What's today?"

Ventus landed on his head.

"You're leaving to Eldwoods!"

This was new to Simon. "I didn't know it was today."

"You know now!" cried Ventus. "Your *leaf* is on your desk. Get ready! I'll be back in an hour!"

Ventus swooped out of the window and took off into the sunset. Simon stared at the crimson sky. That was a long nap. He was out cold for five hours, extending past dinner. He felt extremely drained, like he had been working outdoors this entire time. Maybe it was because he had been unconscious for too long.

A breeze washed into the room, and Simon shuddered. He needed to dry himself to rid of the chill. He shuffled to his desk to see what Ventus meant. Besides his textbook (*Western Civilization*) he spotted a golden leaf, quite real and brilliant. He picked it up carefully and flapped it. Its texture was rugged, like sand paper. When he twirled it he spotted letters written on the other side.

Simon Dreamwalker

Something like an identity card, Simon assumed. He checked his watch; quarter past seven. His stomach was groaning for a warm fill, but all he had was cereal and a pack of nearly expired milk. That was not going to do. He instead went to the bathroom and washed down his filth. When he dried himself, he looked into the mirror. He spotted something that aroused a thought. Simon took out a bandage from the bathroom drawer and pla-

ced it right below his left eye, concealing his tear-drop-dot. He wasn't going to draw any unnecessary attention.

He preciously slipped the golden leaf into his jeans and started pack-
ing. His bag was packed with a few shirts, two jeans, three sweatshirts,
some underwear, and socks (there wasn't really any meaning to bring text-
books or notes). The next few minutes Simon took the effort to clean his
room. The laundry was already done last night. He dusted the place down,
folded his sheets, cleared his desk, filed his shelf (this was easy, since he
had only a few books), and scrubbed the stove and countertop. Perspiring
a little, Simon now sat in the middle of his completely organized, spotless
room. He hardly recognized it himself. It was quite some time since he had
the resolve to clean. The wind streaming into his room was doing a great
job carrying whatever excess dust remained. It felt good. It was a good
time for a departure.

"Yo, Magnus! *Magnus!*"

The breeze had brought voices up into his room. Simon listened to the
talk carelessly.

"Can't you be any later, *Lent?*" said a second voice. It was much colder.

"S-sorry," panted the first voice, a bit high pitched. "Dad's not really
around —"

"Like any of our fathers have the time to see us off," said the cold voice.
"Father already left for Eldwoods two weeks ago."

Simon almost choked in his own spit. Did he just hear *Eld-woods?*

"So that's all, then," said another voice, this one a tad gruffer than the
other ones. "Mag, Lent, Celsis, and me. Right?"

There were snickers. The cold voice came again. "It *was* four. Latus is in
the circle, now."

"You do know what it means to be acquaintances with Bloods, right?"
This one was obviously not from around here. He had a few punctuations
in his accent, most likely raised from overseas until recently.

A fifth boy spoke, rather quietly, "Yeah, I know . . ."

The crisp laughter spread like a winter breeze, getting past Simon and
reaching all the way down to his guts. "Mind your steps from now. Better
listen to what we tell you onwards. It'll . . . *help* your family, see."

Simon quietly got up and leaned against the sill. Boys, no older than
himself, were slowly prowling the street. They looked pretty normal. One
had muddy-blond hair, while the rest had strikingly brilliant gold; the boy
leading the group, in particular, was ghostly platinum, making it look
almost ghostly. Just by a swift observation, it was apparent the ghostly-
platinum-boy was the ring leader of those five. The one with the darker

tint, whether from looks or atmosphere, appeared out of place, and his eyes were casted earthward.

"Pfft, whatever." The boy on the right, slightly taller than the rest, shook his head haughtily. "If you don't fit in, feel free to leave anytime. Our fathers are hard men to impress. Not to mention *your* father is already having hard time impressing the Luminaries."

The boy upfront smirked before adding lethargically, "Come on, I want to check out the bunch before we get on the *Explorer*."

"They'll all be just a bunch of idiots, Mag," said another gold-haired boy, the owner of the accented voice. "Father always told me most of them don't even know until they are recruited. Like that's going to help the —"

"And my father always told me Bloods are always there to *command* those bunches," said the ring leader, pushing his bangs out of the way with one swipe of his palm; they ran down right over his ears and down to his neck. "Got to keep them in line, don't you think? They're still useful." Besides the odd-colored boy, the rest sniggered. "Come on."

Simon watched them go past the first block. Simon leaned out and surveyed them. They didn't seem the pleasant type. But he wanted to hear more. Eldwoods had come up, and now he had heard Bloods, Luminaries, and Explorer. They didn't seem to care talking aloud. This was a good opportunity to eavesdrop.

Quickly snatching his bag up, Simon slammed the window shut and darted out of his apartment room. He hissed impatiently as the lock resisted a few attempts. He literally jumped down the flights of stairs before jumping out of the complex. He found the boys, but they took an immediate turn and vanished two blocks ahead. Simon rushed up north with every fiber in his legs strained for maximum performance. He was quick to catch up. But instead of tailing their footprints, Simon crossed the road and concealed himself in the midst of brambles aligned upon the lane divider. He was barely four yards apart, and their carefree voices were no trouble listening to. Simon stealthily crept along with poised concentration.

"Isn't that Ashblood family also sending one this year? What was his name again?"

"Hmm . . ." A thoughtful pause. "No clue."

"Like it matters, does it? They're not Luminaries anymore."

"That woman from Passion is still fond of them. She's been getting on my father's nerves recently."

"They're a house of failures, Mag. All four of their kids, really. Like we have to care who likes them or not. They should just take out the Blood from their surname if I had anything to say. Marrying that common *Devolver* already made them unworthy."

"Still, they're sometimes . . . *dull* about their position. I'd like to remind that Ashblood where he stands and —"

Clatter!

The group halted, and the honcho-boy grunted unpleasantly.

"*Ugh*. Oi, watch where you're going!"

Simon peered through the twigs. Another boy was present, on his bottom before the gang. A cane was abandoned a few feet right from the new arrival. Simon immediately noticed the pale eyes, having neither movement nor focus.

"Sorry," said the boy kindly, slowly fumbling for his cane. As he did so, he remarked, "Excuse me, but I couldn't help but hear you guys talking. Are you perhaps new pupils for Eldwoods?"

There was mild amusement from everyone (Simon more so than others). The boy with the accent replied with a question.

"And who might you be?"

The boy, still searching, answered, "Fortis Goldstone. I'm one, too, but I didn't know about Eldwoods until my brother got in." Fortis Goldstone gave a sincere smile and added, "I'm sorry, but could you perhaps help me find my cane? I can't see."

The platinum honcho scanned the boy. He abruptly brought his hand up close, almost smacking the blind boy square in the nose. There was no physical response. The honcho then smirked and lightly tapped the ground where the cane lay. The boy reached rightwards. Just before the fingers made contact, the guiding foot nudged the cane, making it roll an inch further. The gang, excluding the muddy-blond, pressed their hands over their mouths as they suppressed their snickers. The boy continued to stretch rightwards, and the foot continued to send the cane further and further.

"Is it far?" said the blind boy.

Honcho-boy said nonchalantly, "No, it's just there. Just — no, to the right — no, that's too far — yup, just keep going — almost there —" One of the gang failed to contain his amusement and hid his laughter in overdrawn coughs. Having his fill of merriment, honcho-boy ceased his deception and kicked the cane towards the blind boy. "Yup, there it is."

The sightless kid finally got to his feet. He grinned. "Thank you. It's hard for me without this."

Honcho-boy curled his lips maliciously and replied, "Sure you can find your way to the boarding dock?"

"I came a few days earlier to remember a few spots. Helps me navigate through town on my own." The sightless boy then asked, "But you know, it's not good to talk about Eldwoods in the open streets. We aren't allowed to spread the secret."

The group snorted. The gruff, haughty kid that stood taller than the rest replied roughly, "Keep your thoughts to yourself. Might get you out of trouble."

"But haven't you heard?" The blind boy continued, insisting his opinion firmly. "It's against the rules. You might get deported if —"

"We're *Bloods*," the accented boy cut across loudly. "We're much too important to be trifled with. So like Vass said, *keep your thoughts to yourself.*"

It must've meant to be a powerful, intimidating message, but it went right through the blind boy as much as it meant nothing to Simon.

"Oh, then you must be familiar with what I'm saying, then," said the boy, striking a confused crease upon all the others except Honcho-boy. "You mustn't act so irresponsibly. It was your ancestors that set that regulation isn't it? It could also get your fathers in a difficult position if you neglect the rules."

Now that, judging by the scowling faces of the group (excluding Honcho-boy), was a truly intimidating message. Of course, the boy didn't seem to have any ill will, but it was born anyways. The tall boy named Vass had a locked jaw, muscles twitching beneath the facial skin. The remaining two gold-haired mischiefs surveyed the blind boy as if he was a dimwitted fool. The oddball of the party remained mute. Honcho-boy, who was the only member to have a tiny smile etched in his face, closed in on the boy until they were just a foot apart. "You said you had a brother?" he whispered softly.

"Yes," said the blind boy.

"What's his name?" asked Honcho-boy, even softer than before.

"Ami. Ami Goldstone," said the boy.

"He must be just as funny as you," Honcho-boy said mildly. "I'd like to meet him when I get to Eldwoods. But first . . ." He raised his hand. Simon felt an abrupt chill creeping across his flesh. Something bad was about to happen. "I'll have to see what I can do with you."

"HEY!"

All heads turned. Simon had abandoned his cover. His sudden emergence was obviously a shock to the scenery. Even the blind boy had a change in expression. Marching out of the brambles and across the road, Simon pulled the boy a step back and stood in between him and honcho-boy. Those eyes were a stunning tint of metal-grey, fallaciously shrouded, yet solid and cold as iron. It was an extremely difficult gaze to read.

"Leave him alone," said Simon stiffly. "He's blind, for crying out loud."

Honcho-boy observed Simon thoroughly, eyes darting on every line and edge. The group behind him was doing the same, but they appeared more troubled than observant. A boy farthest to the left stepped forward, his plump face and belly suggesting he came from a wealthy household that spared no expenses when it came to food.

"It's a Devolver," whispered the pudgy boy. "He could've heard everything."

Honcho-boy appeared not to have heard a single word. He was absorbed in his own thoughts. Simon abruptly grew conscious of the band-age hiding his dot. Would it make matters worse if he decided to peal it off? Maybe showing it would somehow scare them off?

"We have to tell *someone*. They'll sort this out. We can make something up. Maybe blame it on that one, say he spilled the beans." The chubby boy chinned at the blind one, who was standing serenely since the begin-ning.

Now holding a stable eye contact with Simon, honcho-boy cocked his chin up, barely looking down through threaded gaze. His smile widened. He slowly began, "You're not a Devolver, are you?" A Devolver? What in heaven's name was that? Reading Simon's mute confusion, honcho-boy snorted and added, "You're a *pupil*. Right?"

Simon got the gist of the question. He replied, "Yeah."

"Then where's your proof?" Honcho-boy reached over his chest. He tapped a gold leaf ornamenting his shirt. It was named as:

Magnus Trueblood

"You should be proud to be one of us, you know? It's a memento saying you were chosen."

Simon hardly regarded *proof* or *being chosen* to be of any significance. But, with a party of five glowering upon him with their chest flashing gold decors, he knew showing them his *proof* would absolve the matter peacefully. He slowly extracted his nametag and flashed it before them. Magnus Trueblood caught a swift look.

"Dreamwalker," he said. "Simon Dreamwalker." He muttered thoughtfully, "Dreamwalker . . . *Dreamwalker* . . ." A tiny crease appeared between the brows. "I've never heard of that name. You're from a sub-family?"

The tone was demanding, like it was an everyday routine to exercise authority without qualm. Simon found that attitude very unpleasant, and he coolly snapped, "I don't have to tell you that."

Magnus split an exhilarated laugh. He waved a hand and said, still chuckling, "Right, I probably won't remember you anyways. You're not that important."

"Excuse me," said the blind boy all of a sudden. "But are you all wearing your leaves? You shouldn't be doing that, either. We were told to only attach them after we get to the dock."

Magnus was entertained for the second time, but more condescendingly than before. Once he stopped chuckling, he brushed past Simon, but not before adding, "Might want to keep your friend over there on a leash. He's the type to *ask* for trouble, you see . . ."

With that final remark, the group advanced past Simon and the sightless boy. Simon took the precaution and check over his shoulder. The party of five continued their prowl, cackles stirring the air. At the first block, they turned right. Once Simon watched the last member (the muddy-blond) stroll out of sight, he faced the boy and asked, "You okay?"

"Yep, I'm fine," said the sightless boy. He was very sprightly in nature.

"Watch out for yourself next time. They were being mean to you." How odd . . . Simon thought he sounded more like Rachel when he said that.

"Were they?" The boy smiled. "I'm Fortis Goldstone. Nice to meet you."

"I know, I heard you talk," said Simon, taking the boy's hand and shaking it. "Simon. Simon Dreamwalker."

"I know," said Fortis, grinning even wider. "I heard you talk, too."

They shared a short laugh.

"Are you new?" asked Simon.

"No, not really. I moved when I was young, but I was born in Nocville. Wish I could see the old school. Shame . . . ." Fortis was still grinning, but looked slightly sad. He quickly brightened up, however, and asked, "Well, we better get going. Can I ask you a favor? Once we get there, can you perhaps explain how it looks?"

Simon was taken aback. What made him think they were heading that direction?

"Uh . . . well, didn't you say you were heading to this . . . this *boarding dock*?"

Fortis stood there for a moment, looking mildly surprised. He slowly asked, "But the school *is* the boarding dock. Didn't you know?"

He did not. Simon shook his head. "I . . . never knew."

"Eight thirty pm."

A withering voice vibrated from Fortis. Fortis put a hand in his pocket and drew out a pocket watch. The casing was wood, but the single dial on top was gold. When he pressed the dial and opened the cover, Simon almost gasped. A pair of eyes was blinked up at them, a bit bloodshot and wrinkled. There was a mouth also, beneath the *nose* where the arms stretched and indicated the time. It spoke, in a soulless voice, "*Thirty minutes until your appointment, sir.*"

"Thanks, *Chrone*," said Fortis, closing the lid. He put the watch back into his pocket and began tapping the ground with his cane. "We should get going. We don't want to be late."

Taking a liking of Fortis, Simon joined him, and both boys began heading towards Nocville School. For a blind person, Fortis was quite skilled in pacing himself. Not once did he stumble, and he never missed a curb. Whatever his cane felt, he appeared to have a predesigned formula to follow.

"Are you really blind?" asked Simon, struck with awe as he watched Fortis hop over a collapsed pavement with ease.

Fortis laughed and remarked merrily, "Yup, *totally blind*. It took me a long time to get to where I am. Couldn't manage myself when I started going dim, but my brother helped me a lot. Told me what kind of bumps I was feeling every day, or if I was veering off onto the road. Taught me how to walk straight, too."

Simon carefully asked, "How . . . how did you go blind?"

Fortis shrugged his shoulders. "Bad luck, I guess . . . I don't know actually *when* it started, but one day I noticed everything seemed darker than usual. The doctor said I had retinal degeneration. That was when I moved; it was closer to the bigger hospital, and my parents were really desperate I'd get better. But it didn't really work out. One night, I think I was still six, I was drying myself (I could still barely see at the time), and when I dried my face and looked up, everything was black."

Maybe it was a bit of a stretch to assume such things, but Simon asked, "Couldn't you have gotten help from . . . *magic*?"

Fortis cracked a pained chuckle. "No. That's what most people think, but there are things you can't do even with magic. I think it was two years after I was impaired when my brother got a message from Eldwoods they wanted to recruit him, to become a wrangler. My parents got high hopes again and asked if they could help me. Well, I had hopes, too, so I wouldn't say I wasn't excited to hear about it." Fortis let out a quiet sigh and shook his head. "But they said there wasn't a way, and they explained it quite thoroughly. For instance, if you don't mend an open gash, you get a nasty scar, right? Can't get rid of it. It was the same with my eye. I had the degeneration for a long time, just didn't notice it take effect until it was apparent."

"Sorry," said Simon, wondering if bringing this topic up was stirring up painful memories.

"Nah, it's okay," said Fortis, descending from a curb without any trouble. "It's not like I'm having a lot of trouble getting along. Plus, I had my brother. Once he got into Eldwoods, he immediately started looking into different ways. I was getting used to feeling what was ahead already, so he taught me a couple of spells that would help. Of course, it was a secret. Both my parents are Devolvers, so I was using magic without permissible supervision. It was different with this watch, though. Eldwoods gave this to him when he explained my condition. It's quite useful; let's me know of the time and day, and a few other things."

Simon was enjoying their conversation a lot. He was so absorbed in their chat; he barely noticed they were reaching the gates of Nocville School. One by one, children, around his age, were entering the gates. Simon noticed them taking out a golden leaf once they entered the school grounds.

"By the way, what's a Devolver?" asked Simon.

"Common people," answered Fortis. "The rest the world, I guess. I found out what it actually meant only a year ago, too. Most people grew oblivious to magic, slowly detaching from the old world. And then they got scared of it, so that's how magic became taboo in the medieval times. Can't tell you the specifics, though. Hadn't put much thought in it."

They were in the soccer field. The moment Fortis felt the texture of grass; he grinned and said, "We're in school, aren't we?"

"Yeah," said Simon. "We're in the field."

"Can you tell me how things look? I need some reminding."

Simon couldn't really put descriptive words together. It was just shaped like a closed bracket, surrounded by brick walls.

"Uh . . . well, it's old," Simon started. Fortis laughed. "There's the courtyard, just up the stairs. It's between the west and east wing. Third floor's vacant mostly. There's a back gate; that's how I usually get to school. Can't give you more details than that."

Fortis nodded. "No, that's good. I can remember, now. Ami used to take me up the third floor. Pretended the school was our small castle."

"He sounds like a good brother," said Simon, feeling a bit jealous, but in a good way.

"Yeah, he is. You'll probably meet him when we get up —"

"OW!"

Simon felt a sharp rap against his temple. He noticed frantic rustling of feathers and an angry screech. He was being attacked by Ventus.

"Simon! Simon!"

"Argh, stop! What are you doing?" yelled Simon, cradling his head.

Ventus hovered before Simon, looking absolutely distraught. "You vanished! You forgot! Why?!" she cried.

And then Simon finally recalled. He was supposed to wait for Ventus at home. She did say she was coming back within an hour. Distracted from eavesdropping, confronting, and conversing, Simon had completely forgotten about her.

"Oh . . ." mumbled Simon, truly feeling guilty. "Sorry. Got carried away."

In a blink of an eye, Ventus began to cry. Tears poured like rain. Simon was a bit overwhelmed. Her rapid transition from one mood to another was far beyond predictable.

"I'm telling on you!" cried Ventus, turning away and ascending. "So mean! I'm telling! *I'm telllllllllliiiiiiiiiiinnnnnnnnnnnggggggggggggg!*"

She flew off, her obvious frustration reflected upon her furious flaps. Ventus was probably going to the white haired girl, Cybele. Simon watched. He would have to make up for this. How, he was going to need to think.

"Who was that?" asked Fortis, looking a bit taken aback as well.

"Just a . . . friend," said Simon awkwardly. He hastily added, "Where do we go from here?"

"To the roof," said Fortis. "That's where everyone will be."

Simon led the way, Fortis having no trouble following up the steps. The door was unlocked, despite being the weekend. Once inside, they turned to the stairs. By an upward glimpse, Simon noticed two other kids already halfway up to the third floor. Simon and Fortis slowly followed. It was strange to visit the school during the absence of teachers and students. It gave Simon comfort. There was no one to lookout for, and no bells to force him to classes. The dense sound of his feet calmed him. It was shocking how an empty building could comfort a person.

The third floor was a bit dusty as usual, since it wasn't cleaned as often as the lower floors. The door leading to the roof was ajar, and Simon heard voices traveling into the corridor. So the school really was the boarding quarters. Simon was beginning to feel his guts freeze as anxiety began to spread downwards to his legs. He was bobbing almost comically as his toes refused to bend.

"It's on our right," said Simon hoarsely, reaching the door. He felt a tug, and he looked around. Fortis had a hand on Simon's shirt. Simon hadn't noticed because of his nerves buzzing.

"Sorry," said Fortis apologetically. "Doors are harder to locate for me."

Of course, it was different than navigating through an open corridor. Simon cautiously led the way, making sure Fortis knew where the threshold was. The stairs creaked as their feet pressed upon the plush dust. They ascended, and the door up top was just ten feet away. Five feet . . . two feet . . . Simon turned the knob and pushed.

The roof was crowded with people. Everyone had a golden leaf displayed above their chests. The shortest of the lot, which were all around Simon's age, were blinking blankly like lost hatchlings (none of them were talking much, which meant these *new recruits* hardly knew one another). The teenagers, on the other hand, were leisurely huddled in small groups, exchanging hearty words and joyous laughter. Simon assumed they were all upper classmen.

Simon recognized a group composed of strikingly radiant hairs (spare one, which was muddy-blond) and pale skins; Magnus and his equally distasteful comrades. They were taking center stage, and to Simon's astonishment, not a single person dared to approach them. The surrounding people took quick glances at them, their hushed whispers sounding spell-bound. Magnus seemed to be enjoying the attention, and his shoulders broadened whenever he heard his surname in the crowd. Simon met eyes with Magnus. Magnus sneered across the crowd of people and began to whisper to his fellows. Not wanting to engage in a second conflict, Simon slowly pulled Fortis away to the left. A girl was kindly greeting a boy who was leaning against the parapet, gazing at the distant view. The boy had intriguing brows; they were rosy red, a contrasting comparison from his caramel hair.

"What's wrong?" asked Fortis.

"It's those guys again," muttered Simon grimly. "Stay with me. There're a lot of people, now."

"I can tell," said Fortis, turning his head and listening. "Ami should be around here. By the way, how do the new recruits look like?"

"They look scared," said Simon, glancing around. "Like me."

Fortis laughed. "That'll change. Ami said once you're at Eldwoods, you'll be so excited —"

"Simon?"

Simon knew that voice. He looked up, and then went totally blank. Rachel was standing before him, looking equally shocked as Simon. A moment of Peace and Zen crept along. The boy who was by the parapet was watching from Rachel to Simon. Rachel, who now seemed to have completely forgotten she was just conversing with the boy, almost ran towards Simon and launched herself over him. Simon buckled as he felt her arms press over his shoulders.

"Simon! You're okay!" squealed Rachel, almost breaking Simon's neck. "They didn't do anything to you, did they? Are you hurt?"

But Simon was experiencing an explosive headache. His vision blurred as he saw memories flash before him like a movie film. He was dragged out of the water, and Rachel was slapping him conscious. Vel was watching over him as he sat in the barn. She and Simon were engulfed in the illuminating disarray, having been thrown off their feet like some ragged dolls. Mr. Fairburn, who was windswept from head to toe, was bowing to show his courtesy to Cybele.

"No way . . ."

The pain left, and so did the flashbacks. Simon got up breathlessly, cold sweat running down his back. The missing puzzle was finally filled. Rachel and Vel were there, and so was Mr. Fairburn. They knew. They knew all along.

"Simon?" Rachel was calling him, looking into his pupils. "What happened? What's wrong?"

This was wrong. He felt a surge of betrayal. How could she have known, for all this time, and not tell him anything? How could she. How could *they*! Out of nowhere, Simon recalled the moment when he was at the clinic. He could hear through the crack as Mr. Fairburn spoke quietly to Mrs. Fairburn. They were in serious debate his mother's sickness was permanent. Simon at that time heard his name being mentioned, beckoning they needed to scan him as well. He was afraid they would cut open his brain and proceed in some grotesque rearrangement. He was afraid they'd do that to his mother. He hated them that time, and that unjustified anger was rekindled right now.

Without warning, Simon pushed Rachel away, glaring at her. Rachel looked perturbed.

"Simon, are you —"

"Don't bother," snarled Simon, grabbing Fortis and moving backwards. "You obviously didn't care. That's why you didn't tell me, didn't you?"

"Wha — no —!"

"I said don't bother," grunted Simon, walking away. "I don't want to talk to you."

He half dragged Fortis away, leaving Rachel behind. People were now watching him, momentarily distracted from the Magnus-group, but Simon was too heated to care much about what they thought. Fortis, who was calmly following him, said quietly, "Is something wrong?"

"No, nothing's wrong," muttered Simon, squeezing between two older girls. "Everything's perfectly fine."

"I'm glad to hear that, Simon."

This was another voice he recognized. But the shock was too much, Simon was almost exasperated. Oh, no. This could not be. This just couldn't be.

He gazed upwards. A woman was standing before him. She had greying hair, cut short. Her features were acute, and her lips were thin, naturally giving her a very strict, overpowering impression. She held herself with dignity, not so much as a hint of weakness in her stance. It was Mrs. White, Simon's English teacher, except she appeared nothing like it. She was wearing a very extrinsic coat; it was red, elaborate, but not too much to be considered ceremonial. The arms were loose and baggy. The bottom hems went all the way down to her ankle. Her top looked more like a vest, and the exquisite imagery on the surface danced like fire as the dying sunlight skid across.

Simon couldn't keep his mouth shut. He felt like being bashed with a sledge hammer across the face, shattering his thoughts like a shower of broken glass. Mrs. White, who was acting like any other day, scowled and commented, "Get ahold of yourself," and made a closing motion with her thumb and index finger. Simon obediently shut his jaw.

"Thank you," she said, and then continued, "I was about to discuss this matter with you in my office the other day, but it seems it will work out just fine like this. Nothing changes from what you know of me, except that I have resigned my post from Nocville School, and am the Head Scholar of Passion."

Simon blurted out, "You're a Head Scholar?!"

"Of Passion, yes," said Mrs. White, putting her hands on her hip. "Fortunately for you, there is Rachel Fairburn and Velox Windly who can help fill you in, though I can see you've started forming communions without problem (Fortis grinned). You can put aside all common knowledge you've gained throughout your history; you will soon learn that having special powers comes at a price, and I hope you do appreciate whatever you learn henceforth." She looked ready to continue, but then she stalled for a brief thought and appeared to consider there was no need. She instead changed topics. "Ms. Bluebell has been informed, so there's no need to worry. I congratulate you. You will be transported to Eldwoods shortly."

Simon thought he heard wrong. He breathed weakly, "Vel is here, too?"

"Very much so, yes," said Mrs. White, and she pointed out to the furthest corner from the door. Sure enough, Vel was standing solitarily as she watched Simon. The moment Simon found her through the thicket, she coldly looked away. "Our method of transportation is the Explorer. And speaking of which . . ."

Heads had turned as a serene wail caught everyone's attention. The new recruits were squirrelly turning from their spots, clueless as to what to look for. The older people, on the other hand, began turning southwards, all staring in one direction. Fortis, who appeared to share his excitement in a contrastingly reticent manner, pressed his fingers tighter around Simon's arm.

"It's here," Fortis whispered, the joy flushing his cheeks.

"What? Where?" said Simon, obviously not looking in the right direction.

"The ghost of the sky," breathed Fortis, his head facing up at the sky. *The Explorer!*

"Look!" screamed a girl, pointing at the sky. "Look over there!"

The youngsters scrambled towards her, but Simon saw no need to, for he could see what the girl had spotted. A gigantic dot was sailing towards them. At first, it looked like a fat airplane, but that imagination was quickly discarded as Simon noticed the rear of the mass was slowly flapping up and down. As it drew nearer, the younger children began to scream in awe as the flying shadow gradually began to reveal its true nature. Simon, who felt his fingers and feet go absolutely numb, dropped his jaw at the presence of a colossal whale, tranquilly cruising the sky with a ship suspended below its bottom side. A flying whale. A *flying whale!* It was larger than any humanly vehicle Tip could imagine; cars, trucks, boats, ships, submarines, or even planes. And what grace it was showing! It was a magical moment for everyone. The youngest bunch was screaming their heads off, while the rest shared their appreciation in mute silence.

The behemoth mammal slowed as it neared the school. The ship was twice the size of Nocville School, and the whale was at least four times the size of its cargo. Simon thought he would get crushed just by looking up at the creature; it literally casted a shadow so thick, he thought night had already come. The ship sluggishly crept towards the school, until it finally made port at the west wing. Two planks were thrown from the ship. Out from the highest deck a man emerged, his mangy beard rustling as he straightened his jacket and threw on his hat. In a booming voice, he hollered:

"ALL ABOARD THE EXPLORER!"

chapter ten ～～～～～～

Eldwoods

"New pupils! Line up here!" Mrs. White commanded charismatically. "To the left, quick march!"

Simon jumped to his senses. The older pupils were already bustling towards the first plank. Simon put Fortis's hand on his shoulder and squirmed forward. Out from the crowd, a voice called, "Fortis! *Fortis!* You there?!" Simon saw Fortis grinning from behind. Fortis called back, "I'll meet you on the ship, Ami!" They heard a distant, "Right!"

"Was that your brother?" asked Simon.

Fortis had a guilty smile on his face. "Yeah. He wanted to take me up here with him, but I told him there was no way I'd let that happen. I wanted some time to myself."

"But that's kind of dangerous, don't you think?" Simon asked, astonished.

"Nah, I barely get to do anything on my own most of the time. I didn't want today to be one of them."

Simon found the line of chirruping kids, all too excited to stay in a straight file. Simon and Fortis were the last. Mrs. White, who confirmed their arrival, began to demonstrate her authority over the children.

"In a *single* file, everyone!" She was definitely born to instruct. Upon command, the new pupils squirmed into their places. Mrs. White nodded and yelled, "New pupils, you are to remain on the deck and seat yourself on the benches. A short announcement will be made before you can proceed to the banquet." She then clapped her hand and indicated the plank. "Up you get!"

Nearly everybody began to run. It was a miracle how none of them broke off from the straight line. Since both of them were last, Simon and Fortis took their time. Simon abruptly spotted something at the front gates. A man was standing just beyond the school grounds, gazing heavenwards at the Explorer. His heart skipping, Simon spat out, "There's a man down there!"

Fortis, in contrast, said calmly, "He must be dazing out, right?"

Now that he mentioned it, Simon did find the man a bit off. He was neither moving nor screaming. He was just standing there, limbs completely relaxed as he barely kept his balance. "What's wrong with him?"

"Magic, I assume," said Fortis, following Simon up the plank. "Ami told me people who haven't awakened, or just regular Devolvers, are put into fake sleep when the Explorer passes. Nocville is one of the few boarding docks in the entire continent, so the wranglers probably needed to make precautions.

"When did you awake?"

Simon said honestly, "A few days ago . . ."

"So you've never seen the Explorer make port, have you?" This was true. All his life, Simon never saw a flying whale before. "You'd be surprised. There're more of them. *Wild* ones."

"There are more Explorers?" gasped Simon, reaching the deck.

"I heard there's three more. Just roaming the world. Like a ghost."

After helping Forits off the plank, Simon took a vacant bench at the furthest back. Mrs. White was present up front. The new pupils ceased their chirping when she raised a hand. The captain took a quick scan. Puffing his chest up, he and roared, "*ALL ABOARD!*" The Explorer, wailing for the third time, beat its mighty tail once, and the ship left port and set sail. The bottom skimmed the treetops before they ascended.

"New pupils!" called Mrs. White. "As you are aware, the Explorer will dock at Eldwoods where you will study and practice in order to become a wrangler. You are now *seedlings*. As the years progress you will enter *sproutling*, *blooming*, and *ripeling*. It takes years to gain your title as wranglers, and thus I expect you work diligently at your field of major.

"Upon arrival you will attend the *Blood Avowal*, where we will draw your blood and establish your proper majors."

There were nervous whispers, some pointing at different parts of their bodies. Fortis leaned closer and muttered, "Ami told me they pierce your ears to take blood. Don't know if it's true. He did pierce, but I think it was from an art shop . . ."

"That is all for now," said Mrs. White. She had not specified how they were extracting blood. Simon and Fortis both crossed their fingers. "The banquet will commence in an hour. Enjoy the rest of your evening."

The seedlings scattered. Most ran amok, climbing ropes and pointing at the horizon. Out of the crowd, Simon saw a few descend to the lower level, including Magnus. Preferring no conflict, Simon decided to stay on deck. He began pacing the boarder rails as the majority of the children decided to assault the captain, who in merry spirit replied by hoisting them onto his muscular shoulder. There were a few sailors present, checking the lines and the wheel. Simon grinned.

"Why don't you join them?" asked Fortis, who was just behind.

"I'm fine here," said Simon. He then said, "You should find your brother."

"He can wait," said Forits.

Nocville was nothing but a dot, now. The Explorer sung its beautiful notes and veered north. The ship sailed over the mountains until the woods came in between, shrouding the town. Simon lingered. He was really going. He abruptly remembered he had not spoken to Ms. Bluebell. She was probably just as clueless as him, or perhaps more. He really needed to go visit her. She was one of the few who graciously gave all the support she could muster.

"You have any brothers or sisters?" asked Fortis.

Simon shook his head, and then remembered Fortis couldn't see. "No."

"The only child?"

"Yeah."

"What do your parents do? They must be proud."

Simon hesitated, but with Fortis he thought he had no problems sharing his past. "Mom's gone. I never knew my dad. I live with Ms. Bluebell. Well, kind of. She comes by once a week."

Fortis stopped dead. Simon looked around. The grin Simon usually saw was wiped clean. Fortis solemnly inclined his head. "I'm sorry . . ."

"It's fine," Simon quickly said, leaning against the rails. "I'm better, now."

"It must've been tough," said Fortis slowly. "I had people helping me along. Did you learn about Eldwoods on your own?"

"You could say that. I had . . . uh, paroxy-whatnot . . . and then a bunch of different people showed up. Like the Head Scholars and Governors of the sort. And the girl, Cybele."

Fortis raised his eyebrows sky high. "You saw them? All of them? Ami told me the Governors and Lady Cybele did come back after missing for three years. Do you know anything about it?"

Simon sighed as he began organizing his thoughts. "Well, it's a long story . . ." But he still told Fortis, how he fell into the water, find the Tome, scattered the Runes, lost all memories, succeeded in retrieving them, and then going into paroxysm before being informed by a bunch of odd looking people that he was a Philosopher. When he got to that point, Fortis turned his head slightly, wondering if he heard right.

"Philosopher?" asked Fortis, his brows gathering into a tight knot. "*An Eld?*"

"Crazy, right?" said Simon, laughing in doubt himself. "Like that's ever possible."

"Was your mother . . .?"

"No," said Simon right away. "I saw things, but they weren't the same as to what mom saw. It was like . . . she was talking to a ghost. If she was like me, she would've known what I was watching. She didn't."

"What about your father? You said you never knew him, right?"

"Nope," said Simon. "Mom never talked about him. Except that he knew mom was . . . unwell."

Fortis stepped closer and whispered, "Do you have the mark? The Philosopher's mark?"

Simon touched his bandage concealing the dot. "They say I have it. It's there, alright, but I don't know . . ."

"Wow," said Fortis, rubbing his neck. "It's weird, talking to an Eld. Never knew I'd come to know one so close."

"Don't bother about it," Simon insisted. He really didn't want this Philosopher or Eld thing get in between and make things awkward. "I didn't come here because I'm an Eld."

"Fair enough," said Fortis understandingly. They had spent more than an hour talking. Most of the kids had already gone down. Fortis tapped his cane and suggested, "The banquet must've started. Let's go."

The two boys went down the trap door. Simon had to admire the size of the ship, even more since he was now aboard. The stairs led to a channel of separate corridors, and pupils were appearing and vanishing from every single one of them. The map on the wall showed the banquet room was on the second and third level up front. That wasn't too far. Simon lent his shoulder to Fortis once more and proceeded, occasionally halted as fellow seedlings dashed past him. When double doors at the end of the hall suggested they were close, Simon heard a faint shout coming from behind. He looked around and searched. It was muffled, unmistakably from one of these rooms.

"Did you hear that?" asked Simon.

"Yeah," said Fortis, turning his head. "It was a girl."

Rants came through the walls. Simon changed course and reached to the first door to his right. He knocked

"Hello?" called Simon, opening the door. It was a vacant bedroom.

"It's coming further back," said Fortis, pointing with his thumb.

Simon went to the next room. When he entered, the noise was now cutting through the wall. He quickly treaded to the third room and rapped it sharply. The yells died. No one came to the door, however. Taking the liberty to breach, Simon swung the door open.

The first person he noticed was Rachel, who was heated with fiery flushes. And then there were the blonds, Magnus facing Rachel as his chums stood beside him. The last member in the scene was the boy from the parapet, his prominent red brows standing out under the caramel hair; he was sitting against the wall. Something told Simon he had been chucked, or maybe hit.

"Isn't this a surprise," hissed Magnus, sneering. "*Dreamboy* and *Blindstone*. We seem to have natural attractions, don't we?"

Simon ignored the snickering and demanded, "What are you doing?"

"What do you think?" said Magnus, chinning Rachel and the unnamed boy. "Giving a lesson."

Rachel burst out angrily, "Leave him alone!"

Magnus chuckled and breathed menacingly, "Must feel great, Ashblood, being protected by a girl. Like your mother standing for your disgraced father, isn't it?"

The boy was livid. His fists were balled white. Delighted with the response, Magnus pulled out his hands from his pocket and rubbed them together.

"Bring it."

Rachel noticed the boy's retaliation and said warningly, "No, you mustn't!"

The boy got up and growled, "Get out of the way."

Rachel turned to Simon and cried, "Simon, help me stop them!"

"Is there a problem?"

Someone else intruded the room, much older and taller than the rest. He had tanned skin and lean jaw, and his nose was perfectly straight. He had two piercings on each ear, and one had a vicious looking nail protruding from it. His hair was short as Simon's, but waxed neatly. He was, in whatever perspective, a strikingly handsome guy.

Magnus scanned from head to toe. "None of your business, is it?"

"Really?" said the young chap kindly. "Sorry if I intruded. But this room isn't for pupils, you know, so I'd advise you skip along to the banquet. Wouldn't want trouble on your first day now, would you?"

The boy opened the way. Magnus, who glared at the upperclassman, slowly turned to the door, but not before commenting, "It's your lucky day, Ashblood. I would've liked to see you cry." He pushed Simon out of the way, who in the meanwhile was keeping Fortis from being touched. With a last glower at the handsome boy, Magnus crossed the threshold, his gang on his heels as they whipped out of sight.

"The same kids?" asked Fortis.

"The same, yeah," said Simon.

Fortis nodded. "Seems you're right about them being dangerous."

Rachel was staring at Simon, although unsure how to start a conversation. Simon spared her the trouble, and he broke the ice by saying, "Is he alright?" He eyed the red browed boy.

He seemed okay physically, since he got to his feet just fine. But there was a dark shadow casted over his eyes, showing intense damage in pride. It was hard to find an expression like that from a kid. But Simon, who had put on a similar face on one occasion not too long ago, could read the anger that was choking the boy into speechless misery. It was *disdain*.

Rachel asked cautiously, "Are you alright?"

The boy turned to the door. "Yes." He left before anybody could stop him.

Now only Simon, Rachel, and Fortis remaining in the room, time slipped by very awkwardly. Rachel appeared have overdeveloped her sense of guilt. She opened her mouth to initiate. "Sim —" But her chance passed as all three of them jumped from the door swinging shut. The upperclassman was grinning broadly.

"You all okay?" he asked. Everyone nodded.

"We're fine," said Fortis, grinning. Simon paid little attention before, but now something hit him. He did a double take.

"Good," said the older pupil, standing before Fortis. There was no mistaking it. It was obvious just by looking at them. "And *you*. I've been looking all over for you. Walking out on me when you know I worry . . . Mom and dad would've flipped if they heard I left you."

"I'm fine, Ami," said Fortis. "I'm not a baby, anymore."

"Yeah, you're a *kid* now. Not much different," said Ami, turning his attention to Simon. He stepped past Fortis and put out a hand. "Thanks for helping my little brother. I'm Ami."

"Simon," said Simon, shaking hands. Fortis and Ami had common traits, like lean jaw, straight nose, and even voice pitches. But it was the grin that made them strikingly similar. If Ami wasn't so tall, the brothers would've been hard to tell apart.

Ami squeezed Simon's shoulder briefly, signaling his appreciation. Then, he turned to Fortis and started leading him out. "The banquet has lots of food. Come after you've . . . finished." He winked at both Simon and Rachel.

Fortis, wearing the same grin as his brother, nodded. The Goldstone brothers stepped out of the room, and Ami softly closed the door.

The moment they were left alone, Simon turned away. Rachel quickly stepped forward and grabbed his arm. "Wait, Simon!" Simon said nothing. He stood there waiting for the explanation to come.

"Simon," started Rachel desperately. "Could you listen?"

"I am," said Simon shortly.

Rachel let go. "I know what you're thinking. I should've told you, but the Head Scholars said they needed to hear things from your end, too. Head Scholar Altum also told me . . . well . . . if I got together with you *right after* it happened, I'd just put you in more trouble. You were a suspect; a crime suspect."

"You could've come to me after," snapped Simon. "You should've known. They wanted to recruit me, said I'm innocent. I wasn't a crime suspect then, was I?"

"*I tried!* But when they said you weren't charged, they still wanted to keep people away from you. They didn't know how you'd react. Mrs. White thought it would most likely develop negative perspectives."

Which was a keen hypothesis. Simon did feel betrayed at the beginning. He finally did the honor of turning around and facing Rachel. The moment they met eyes, she looked down. She was at the verge of tears, but barely suppressing it. Simon's anger towards Rachel was slowly fading. Before it went entirely away, however, he had questions that needed answering.

"How long did you know?" Simon asked flatly. "Since when?"

Rachel quickly dried her eyes and tentatively confessed, "Since I can remember. Daddy isn't like us, but mom was always a wrangler. I knew magic and Eldwoods because she taught me. Of course, I could only practice when mom was around, but it didn't take too long for me to awake. And then I started seeing . . . well . . . what you . . . you know . . ."

"*Things,*" finished Simon, knowing exactly what she meant.

"They're magical creatures," explained Rachel. She looked at Simon after a pained sigh. "Why didn't you tell me? Since when did you start seeing them?"

"You know why," said Simon, staring into her eyes very hard. "Mom was diagnosed, Rachel. By *your* family. Mom thought I was going crazy, too, so she told me not to speak of it. How was I supposed to know those things were real when I never heard about all this? Your mom knew, alright, but my mom didn't. She wasn't like your mom. She was hallucinating. So tell me *how* I was supposed to tell you?"

Rachel was speechless. A tear managed to escape and trickle down her cheek. She quickly hitched it away. "I'm sorry . . ." she mumbled. "I'm sorry. I should've known."

Simon wasn't interested in apologies. He knew, deep down inside, there was nothing to feel guilty about. She could not have known he was seeing monsters, and at the same time Simon could not have known Rachel was conscious of magic. Neither of them had reached out that far, and thus there was no fault. He let the bitterness in his mouth wash down as he looked away.

"I'm not blaming you. She wasn't sick because your family said so."

Rachel shook her head. "No, daddy later started regretting. Once he saw what happened at the barn, he started saying there might've been a chance that she wasn't sick, and —"

"I told you it's not anybody's fault," Simon cut across forcefully. "She didn't see what I was seeing. She was sick, so don't go blaming yourselves." Truth be told, Simon was already trying real hard to commence this *moving on* adventure. Personal grudges or accusations needed discarding. Simon turned to the door and pushed it open. "Come on," said Simon. "I'm hungry."

Appearing ten times more relieved, Rachel followed Simon out of the room. With past misunderstandings out of the way, their footsteps were lighter and much more vibrant. Especially for Simon, the resentment cooped up inside him was cleansed clean. He felt very refreshed, a lot better than these past few days.

He quietly asked, "And Vel? What's she? Her family's involved, too?"

Rachel hesitated for the longest time. When she did speak, her voice lacked solidity. "She's . . . well, I can't really tell how long she's been awoken, but it was way earlier than me. But I can't tell you about her family, only that her father's not with her. That's all I know."

So Vel was also a part of this, perhaps longer than Rachel or Fortis. Surprises were around every corner. Simon couldn't help but snort. If this was going to be a common routine, he might as well get used to it.

When they reached the banquet room, the feast was already at its peak. Simon got his own share of food; mashed potatoes, chicken legs, roasted salmon, and apple pie. Out from the corner of his eyes, Simon found the person he was looking for: Ami and Fortis Goldstone. They were occupying a smaller table out on the terrace. Simon nudged Rachel and led the way to the outdoors. Once Ami spotted them, he whispered to his young brother. Fortis grinned the moment he heard the chairs draw back.

"Hungry?" asked Fortis politely.

"Yeah," said Simon, ripping a chunk of chicken leg off the bones. "*Famished.*"

"Ami!" Someone from the distance called, waving his arm. "Ami, come on!"

Ami rose from his seat. "You three enjoy." He tapped Fortis's shoulder and added, "Holler when you need me. I'll be close by."

"Won't happen," said Fortis, but nodded still.

Ami went away. Rachel, who was observing Fortis closely, slowly asked, "Ami? Ami Goldstone?"

"Yeah," said Fortis. "You're Rachel Fairburn, right?"

"Yes," said Rachel.

Fortis grinned. "Ami remembers you. He used to come by your place when we were still in Nocville."

"So I was right!" exclaimed Rachel, a beam blossoming. "Ami used to take me to the ice cream store. He even babysat me a couple of times."

"Yeah, he was surprised how much you changed," said Fortis, equally entertained.

"I remember he had a little brother, but I never met you back then, did I?" asked Rachel.

"You did once," said Fortis, his voice turning soft as he jogged through his memories. "We were six. I saw you at the clinic. You were a bit taller than me. You had a ponytail, too. You found me in the woman's restroom."

"Ooh!" whispered Rachel, memories coming back to her. "That's right! Weird how I couldn't tell . . . You two look so much alike. "

"Not so much back then," said Fortis.

"I'm sorry for what happened to your eye," said Rachel sadly. "You were there that time for an eye examination, right?"

"Yeah," said Fortis, smiling cheerfully. "It's alright. It was bad enough for me to mistake men's and women's restrooms, so I kind of knew it was going to happen sooner or later. Felt almost natural."

The food was perfect under the darker sky, and their conversation stretched for another two hours. Simon, who was now becoming a bit drowsy, leaned back and put a hand on his bulging stomach. He had consumed too much. It was a long while since he had taken the pleasantry of plentiful food. Rachel was also displaying some relaxed blankness. Fortis had taken out a book and was skimming the dots with his fingertips. It was a calm night, or perhaps it was magic that was blocking the wind. Not a sound bothered them, and even the rest of the passengers were taking their leisure time peacefully.

Simon was literally craning his head backwards as he passively watched a boy and a girl huddled in a corner. They were giggling. Whatever they were doing, it looked fun.

"Pupils." Simon jerked back up, Rachel stirred, and Fortis stopped. "Attention, pupils. The Explorer will be arriving at Eldwoods. Please assemble at the deck for prompt disembarkation."

"We should hurry," said Rachel, double checking her leaf as she got up.

The three of them joined the crowd as they sluggishly made their way up the corridor. As it turned out, the number of pupils was too great to fit everyone on the deck. Fortis barely made the cut line as Simon and Rachel pulled him up to the top of the stairs. The rest of the pupils remained in the second level.

"Do you see anything?" asked Fortis eagerly.

"Yeah," said Simon. They were cutting through clouds. "But nothing really interesting."

"How long?!" yelled a young seedling, leaning against the rails. "Are we there yet?"

"HOLD YOUR HORSES!" roared the captain. "YOU'RE SECONDS AWAY!"

The Explorer turned hard left. The weight of the crowd pushed Simon as the clouds cleared. There were excited cries, but Simon was too busy saving himself from becoming a human pancake.

"Do you see it? What does it look like?" yelled Fortis through the crowd.

"It's — it's wonderful!" cried Rachel, who had managed to untangle herself. "It's the *Elder Tree!*"

Finally wrestling back to where Rachel and Fortis was, Simon spotted what everyone was screaming about. In the forest of mountains and nuggets of clouds, a single, outrageously huge tree was rooted like a skyscraper. It spiked past the clouds and towards the heavens, and the body twisted and whirled until it accumulated to a single point at the highest peak. Light escaped from thousands of windows, manifesting a peculiar image like a greater beehive. Simon conjured a brief fantasy of countless people with insect wings swarming out of the tree to attack the Explorer.

Fortis was listening as Rachel gave every detailed description of the scenery; he was sure there had to be a powered motor somewhere in that throat. Out from the corner of his mouth, Fortis whispered, "How is it to you?"

Simon took a moment before admitting, "Yeah, it's really something . . ."

The captain of the ship roared over the crowd, "FEAST YOUR EYES, LADS! WELCOME TO ELDWOODS!"

chapter eleven ~~~~~~~~~

The Avowal of Blood

Simon hopped off the plank and helped Fortis descend. The ship looked puny now that it landed. It was docked by the south side of the tree, and the pupils proceeded like prancing donkeys. Simon stared at the Explorer, to the Elder Tree, and back to the Explorer. Yes, the tree was just too big. He couldn't even see the top from where he stood.

"Simon, come on!" They were the last ones, and Rachel pulled Simon towards the great entrance cavity. Fortis was waiting with his cane placed comfortably before him.

"Sightseeing?" asked Fortis.

"You could say that," said Simon.

"Let's go," said Rachel. "We'll get lost if we don't join the rest."

The three of them entered the fissure and into the titanic entanglement. The inside was spectacular. Thick channels of hundred different steps webbed the vacant inside like a spider's den. The bright illumination was coming from a system of vines that spread like blood vessels, some thin as threads while others vast as tree trunks. The inside of Eldwoods was more humid than the outdoors, and a natural stream ran at the bottom of the plant. It was a beautiful work of nature, perhaps the finest in the world.

Many people were watching from above, and most of those many were lightly applauding them, shouting vague greetings such as, "Welcome, pupils!" or, "Evening, seedlings!"

"So many of them," muttered Simon, missing a step due to his lack of vigilance.

"They've been around for thousands of years," said Rachel. "And the Elds before that, maybe the longest ever. It was the Primals Atta and Madrem who built this place. It's said they used the heart of a dead Primal and the tears of Atta and Madrem to build Eldwoods."

The main staircase ended, presenting before them a monumental gate. It was ajar, and past it was a foyer with additional smaller exits at the right and left wall. Giant plant pillars were suited with glowing vines. The floor, unlike the rest of Eldwoods, was a flat surface of mineral composition, and Simon noticed footsteps echoed rather discreetly. There were rows of seats settling the hall, and excluding the seedlings all pupils filled them up.

Simon was more curious of what was being promoted at the other end. On top of the elevation of steps there was a fountain with a bud the size of a soccer ball sitting on the top. Three people were present by the fountain, and Simon immediately recognized the Head Scholars: Altum, Venator, and Frao, all wearing their enticing coats of blue, teal, and brown. And behind those three was a throne of a sort, an accumulated production of the radiant vines. On the throne, which oddly suited her, was Cybele, still tiny and godly. She watched over the seedlings (whom were dazedly staring back at her) lining up behind Mrs. White. When her eyes found Simon, Cybele inclined her head ever slightly.

The last of the empty seats were taken, and Mrs. White made a last headcount of the seedlings before marching up the steps. The four Head Scholars looked down upon the children, Mrs. White composed and unwavering, Altum all the more merry, Venator slouched and predatory, and Frao like a fatherly pastor.

"Dear, Seedlings!" shouted Mrs. White, and the crowd of pupils was silenced. "You have been recruited to Eldwoods because you all have, purposely or accidentally, awoken. In the history that is unwritten to the rest of the world, there were the Elds; Primals, Governors, and the Philosophers. Through great effort and strife, they found sanctuary for the epitome of magic. Many turned away, chose to forget, and became Devolvers. You, however, are the few who have opened your eyes, recognized there is more to life than just living. Cherish your opportunity, and we will teach what being a wrangler means."

The pupils applauded, and the seedlings jumped and quickly followed along. Mrs. White waved her hand curtly, and the audience silenced.

"The legacy of Eldwoods runs deep within the Elds. The Primals —"

And she went on, repeating the tale Simon already heard. Rachel was listening very intently, almost on her toes. Fortis was also taking heed of the story. Simon looked about, a bit bored. He spotted Magnus and his gang up ahead. They seemed disinterested in all the ceremonial talk. Minutes passed.

"We will now commence the *Blood Avowal*." Mrs. White had finished, and most of the seedlings shifted nervously, some clutching their wrists, ears, and even stomach. "You will orderly proceed up and contribute a blood sample to determine your major, and you will receive your *Pupil's Cloak* afterwards. First in line, please come up!"

A tiny young girl, short for even a seedling, trembled as her eyes bulged in terror. Breathing rather heavily, she ascended one step, but was unable to summon the courage to continue. Simon saw Ami, sitting at the front row, get to his feet and caress the girl's head, whispering inaudibly. He kindly pushed her forward, and from then on the girl made her way like a terrified puppy. In the meanwhile, Mrs. White had prodded the bud besides her. A beautiful white flower, petals the size of Simon's hand, blossomed.

"Your leaf," said Mrs. White. The girl took off her golden leaf and offered it. Mrs. White looked at it and announced, "Mary Shyhand!" Mrs. White pointed at the pedestal behind the fountain and said, "Up." Mary climbed and faced the entire foyer, the fountain and flower just below her chin. She shook like a leaf in a rainstorm. She had seen something the moment she looked down at the flower, and her face turned pale chalk.

"Hand," demanded Mrs. White.

Mary was strangling her sweater with iron grips. Very slowly, she offered her right hand, and Simon could see how fiercely it fluttered. Mrs. White took it and spoke, maybe a bit gentler than what she used to sound, "Nothing to worry. It'll only be a prick." And she held Mary's hand and offered it to the flower.

What was hidden to the crowd, but foreseen by Mary, emerged; tentacles, or arms, or whatever they were slithered up from the core. Mary squealed and shut her eyes, tears streaming down her cheek. The seedlings were screaming various impressions, some finding it utterly awesome, other speechlessly shocked, and most giving out an exclamation of disgust. The seated pupils, however, broke into laughter, clearly enjoying the reaction of the new recruits. Mrs. White barked, "Silence!" and then added, "They are feelers. No need to be frightened."

Indeed, the so called *feelers* weren't exactly harming Mary. They prodded her tentatively, some bothering to loop themselves around her wrist. Simon began to wonder in what manner were those feelers going to extract blood, when one of them tickled the index finger before jabbing it lightning fast. Mary squeaked, but took a glance when she realized the pain was nothing but instant. A drop of blood gathered and descended into the core. The feelers caressed the wound as the petals shuddered. The whiteness of the flower converted into sky-blue.

"Wisdom!" announced Mrs. White, and there were a round of applause. A few enthusiastic clappers suggested they belonged to Wisdom as well. "That'll do," said Mrs. White, and she led Mary off the pedestal. Mary rubbed her healed finger before accepting folded clothes from Altum. She shyly scuttled to the side where she was pointed to and stood there. Mrs. White faced the pupils again and called, "Next in line, please!"

Attitudes transformed from disgust to enthusiasm. Seedlings eagerly advanced towards the mysterious flower, anxious to discover what it felt like to be encased by the feelers. Some were bold enough to lower their hands into the core.

"How does it look like?" asked Fortis, who was inevitably missing all the details.

"Like a sea urchin," muttered Simon, watching those feelers crawl up a boy's hand. "Except really flexible."

"Oh, don't be such a killjoy," said Rachel excitedly. "You get to do this only once. I never thought the flower would be so big, though. Mom never told me what it was like. Ooh, there goes Vel!"

Vel was climbing the steps, her ivory hair hard to miss. She got up the pedestal and (neither excited nor bored) let the feelers probe her skin. One jab, and a drop of blood fell. The moment the blood touched the core, the petals shifted colors to rich green.

"Expression!"

Vel came down the pedestal to receive her Pupil's Cloak from Venator. Despite the hawkish glare, she stared straight into those circular keen eyes. There was a pause when both pupil and Head Scholar exchanged thoughts. And to Simon's astonishment, Venator curled his lips (he didn't look kindly, despite the gesture) and mumbled a few words. Vel's eyes widened, but as Mrs. White shouted, "Next!" she turned away and descended. What had they talked about?

The Blood Avowal was now half way through after dispatching Jamey Downriver to Belief, Aro Clearmen to Wisdom, Uro Clearmen to Passion, Claire Watcher to Belief, and then Simon heard "Aemulus Ashblood!" There were hushed voices all around, the sort that was heard when people got wind of something sensational. Rachel said, "Oh . . ." and held her breath as she looked at the kid that stood before flower.

It was the red browed boy. His somber glower that mismatched his age hardly showed signs to vanish. He promptly put out his hand and let the feelers drape his arm. When the blood dripped into the core (feelers going mad as they began their healing process) the petals instantly turned scarlet, almost as thick as the color of his blood. "Passion!" shouted Mrs. White, and the pupils clapped along (a bit more wildly from a good number of them) as she presented Aemulus with his clothe. Rachel breathed freely.

"Well, I figured so. His entire family is devoted to Passion."

"You know that guy?" said Simon.

Rachel frowned. "He's an Ashblood. The ones living at the side of our town?"

And it finally came to him. "Oh," said Simon, "the really rich folk?"

"You can put it that way," said Rachel as she rolled her eyes at Simon's over-simplicity. "They fund Nocville School and also the townspeople that are in need for a living. For example, *you*."

Simon was taken aback.

"I only get some from Ms. Bluebell."

"Where do you think she gets that from?" snapped Rachel, this time not ignoring his stupidity. "She can't afford to pay for your rent at the same time, you know. The Ashbloods pay your rent, food supply, and education. They do more than what people know of them."

Simon found this fresh news a bit amusing for a few minutes until he was distracted again when he saw Magnus ascend. There were already whispers channeling about. When Mrs. White read the name, "Magnus Trueblood!" conversations were no longer hushed. Simon recalled something from his memory and quietly asked, "Hey, what's a *Blood*?"

Fortis shook his head. "First time I'm hearing about it. Can ask Ami about it."

Rachel looked grim. She said in a low voice as Magnus went up the podium, "They're the high born, the descendants of the Philosophers that kept their bloodline."

"Descendants?" asked Simon, watching the feelers caress Magnus.

"Not direct, though. They're human, but they have the blood of Elds. I guess some of the Philosophers developed intimate relationships with humans. Being related to the Philosophers gave them a superb performance and advantages. It helped restore the damage and reestablish order, and since Lady Cybele was not exactly at the age to rule, they formed the Luminary to do what was necessary in her stead. And that's how the linage of Bloods started. They're powerful people, the closest thing to a Philosopher."

Fortis inched closer to Simon when Rachel finished. From the corner of his mouth he muttered, "There you have it, they're your distantly related cousins."

"I can't think of anyone less I'd consider as cousins," Simon grunted back, clearly not enjoying the thought of him and Magnus sharing a cup of tea.

"Still, they're the closest thing you have as a family. You're a Philosopher."

"I told you I'm not," said Simon firmly, glaring as the feelers poked Magnus's finger.

"It won't matter what you think," said Fortis. "Once people find out, they'll start relating you guys."

The moment the blood hit the core, the flower turned startling green, maybe as much as Vel. But a different phenomenon was discovered; a few petals, maybe a dozen or more, became muddy brown, like the coloration decided to change at the last second. Mrs. White exclaimed, "Expression!" Magnus appeared exceedingly proud with himself, and he puffed up his chest when the crowd applauded. Simon stared at Rachel for an explanation.

"What happened?" asked Fortis.

"There were two colors," said Simon.

"Mom said there are people like that," explained Rachel as Magnus received his coat. "Very few, but the Bloods are mostly the case. They have the potential to annex more than one major, like a double major."

"Yeah, I heard about that, too," said Fortis thoughtfully. "But you can naturally develop a second major over time and practice. Having that as a kid just gives you a better start."

"Why are some people's tints darker, though?" asked Simon. "Does it mean anything?"

"It means you're more tuned into that major," said Fortis analytically.

The rest of Magnus's crew went up, starting with the pudgy Lent Bloodluck to Expression (he had green with blue), the tall Vass Moonblood to Expression (green and brown), the muddy-blond Latus Goodwill to Expression (lime green with pinkish red), and Celsis Bloodmark with the heavy accent to Expression (green with brown). Each time their majors were announced the applause and cheers grew louder from the same group of people. Simon was astounded all five got into the same major.

"Funny," said Fortis, echoing Simon's thoughts.

"Yeah," said Simon. "What's up with that?"

Even Rachel looked a bit confused. "I don't remember hearing about this . . ."

The remaining seedlings proceeded in order. As the line grew shorter, Simon noticed his anxiety rise. Watching the event was different from facing the actual thing. Fortis, appeared to be experiencing similar sensations, but he was handling it much more calmly. Rachel, too, seemed resolute and considerably cooler than Simon.

"Roth Mayberry . . . Passion! Brendon Oathrun . . . Wisdom! Claire Sharpcliff . . . Belief!"

"Have you thought about your major?" asked Fortis quietly. "Where you might belong?"

Simon lost his head there for a moment. No, he was so absorbed in the ceremony he had not what would happen *after* he had gotten to the pedestal. What coloration was he going to be?

"Next, please!"

It was Fortis's turn. He whispered, "I'll be fine on my own." He left Simon and Rachel, his cane gave him guidance. To the crowd's surprise, Fortis made it up the pedestal without so much as a bump (Simon felt oddly proud). "Fortis Goldstone!" The feelers grazed his hand. Fortis flinched from the alien touch. Out to the side, Simon saw Magnus snicker. Fuming, Simon did his best to ignore and looked back at Fortis. The flower altered brown. "Belief!" To his left, Ami was grinning very broadly, and his hands were flushed from clapping hard. The brothers were without doubt in the same major. Frao delivered Fortis his cloak and gave short compliments.

"Next!"

Rachel exhaled sharply before stalking up the steps. Simon kind of knew what her major was going to be; she was the *smart* type, after all. Once Rachel gave her leaf to Mrs. White — "Rachel Fairburn!" — she stationed herself before the fountain and let the feelers do their work. A quick jab, a drop of blood, and a transformation to a navy flower. "Wisdom!" She appeared pleased of her major, and she looked up at Altum with admiration. Altum in return smiled behind his beard.

"And last!"

Breathe, Simon. He thought to himself as his feet felt very heavy and unresponsive. *Just breathe.* The journey to the fountain felt like a million years. He barely heard Mrs. White command the pupils silent. The warm smiles of Altum and Frao did not help. Venator's acidic glare just made things worse. Cybele, sitting in her vine throne, was watching over him. Simon had the queerest feeling she knew what was going to happen. Maybe he should ask.

"Simon Dreamwalker," said Mrs. White. Simon noticed he was getting onto the pedestal without submitting his name. He quickly took off the leaf and passed it to Mrs. White. The crowd laughed. "Hand," she said, and Simon tentatively reached out before him. He couldn't find words to really describe what he was seeing. Within the flower, there was a stigma, but looked like a mouth than anything. Hundreds of feelers were batting inside the core. The moment the flower detected a new arrival, it stretched as if yearning for the flesh. Simon understood why the first girl was so alarmed. It was kind of creepy.

At the moment of contact Simon felt a shiver run all the way up to his temple. There was no oil on them, but the feelers were slick and fluid. They tickled him to the point where Simon kind of wanted to yank his arm away. When his arm was grotesquely enveloped by hundreds of wormlike strands, Simon felt a sharp prick on his index finger; followed by an immediate mobilization of feelers around it (Simon thought he was getting sick from the squirming). A drop of blood spilled to the core, and an abrupt coolness settled into his finger, as if he was experiencing mint refreshments in the wrong body part. The blood landed straight into the stigma. Simon noticed the stigma make a — what appeared to be — swallow.

For a moment, nothing happened. The petals stirred, shuddered, batted like wings. The feelers released Simon's arms as they flailed in harmony. If it had a voice, Simon thought it could be crying, maybe even screaming (he had an alarming impulse to just run away). The jaded pupils were gathering their attention to the fountain again. Under the fixated surveillance of the entire foyer, the flower gave a mighty twitch and reacted so suddenly nobody quite comprehended what the color was until the petals turned deep, solid, onyx black.

Simon was greatly confused. Most of the pupils appeared the same, sparing a few who were gasping wildly. Simon searched for the faces he knew. Rachel looked a bit worried. Vel, who was always so calm, observed Simon with an eyebrow raised. Hard to miss the red brows, Simon spotted Aemulus Ashblood; he looked surprised, and twice more acute. The Bloods were open jawed, and Magnus stopped snickering as his face went blank. Fortis, who was nearest, was grinning; even blind, he was the only one who knew what was coming.

"It's a Philosopher!" cried a pupil, pointing at Simon. "It's an Eld!"

"No way! Don't kid us!"

"Where's the mark? Where?"

"He has a bandage! It's covering it!"

"Let us see! Let us see!"

The response was pretty chaotic. Pupils were standing, some even on their seats. Simon felt like he was in a zoo or something. They wanted to see his dot. He wasn't fond of that idea, and thus he kept his hands right by his sides. Like a pair of cymbals, Mrs. White cut through the air and disciplined the crowd. "*SILENCE!*" Raising her hand, she clicked her fingers, and Simon almost tripped backwards as a column of wild fire roared out of her palms and ascended thirty feet high. Pupils as unison gasped as her magic bellowed and danced for a moment. Mrs. White closed her hand, and the flames dissipated.

"Now," she continued, as if nothing had, "a word from Lady Cybele, who has also returned from her forced absence."

Cybele got to her feat. She was tiny, and thus it made her smaller than when she was sitting. Most looked perplexed by her miniature looks. Regardless, her presence was of great interest amongst the pupils. Cybele's crystal voice chimed above all sounds.

"Seedlings," she said, "I greet you to Eldwoods, the home of Elds. You will learn beginning tomorrow the ways of Passion, Wisdom, Expression, and Belief. As you have seen, Passion is fierce as fire. Wisdom —" she directed Altum, and the old man twirled his finger. The fountain water that poured like a stream splashed and tossed before weaving upwards. Altum continued to conduct his articulate magic, and the water splurged, spiraled, spread, and raced in the air as if painting a multidimensional canvas. "— is vast as water, and thus the most articulate. Expression —" Venator did not present much subtleness in his demonstration. He flicked his wrist as his spidery fingers spread. A mighty gust tossed the pupils in disarray, but it died as quickly as it started. "— is true as wind. It could be unforgiving, or charitable. Belief —" Frao was already performing his own show. Rocks, the size of his head, were revolving around him like a miniature solar system. "— is stout as earth. You will experience the weight of your own faith as you progress.

"Be proud of whatever major you have been selected to. You are now a significant member of hidden history. Keep in mind, the world may not remember you, but you will be of great part of it."

Cybele sat back down, and a rather solemn round of applause followed. Simon joined in. When the claps finished, Frao moved before the fountain and drew everyone's attention.

"Seedlings, you will have a brief moment of choosing your sentry. The remaining pupils may return to your living quarters; your sentry is waiting for you.

"Good work, and good night!"

It was like everybody had a thorn on their seats. The pupils scattered like ants, stalking past the pillars and migrating into the smaller thresholds. The seedlings remained in the foyer. Only a few of them looked like they knew what was about to happen. Altum the ancient merry-mind stalked towards them rather actively for his age. He smiled kindly and addressed to the seedlings, "If you would follow me . . ."

chapter twelve ~~~~~~

Agilis the Chained

They headed further up the webbed steps. At the elevation they were at, looking out a window provided wonderful scenery of the wilderness (of course, not as spectacular as the moment on the Explorer). If there was a major problem, it was the size of this place. Simon knew for a fact he was going to get lost if he wasn't with the group, and that was for everyone else. Altum was there beacon, and they followed him like chicks chasing after their mother.

Altum stopped before a threshold that was poorly constructed with jagged edges as if someone had hammered and hacked their way in. "Would anybody suggest minding their footing?" he remarked gaily as he ducked across. Since everybody was so tiny compared to him, the rest had to jump. Simon, Rachel, and Fortis were the last. Upon entrance, the same vessel-like vines were pulsing. Seedlings oohed and awed as they all spun in one spot. There were knots all around them, like hundreds of bird nests.

"My dear seedlings," said Altum, spreading his arms. "This is the home of sentries."

Simon heard mighty strokes of countless wings. Creatures swarmed out from their holes and flew in counterclockwise. At first, Simon thought they were giant bats, but then it turned out they weren't bats at all. They were all of different bulks and colors. Some had tails, some had hair, and some had both. Their eyes glowed in the nocturnal bleakness. It felt a bit creepy to be watched over a couple hundred foreign creatures.

"What are they?" whispered Simon.

"Gargoyles," said Rachel immediately, but despite knowing so, she still appeared equally spooked.

"They will be your companion for the years you spend as a pupil," said Altum. "They will prioritize your wellbeing and education. You can be sure to develop intimate relations with your partner. Choose to your liking. They will cherish you, and you will cherish them."

Simon already saw a few pointing out their finger. At indication, the gargoyle addressed swooped down and greeted the seedling. In general, they were not even two feet tall. They all had four claw-like fingers, but the number of toes varied from five to three. Horns were almost a common feature amongst them. One in particular grew a vicious spike from its nose.

"I guess it's really just picking one out?" asked Fortis, who was intently listening to the campaign of wings. "Fancy that."

"Which one do you want?" asked Simon, observing very carefully to provide assistant. "There's a fanged one . . . or a one with manes. Oh, there's a big — no, he's just fat."

Fortis grinned and raised his cane sky high. "I choose whoever picks me."

A gargoyle from the furthest left of the chamber came spiraling down. When it halted before Fortis, Simon noticed its face was heavily lined into a frown, like a tiger bearing its teeth. It looked promising . . . in some aspects.

"My name is *Vigil*," said the sentry in a harsh growl. "I can be your guide and shield. Will you give me the honor?"

Fortis grinned even wider and said, "Nice to meet you, Vigil. You can call me Fortis Goldstone."

"Interesting taste," muttered Simon as Vigil bowed.

"He sounds resolved. I like that," said Fortis.

Simon looked over to Rachel. She was already in the bonding process with a blue sentry, rather muscular with a square jaw and two tiny horns protruding above both eyes. Its wings were strong and powerful, and each time it flapped it bobbed a few inches up and down. Its arms were lengthy and strong, and its hands were big enough to lock over Simon's face.

"*Tutela* is the name," said the sentry, its voice deep and rumbling. "You require caring, and I shall provide it to you. Let me assist."

Rachel seemed unsure if she should accept the offer, but in the end she nodded and said, "Rachel Fairburn. I accept." When Tutela bowed, she said from the corner of her mouth, "Caring? From that bulk?" Simon laughed.

Others seemed to have mated with their partners. Vel was accompanied with a grey sentry; it had a face with nothing but eyes. Aemulus nodded at a scarlet sentry that had a white beard and a few scars. Brendon Oathrun from Wisdom was in a complicated dilemma; rather than he choosing a sentry, it appeared a sentry was demanding selection, and the bat-sentry shrieked, "You require assurance, confidence, and dignity! I shall change you into a man!" while Brendon cried, "No! No,

I don't want to! Please!" Aro and Uro Clearman each had feminine sentries, both long necked and reptilian featured. Magnus was conversing with a bronze sentry that looked hawkish; he looked extremely pleased on how it stood tall like a human.

Simon left Fortis at Vigil's care for a moment and dawdled around the chamber, searching for a particular sentry that stood out. But there seemed to be none. Making two laps around, Simon was beginning to lose focus from the fatigue that was settling in. Intending to resolve the matter just like Fortis did, Simon inhaled and was about to give command, when he discovered a pair of glinting eyes, looking back at him from a hole a few yards ahead. He squinted. There were thin chains blocking its exit. Why wasn't that sentry out and flying? Simon went closer and peaked into the knot.

"Hello?"

The eyes closed. Simon pushed the chains up for a better look.
"Think carefully, pupil."

The eyes reappeared. Finally adjusting to the bleakness, Simon saw that the sentry inside was dark as night. It had slender limbs, cuffed with identical chains around the knot. It had fangs, antlers, and pointed ears. Ebony hair grew from head to all the way down its arrow-head tail.

"I would deem it wise to search for another sentry," said the sentry in a funereal voice.

Simon asked strangely, "Why? What's wrong with you?"

The sentry shifted, turning its chains so it clinked.

"I am not fit for service."

"Why's that?"

The sentry looked down. "I have stepped beyond my assigned obligation. I am a branded failure."

That was an interesting story. Simon asked, "What did you do wrong?"

The sentry looked a bit pained to continue the conversation. It simply spoke, "I assisted my master into an endeavor I should have forestalled for his sake. He was dismantled of his honor. Bringing disgrace to a master is the biggest insult to a sentry."

Simon found this account a bit odd. If the sentry treasured oaths and honor, did it mean they always disregarded their own opinions? If that was the case, they were more like puppets than actual beings. That was a bit cruel. Simon slowly asked, "But what about you? What did you think about it?"

It seemed the sentry was never asked that question before. He quietly dismissed, "Sentries are in no position to defend their wrong. They guide their masters, nothing more."

"Yeah, I know, but you helped him anyways, didn't you?" Simon pressed on.

The sentry glowered at his chained feet. He admitted gravely, "I believed it was the right choice . . . and I still do." There was a solemn pause. The sentry looked away and croaked, "The selection is about to end. Make haste and find a suitable sentry, pupil."

But in truth, Simon already found a sentry he wanted to bond with. He didn't need a servant. If it was a companion he was choosing, he wanted a partner, a friend, just like any other person he was close to. This sentry seemed just the thing.

"A sentry is *chosen* by a pupil, right?"

The sentry nodded and said, "Yes."

"And they can't object?"

"No, they cannot. They *will not*."

"And once the bond is done you can't revert it, can you?"

"It is up to the pupil, no one else."

Simon shook the chains. "And it's not like you *can't* serve, is it?"

Finally realizing where the conversation was going, the sentry peered at Simon very seriously.

"I am not fit —"

"But you can serve, still," Simon insisted earnestly. "You said it yourself. I get to choose, and you can't say no."

The sentry stalled, tied down by the predicament Simon was keen to use. It rubbed its cuffs and elucidated, "You're correct, I cannot reject. But if I can give you my advice, pupil, there are better sentries that are more reputable. There are many that remember me, and they will be watchful. They will suggest to bond with another."

Simon could hardly care about that. As a pupil, he assumed his freedom would be the same as any other regular student. Go to class, and be a good boy. What were they going to say as long as he behaved?

"I'm fine with that," said Simon casually. "What's your name?"

The sentry sighed, eventually acknowledging Simon was not to be persuaded. It crawled forward and came face to face with Simon. "*Agilis*," it said, sounding more resolute than before. "Might I ask whom I'm serving?"

Simon grinned and said, "Simon Dreamwalker. So you'll be my sentry?"

"Until your ascension to wrangler," said Agilis.

The chains promptly followed in sequence by shattering to tiny pieces. The cuffs restricting Agilis snapped open. Agilis crawled out of his den and spread his wings, expressing his liberation. He was considerably more fabulous than how he looked cramped up and chained down. Agilis took swift flight around the chamber before residing next to Simon.

Many of the other sentries were averting their gazes at him. They looked repulsed. A gargoyle swooped down from above and hovered. It glowered at Agilis and hissed, "Agilis! You should be ashamed of yourself! Luring a pupil into your service; what disgrace is this?!"

"I did not lure him, Temptis. He came to me, and I will serve whoever asks," responded Agilis calmly.

Temptis directed her attention to Simon and started speaking, "Pupil, you must reconsider. Irresponsible sentries are capable of dangerous deeds. Reconsider. I can be of greater service. You mustn't suffer from —"

"No, I'm fine," said Simon bluntly. "I like him. I don't need anyone else."

"Pupil, I must insist —!"

"Seedlings, the selection is at an end!" Altum spoke out loud. "We will make our way to your living quarters, soon. I could only assume you would be exhausted from your eventful day."

Temptis the sentry gave a last reproachful look at Agilis before spitting out, "Your wrongdoings have not been forgotten!"

"I do not ask for forgiveness. I will bear the pain for eternity," said Agilis, sounding a bit obstinate.

Temptis flew away. Simon and Agilis joined the rest of the seedlings. Fortis and Rachel were waiting for him. The two of them seemed delighted to hear his voice. Their sentries, however, appeared discontent.

"Agilis . . ." growled Vigil, contorting his face into an ugly knot. "The pupil has selected you?"

"Vigil, Tutela," Agilis greeted, though a bit coolly. "Yes, he has."

"And you see yourself fit to do so?" demanded Tutela. "You have a history of leading your master astray."

"I do not mean to discriminate, but your expertise were *pampering*, if I recall," responded Agilis.

Rachel inched closer to Simon and breathed, "Why're they fighting?"

"I'll tell you later," mumbled Simon.

Altum swiftly searched through the seedlings, reaffirming all of them had a sentry by their sides. When he reached Simon, he eyed Agilis. It was a warm smile that was made, quite the contrary from what Simon was expecting. Altum whispered in a low whisper, "An interesting choice . . ."

as he passed Simon. Altum stalked back to the exit and called out, "Follow me, if you would please!"

Another march took them downwards, a few levels below from the sentry room. In this particular level, the channels of stairs were significantly less lengthy, and there were corridors that were filed with doors like hotel units. It had a cozy atmosphere, especially with the vines delivering light from above.

"This is the living quarter for pupils. You can find your designated units by the leaf indicated on each door." Altum gestured a door, and sure enough a golden leaf everyone had handed over at the Blood Avowal was pinned on it. "You young gentlemen will find your quarters here. The rest of more graceful and feminine nature may follow me to the opposite direction."

The boy named Uro Clearmen yelled out in despair, "No! Why?!"

Most of the boys laughed. Altum chuckled along, but commented, "So they may have a good rest at night from boys with much . . . impulsive curiosity."

It was the girls' turn to laugh, and his younger sister, Aro Clearmen, said in a mock mewl, "Oh, mom's going to be so proud they're finally putting a leash on you. What would you have become if it weren't for coming here?"

The girls giggled even harder as they disentangled from the boys and followed Altum. "I'll see you later," said Rachel, and she scuttled off as she called after Vel. The boys began to disperse, yawning as they dragged their feet to their awaited quarters. Simon said to Fortis, "Let's go. I think it's in alphabetical order."

"Fair enough," said Fortis.

They strolled down, watching others discover their units and vanish behind the door. The sentries did not enter, however. They perched themselves on a small platform just above the doors. Once they touched base, they immediately calcified into wooden sculptures. As more sentries settled in, the more Simon thought the corridor was looking like an ancient castle.

"Here it is, Master Dreamwalker," said Agilis.

The leaf with his name labeled was to the right. Simon turned to Fortis and said, "You sure you don't need help?"

"I have Vigil for that," said Fortis, grinning. "See ya."

"Night," said Simon.

Fortis walked ahead, cautiously guided by Vigil. Agilis found sanctuary above the door and nodded.

"I shall wake you, Master Dreamwalker."

"Yeah," said Simon. "Sleep tight."

Agilis solidified. Simon split a mighty yawn as he turned the wooden knob and pushed the door open. Whatever he imagined to be in there, it was nothing what he could've expected. Apart from the bed, the closet, a bathing room, a window, and a desk, there was nothing. Everything was made of wood, and the room even *smelled* like wood. Simon was glad there were at least thick blankets to make his sleeping den all cozy and soft. He threw himself onto the bed. Yes, it was a texture beyond fantasy. He felt like he was cuddling in clouds. He rolled and wrapped himself like a burrito. He felt like falling asleep any second.

"Boy."

But an all too familiar voice forced his eyes open. Shirking through the slim crack from the nearly closed door was Ignis, followed by Terram, and lastly Aqua (Aqua taking ages). Simon jumped when he heard a sharp crack. Ventus had crashed in from the window; she floundered as she lost directional coordination. Simon sat back up.

"Why are you guys here?" groaned Simon.

"To see if you're finding this place to your liking, child," said Terram generously. "Do you require anything else?"

Simon shook his head. "I'm not looking for special treatment. I'll be fine."

"Simon! Simon! Simon!" cried Ventus pointlessly. She looked more deranged after the crash-and-entry.

"You . . . must . . . be . . . overtaxed . . ." croaked Aqua.

Simon rubbed his eyes. "Yeah, really . . ."

"This will be brief," said Ignis stubbornly. "You will —"

Ignis abruptly stopped and looked about. There was someone lurking behind the entrance. Simon saw a gray eye and the flash of platinum hair before it slid away.

"Eavesdropper?" growled Ignis maliciously.

"Yeah, he's new like me," said Simon airily.

"You know the boy," said Ignis sharply.

"Magnus Trueblood. Rachel said he's some high born. Didn't get along too well."

"Oh dear," said Terram casually. She shut the door with her paw. "Well, we can't have him listening to us now, can we?"

"Humph, a Blood, is it?" growled Ignis, whipping his tail suspiciously. "Anyhow, you will be attending your session for Passion tomorrow. I stress that you be prepared."

". . . Prepared for what?" asked Simon blankly. "I have nothing with me."

"Prepared for strife, you fool," hissed Ignis, and Simon winced Ignis lashed his tail. "Tomorrow, you will go to session of Passion. Tuesday is Wisdom, Wednesday is Expression, and Thursday you will attend the session of Belief. Friday, there will be Introduction to Wrangling all day."

Simon failed to record any of that into his brain. He lazily muttered, "Can't you guys print a class schedule or something?"

Ignis pounced, and Simon yelped and tightened the blanket around him. Simon could've sworn the claws were injected deep within the fabric.

"Your . . . sentry . . . will recall . . . your . . . schedule . . ." croaked Aqua as Ignis hissed angrily over Simon.

"Will I be with Rachel and Fortis?" shouted Simon through his blankets.

"We can't tell, child. There is a morning group and an afternoon group. You happen to be in the morning group for all four days," narrated Terram kindly.

"Sounds fun . . ." groaned Simon, wishing nothing more than to sleep.

"Take your sessions seriously. Lady Cybele and us Governors will be watching you at a close distance," growled Ignis, turning away to the door.

Ventus cawed, "Want to play, Simon? Want to play?!"

Ignis rushed up the bed and slashed, and Ventus dodged by a hair's width. Ventus made a few wild circles around the room and cried, "See you later, Simon!" before zooming out of the window and into the night. Ignis hissed and skulked to the door.

"Mind your door, boy," he growled, nimbly undoing the knob. "Whatever conversations we share won't be of light topic."

"Yes . . . young one . . ." said Aqua, sluggishly crawling to the door. "You . . . must . . . be . . . cautious . . ."

"Okay, okay," said Simon tetchily. "I'm going to bed, now."

Ignis vanished with the last flick of his tail. Aqua bobbed his head rather heavily and said, "Good night . . . young one . . ." It was another twenty seconds until he reached the door and crawled out of sight. Now it was just Terram who was to take her leave. But before doing so, she inched closer to Simon and added a final note.

"Have faith in yourself, child. And come to us if you need any help." Terram headed to the door. "Rest well." She left.

Simon walked up to the door and gently closed it shut. He was unspeakably exhausted. Simon dove into his bed and fell right into bleakness.

chapter thirteen ~~~~~~

Complicated Relations

The forest was greeting the dawn. The shadow that he was strangely attracted to was not there. Lesser roots and dirty vines had caved in, blocking the entrance. He drew forward and stared. Where was it? Where were the eyes? He placed a hand, and it slipped right through. Simon was inside. A bloodthirsty scream reverberated from the lightless tunnel. Something was moving. Fast. Long. Violent. Terrible.

"It's here, my love! New ones! Don't worry. Mommy will bring you one! Don't you worry —!"

Simon woke. He was safely in his bed, but a bit hot and perspiring. The sun was announcing a new day; the *first* day. Simon rolled over. Agilis's head was inches from his. He nearly got a heart attack as he jerked back in alarm.

"It is time, Master Dreamwalker," said Agilis.

"Could've shook me awake, you know," grunted Simon as he buried his face in the blanket.

"I did, Master Dreamwalker," replied Agilis, crawling off the bed. "It appeared your dreams were bothering you, hence I woke you earlier."

Simon groaned and began fishing for his watch on his desk. The time was . . . fifteen before seven. He had barely slept five hours. His body seemed apathetic to commands; he was feeling light headed just by sitting up. "Ugh," he groaned.

"Is there a problem?" asked Agilis.

Simon rubbed his eyes. "Just tired."

"Cleansing might help," said Agilis. He pointed at the restroom. "You will find everything you need in there. You can take your time. Breakfast is not ready for another hour."

With nothing better to do, Simon slid into the bathroom. A vague image popped into his head. A cave. Yes, a cave. Was it from his dreams? What

did he see in there? There was a woman's voice, also. A faint echo of it made his blood run cold. Simon lost himself in the warm shower for a while.

When Simon finally came out drying his hair, there were guests waiting for him. The most noticeable was Ignis, sitting rigidly on top of his desk. Frao was peacefully waiting by the window, his glasses blinking as the sun hit it square on. The last visitor was not an acquaintance; the man was covered in a black cloak, and his hood concealed most of his facial mask except for his eyes, which glared back at Simon unblinkingly. Simon was unnerved a bit.

"Good morning, Simon," said Frao, straightening himself. "How was your night?"

"Good," lied Simon.

"Splendid," said Frao energetically. "Would you mind sparing a moment?"

Simon hardly saw how he could refuse. They were in his room already.

"Sure," said Simon.

Frao smiled and pulled the chair back. Simon sat down, and Frao sat on the bed. Now that he was facing away from the hooded man, Simon felt at complete ease before Frao. The man surely generated a comforting vibe.

"Simon," Frao started out kindly, "might I ask if you have picked a sentry?"

"Yeah," said Simon. "Last night. Didn't everyone?"

"Was it the one addressed as Agilis?" asked Frao.

Simon finally knew where this was going. He slowly nodded. Frao crossed his arms and released a thoughtful sigh. From behind, Simon could hear the cloak shifting.

"You may not be aware, but that sentry has been reputed for assisting unethical deeds."

"Yeah, I know about it," said Simon calmly, and Frao widened his gaze.

"Then you must understand we advise you to void the contract. We can give suggestions on who might be of better worth."

Agilis' prediction was true. Whatever he had done, people were concerned enough to come visit and protest. In truth, Simon was curious what this *unethical deed* could've been, but it didn't seem nice to bluntly ask for details if Agilis was feeling personal about it. Besides, Simon liked him. Simon wanted to hear the story at his perspective, not the filtered, prejudice version whispered by others.

"No, I like him," said Simon simply. He turned to the door and called, "Agilis!"

Agilis came shooting through the door. He gently landed next to Ignis. "Yes, Master Dreamwalker?"

"You're not going anywhere, are you?" asked Simon.

Agilis inclined his head. "I serve no one but you —"

"You deceitful creature."

Simon looked around. The cloaked man was glaring at Agilis now.

"Pardon me," said Frao, gesturing the man. "This is Head Warden of Eldwoods. He and his men safeguard the lands."

Head Warden's voice was inhuman, like three or four people were speaking an identical dialect at the same time. Was his voice damaged or something? He continued to patronize Agilis. "You were chained for your and your master's schemes. You should feel grateful your punishment was just that. How dare you show your treacherous face as if you deserve a chance."

Simon screwed his brows. He didn't like Head Warden. Not one bit.

"Scurry back to your hole. You belong in shackles and —"

"I *said*," Simon cut across coldly, making heads turn and converge on him. "I said I like him. He's staying."

The atmosphere turned uncomfortably tense. Those merciless eyes were about to stab right through Simon.

"You dare reason with —"

"Of course." Frao cut across, subtle yet sharp. "If you wish to still continue the partnership that is yours to choose. A bond between a pupil and a sentry is much too powerful to sever by force. You have all the right." Frao nimbly got to his feet. "We can depart, Head Warden. It was agreed we would suggest a new sentry only if Simon wished it."

The Head Warden looked sourly reluctant to retreat. He slowly turned to the exit, every step echoing hostility. He turned back at the last second and growled, "I'm watching you. You may be a Philosopher, but you're freedom is under my surveillance." And then he walked out of sight.

Simon scowled and muttered, "*Really?*"

Frao chuckled. "His duty beckons hostility. Please understand." He leaned closer. His voice dropped a few notches as he added more seriously, "But I would advise not to cross him. Very few cases evade his jurisdiction."

"Right," said Simon, foreseeing he will clash with many of those jurisdictions.

Frao winked at him went to the exit. "I look forward to Thursday," he added before leaving.

Simon put his chair back in place and asked to Agilis, "You okay?"

"I am in your debt," said Agilis, bowing. "This cannot be repaid even through death."

"Well, get used to it," replied Simon coolly. "That's how things work where I come from." He noticed Ignis hadn't left yet. He asked, "What's up?"

"To remind you what I said," said Ignis.

Simon fumed. "I know what you said."

Ignis said sternly, "Make yourself presentable. Your cloak is right here."

Simon had carelessly dropped his Pupil's Cloak on the desk last night, but now it was spread facing up. Agilis picked it up. "I can provide assistance."

It was not hard. Simon had his normal clothes on, and he just needed to pull the cloak over his head and button it down. He went into the bathroom to look at himself. He was pleased he looked nothing like the Head Warden. The bright beige gave a very simplistic look, and the cloak didn't drag. It was light as a feather, too; Simon hardly noticed its weight.

"Is it to your liking?" asked Agilis.

"Yeah," said Simon, flapping the hems like a bird.

"Hurry to the foyer, boy," said Ignis, trotting out of the room.

But before heading down, Simon stopped by another unit. He rapped the door. A few moments later, Fortis pulled the door open. He, too, was wearing his Pupil's Cloak.

"Morning," said Simon.

"Morning," replied Fortis. "Hungry?"

"Yeah, let's go."

The two headed down to the foyer, Agilis and Vigil often exchanging curt words as they led the way. Maybe it was because they were sentries that neither of them showed intentions to harm one another. Their verbal strife, as a matter of fact, was entertaining to listen to. They always had something to come back with. "Your masters never knew their places." "You've always forgotten *your* place." "Being ruthless when it's necessary is a sentry's duty." "I recall you were nothing *but* ruthless." Simon and Fortis snorted numerous times.

When they entered, pupils were already flooding the foyer. Tables that were absent last night filed the space. Warm food was being served at the buffet. Agilis and Vigil hovered behind and bowed. "I take my leave," said Vigil. "I will be waiting, Master Dreamwalker. Midnight is when you must return to your unit," said Agilis.

"Thanks."

"Yeah."

Both sentries flew out of sight. Fortis said in amusement, "Funny folks."

"Yeah," said Simon. "Is he really ruthless?"

"I'm starting to notice it," said Fortis lightly. "But no worries. I'm having fun. I don't think he's used to kids not listening to him."

"What if he flips?" asked Simon.

"I will smite him. I have my plastic cane of justice."

Simon laughed.

The two of them walked up to the buffet (Simon helped scoop food for Fortis). Simon led Fortis to the tables, searching for someone he was earnest to reunite.

"Wish they'd stop staring at me," he muttered.

People were glancing at him again while muttering, "There he is, the Philosopher! An Eld!"

"Can't be helped. You're like a living fossil," said Fortis. "They'd pay to see you if you asked."

Simon finally found who he was looking for and called, "Rachel!"

In the midst of pupils, Rachel poked her head out and waved. Simon wormed through the tables and set both trays on the table. Besides Rachel was Vel, and across from Vel was Aemulus. Simon and Fortis sat next to Aemulus.

"What took you guys?" asked Rachel. "I was looking for you two!"

"Why's that?"

"Well, it is our first day in Eldwoods," said Rachel happily. "And since we're all from Nocville — figuratively speaking — I kind of wanted to get together."

Simon looked at Aemulus and Vel. Both were eating their food mutely, and both of them seemed disinterested in sharing any words at all.

"I see . . ." said Simon vaguely.

"So, let's start with introductions," said Rachel briskly. "I'm Rachel Fairburn, next to me is Velox Windly, across is Aemulus Ashblood, and . . . " she stared at Simon. "You guys can introduce yourselves. Go on!"

Simon was hoping this moment wasn't going to come. He said awkwardly, "I'm . . . uh . . . I'm Simon Dreamwalker."

Fortis followed his lead. "Fortis Goldstone."

Rachel beamed. "Great, we all know each other, now! So what are your schedules?" Aemulus promptly got to his feet. Rachel asked hurriedly, "Aemulus? What's wrong?"

"I'm not hungry," he said shortly. He went off on his own. Rachel looked down from his departure.

"He's nice," said Simon dully. "I feel friendly already."

"Oh, shut it, Simon. It's not like you weren't any different," said Rachel sharply. She sighed a second later. "He's just not used to being around people. He's home schooled and all, you know. I wish he would be more social."

"Sounds like you talked to him before?" asked Fortis.

"Yes, I have, actually," said Rachel. "He came to Nocville, once. His dad was a bit . . . *stiff*. Anyway, it was a long time ago. He was shy back then."

"He still is," said Fortis bluntly. "He doesn't know how to talk, if you ask me. He's a Blood. Most Bloods are raised to act like nobility. Not much of the conversing type."

"He's. Just. Shy." Rachel insisted firmly. "Once we get him to talk, you'll see that he's just like any of us."

"Any of us, eh?" muttered Simon.

Fortis changed subjects and averted his attention to Vel. "Velox, was it? Nice to meet you."

Vel looked up and replied, "Nice to meet you."

"You can call her Vel," said Rachel informatively.

Simon had not talked to her properly since the barn event. "Hey, Vel," he said friendly. To his surprise, Vel threw a particularly cold glare at him. She said a curt, "Hi," before busting out of her seat and departing. Simon gaped.

"What's her problem?" Simon blurted out.

Rachel sighed and shook her head.

"Well, it's a bit complicated . . ."

"Please, do explain," demanded Simon.

Rachel looked at him almost pitifully. "Alright, here it is. You were there with Vel the day at the barn. You remember?"

"Of course, I do," said Simon, clearly conjuring the image.

"Well, everybody who was present was questioned. You, me, daddy, and Vel became prime suspects. *If* Vel or I were prosecuted and charged, neither of us would be where we are right now."

"Yeah, I get it," said Simon defensively. "But it wasn't like I knew what was happening, either. She can't go blaming that on me!"

"Yes, she can," said Rachel painfully. "She was really looking forward coming to Eldwoods, maybe more than me. Finding herself in a tight spot by being with you obviously hindered her chances. She always knew she was good with magic. I'd imagine she would be devastated to be banned, or even held responsible of the account. It's good that things worked out, but she still blames you for all the trouble."

"That's not fair!" exclaimed Simon. "I had no clue! *I* should be the one being angry over all this!"

"Oh, Simon, you're denser than a rock, you know that?!" Rachel retorted exasperatedly. Simon gaped at her, but she snapped, "Just say you're sorry, just once! It's not that much to groan over. She'll be a lot of help to you if you just make a commitment." Rachel pointed her fork viciously. "She saved your life one time, remember?!"

Simon ogled. Fortis, who was listening patiently, shrugged his shoulders and said, "You've got to do what you've got to do."

Rachel's fork was still quivering. "Not just the words. You have to *mean* it."

When the pupils dispersed for their first session, Simon gloomily said good bye to Rachel and Fortis. He was attending Passion alone. Well, not alone; with Aemulus, but Simon hardly knew him. Agilis providing guidance, Simon sluggishly made his way up and into a complicated labyrinth.

"You memorized this place?" asked Simon.

"To the last tunnel, Master Dreamwalker," replied Agilis.

"How?" Simon asked, almost mind-blown.

"I've been serving for centuries. Time is what made it possible."

Simon spotted two girls trotting up ahead rather hurriedly. He pointed out and asked, "That way?"

"Yes," said Agilis.

"Right, I think I'll just follow them. You can go back, now."

"If that is your wish . . ."

Agilis turned and speeded out of sight. Simon leisurely followed the girls. There was only one channel to follow, thus it seemed logical it would lead him to his session. Simon observed the wonderful view of Eldwoods as he passed each window.

"Oh!"

Simon got distracted. It was the girls' voice. Simon climbed a few steps and made a wide curve to investigate.

When he reached another flight of stairs, he saw the two girls stalling. Simon didn't blame them. Aemulus was slouched besides the window, and there was definitely something wrong. His Pupil's Cloak, which was once clean and new, was partly torn around the neck. He had a bruise over his lips as it bled rather abundantly. He wiped the blood off with his cloak and muttered roughly, "Get going, would you?"

The girls scurried away, their offended emotions converting into verbal complaints. Simon waited for the voices to die out before climbing the steps himself. He stood a few feet apart from Aemulus. The blood resumed to spill.

"Need a hand?" Simon was astonished he was offering help. For all his life, *he* denied any help. Now, he was the one providing it.

Aemulus looked at Simon coldly. "Did I say I needed help? I told you to *get going.*"

Simon raised an eyebrow. "Really?"

"Yeah, *really*," snapped Aemulus. "So beat it."

Whatever sympathy he felt for Aemulus evaporated. Simon replied acidly, "Have it your way."

Simon strode right past Aemulus, but only for a few steps before Aemulus called out, "Hey!" Simon looked back. "Don't you dare speak of this."

Simon snorted. "It's none of your concern what I do."

Aemulus got to his feet and approached Simon. Their eyes matched and started blazing.

"You're an eyesore, you know that?" Aemulus snarled.

"You're a jerk," said Simon icily.

"Not a surprise. I get that a lot," said Aemulus, unconcerned. "Let me make this frank. I don't like you, and if you start putting your nose into my business, I'll burn it." He stalked off, leaving Simon in outrage. What a wonderful way to start off his first day in Eldwoods. Head Warden, Vel, Aemulus, and Magnus; he was making great relations, indeed.

chapter fourteen ~~~~~~

Wrangling

His sessions were really just like going to school, and for the first time in his life, he seemed to be doing great in average. After a full thirty minute lecture from Mrs. White in Passion, they spent the remaining hour snapping their fingers to force combustion. Simon was one of the few who got the spark going consistently, and by the end of the hour he was glorious as his thumb was flickering like a candle. "*Passio!*" But, there was a faint aroma of burnt smell, and Simon saw a thin line of smoke slither up. Fearing he might burn himself again, he was quite desperate to put it out after a few seconds.

"It is *passion* that derives flames, not fear," said Mrs. White as she watched Simon flap his hand and distinguish the fire. But then she added, "But, good work." That was a good sign, especially from her.

Wisdom, the next day, was thankfully accompanied by Rachel. The reason Simon and Fortis were thankful was because of the speech. In the midst of a pond (which was strange that one existed in Elder Tree in the first place), where giant lotus leaves replaced regular seats, Altum provided a very philosophical, puzzling lecture to his pupils.

"Sit, and welcome to the ways of fluidity. Wisdom is a character that all life must possess, or else survival would be a bigger challenge from how it already is. As history has proven itself, we learn, think, and remember. Those who choose to step ahead; they show the most magnificent idiosyncrasy of the living brain: they *improvise*. Yes, to appreciate the best of wisdom, you must be flexible, and then questionable.

Open your minds and see the world in a picture that surpasses the naked eye.

"Now, please repeat and memorize. *Sofia!*"

And a large balloon of water detached itself from the pond and levitated before Altum. Yes, it was a magnificent feat, but the problem was he wasn't exactly telling how to do the job. And thus, Simon and Fortis gave their full reliance on Rachel, who was remarkably executing the spell efficiently.

"No, Simon, you've got to imagine scooping it out," Rachel directed him as Simon was at a stall. "Scoop, Simon. *Scoop!*"

"Give me a scooper, why don't you?" grunted Simon, getting irritated with the lack of progress. "I'll scoop the whole pond for you if I could!"

"That sounds fun," said Fortis mildly. "*Sofia!*"

"Exactly like that!" exclaimed Rachel excitedly.

Fortis touched his body of levitating water to confirm if he was indeed good as Rachel praised him to be. "Wow, it's really something. Wish I could see it, you know."

Simon was left to struggle for the entire session.

Wednesday, as it turned out, was his least favorite day of the week. When he arrived at one of the top most platforms of Elder Tree, quite open to sunshine and clouds, the first that caught his attention was Magnus, along with his squad. To the furthest outskirts of the platform was Vel, who intentionally detached herself from the crowd. Up at a higher seat supported by a few lesser branches was Venator. He surveyed the class as if to pick out which one to feast upon.

"May you seedlings heed well," Venator called at the beginning of class, "I rarely make the trouble educating people who lack talent. They are slow learners, and they call for maintenance every too often. Under the unfortunate event that I *do*, I expect them to make swift progress, or," he tossed a dangerous, "they can expect a quick leave. *Permanently.*"

Outright cold. Just as expected, the man had very little empathy.

"Continuing on," said Venator curtly. "The wind does not do your bidding just because you *ask* for it. You must *feel* what it tells you, and in return, you must also express your desires. Of course, I doubt any of your naïve minds have the delicacy to properly appreciate the relentless beauty of the gust. It cannot be tamed, just like your unconscious minds."

Venator threw a sharp glare, and a violent current was summoned out of the blue. Simon shielded his eyes. Venator locked his fingers, and the wind died as abruptly as it appeared.

"Pitiful parodies as if knowing what Expression is are nothing but flukes. I have witnessed simpletons wailing, raging, guffawing, and even dancing to converse with the wind, while their efforts to my eyes are nothing but humiliating idiocy. Fools who believe they have mastered their emotions have challenged the breeze, only to crumble with failure. Commonality of them all: *inept*. Deluded they can achieve great heights by artificiality. Inept to direct their emotions into goals. Lost by chasing a fabricated truth.

"Since you are nothing but young lambs, I will show the benevolence of reminding you all the basics: *acceptance of self is the acceptance of expression*. If I so much as spot fools that veers astray," his tone was deadly, "I will leave them astray, for they have beckoned their demise."

As it turned out, Simon was one of those *inept* pupils. He was making no progress whatsoever. Magnus, who puffed his chest proudly, was one of the most able pupils (the rest of the Bloods were making their paper planes fly like a bird). Vel was also doing a remarkable job. Her plane aviated in measured spirals, and if that was not enough, she sent it far beyond the platform and into the clouds before directing it back into her hands. A longing, satisfied look passed from Venator, evidently pleased there were promises from the Bloods and Vel. But the remaining moments he focused on Simon, who in comparison was staring at his own plane for the full hour and a half. This did not please Venator; he even looked outraged.

"I would've thought you would be more . . . *gifted*, but it looks like you are nothing *but* that," Venator hissed as he passed. "I hope you do not address yourself as a Philosopher."

Simon retorted back rather hotly, "*I don't.*"

"Cheeky, are you?" said Venator softly. "You are *nothing* without us. Make sure to remind yourself every night, and the following morning as well."

Magnus looked extra pleased that Simon was neither doing well nor making an impression. Vel, who was still not in any forgiving sentiment, let Simon be humiliated.

"Have you even tried talking to her?" asked Rachel at lunch time.

"Yes!" retorted Simon, stabbing his food furiously. "Three times! And she just brushed me off like I was some insect."

"She can hold a grudge, I'll tell you that," said Fortis, sounding amused. "And it sounds like you're not too friendly with the rest of the lot?"

"Hard to say," said Simon sarcastically, the image of Venator constantly boring down on him resurfacing. "It's either really romantic, or really unromantic."

Belief, on the contrary, was the most fun of all days. Frao's class was located in the lower level of Eldwoods. Minerals ornamented the layer in every corner, and Simon even thought he saw strange reflections within them. At a business standpoint, it was perhaps a heap of unfathomable wealth, but to Simon there seemed to carry much more value than the exchange for luxury and fame.

"Magic is a complicated source of power. How, where, and when is not the question you must seek to attain it. It is *why*. To bask in its might; to explore infinite possibilities; to aid those that are weak; that is up to you to decide. But all of you have your own outstanding qualities, thus I can confidently say you will find your reasons within your years as pupils."

Frao was full of encouragements and excitements. Yes, Simon *really* was starting to like this session.

"Now, to the fundamentals. *What is belief?*"

To Simon's surprise, and Rachel's as well, Fortis raised his hand.

"Yes, Fortis?"

"It's an idea that is accepted as an unquestionable truth to people."

Frao beamed and surveyed Fortis, intrigued by his ingenious answer.

"Excellent, Fortis. A belief is nothing more than a concept; a thought. But, thoughts can be more capable than weapons. If an idea is accepted to be unquestionable, then that itself can become the platform of how you wish to perceive the world. The more you become attached to it, the stronger the belief becomes.

"In many occasions, belief can often bring joy. In the human world, *religion* is one of the most common, profound belief systems. They bestow their trust into a certain spiritual organization, and as a reward their doubts are washed away, lessening their worries that were once unanswered before their devotion.

"In this class, however, we are in search of *your* belief. A respectable figure is praiseworthy, but it is one thing to follow their footsteps, but another finding your own path. To become a true believer, you must first question if you are in reliance or liberty. If you are in the mercy of your own weaknesses and fears, than it will be wise to question where you have placed your roots. However, if it is the opposite, if your independence in belief is solid, most likely you will develop ideas of your own.

"But take heed, class: independence must not lead to absolute denial or pessimism. If it does, there will be no room for belief. Independence only implies the development of unshackled perception and will. You may reference to others as a guidance, but do not strive to become a duplicate. Find the answer on your own, and it will be as fascinating as Head Scholar Venator's nose."

Laughter echoed, and Simon happily joined in.

"Now putting aside the boring part, I ask you to find a small pebble and repeat after me. *Fides!*"

Nearly everyone was levitating their pebbles by the end of the session. Fortis was the first to succeed, and it appeared he had just as much talent as Rachel. The two of them were making *two* pebbles float while the rest of the class remained with one. Simon couldn't stop watching as Fortis revolved the stones around his head.

"Very good." Frao arrived at their table after helping the rest. "I heard you were a keen student in Wisdom, Ms. Fairburn. I might be questioning if the Blood Avowal was misinterpreted."

Rachel blushed and said in a tiny voice, "Thank you, Head Scholar Frao."

Frao beamed and turned to Fortis. "And Fortis, I can't but say I'm looking forward to your growth. I have your brother, Ami, doing exceedingly well in his studies as well."

"He's better than me, sir," said Fortis, grinning.

"Oh, I wouldn't assume so. Ami was an outstanding seedling, but I can see there is more depth to you. It is a shame what happened to your sight. It is incidents like these that I often question fate, but your effort despite the misfortune restores joy. You should be proud of yourself."

"Thank you," said Fortis merrily.

In the midst of the conversation, however, Simon was facing a predicament. One moment he had the touch, and the next thing the spell slipped away and left the rock motionless. He was feeling a bit miserable as he was comparably doing worse than Rachel and Fortis.

"I see you're facing difficulties, Simon," Frao said kindly.

"Yes, sir," said Simon, picking up his pebble again. "*Fides.*" The pebble quivered, but nothing more.

"Tell me, what do you think of Eldwoods?"

That was an odd question.

"I . . . uh . . . well, it's kind of new to me . . ."

"That also comes into account, but the question that I wanted to ask was not your impression. I am questioning your perception. What is this place to you, Mr. Dreamwalker? Is it a dimension of fantasies? Or are you still confused if it is a dream? Or maybe you're afraid it is a danger zone?"

Simon put his thinking cap back on. There was the hint, he just needed to match the puzzles, and he was good in putting things together. Was Frao asking how he was taking all this in? Well, there were plenty of different feelings. There were already people he wasn't getting along with. Yes, he once thought of things as just a dream, but that was way in the past. Everything was magical, so it was natural to become intrigued. The teachings in Eldwoods were abnormal, and since he was the only one who never knew of Eldwoods until a week ago, he was poor on the uptake. Plus, the shock of Mrs. White, Rachel, and Vel confessing they were secretly a part of the magic world for years still lingered somewhere in his guts.

There were countless more. But there was no helping it since they were all . . . all . . . all . . .

". . . *Real*." Simon said slowly. The pebble sprung off his hand and hit him in the forehead, leaving an angry red mark. Frao complimented the sudden achievement with a warm smile.

"Well done, Mr. Dreamwalker. That's a start," said Frao. "But safety first."

Unlike the rest of the days, *Introduction to Wrangling* had no morning and afternoon groups. It was a one big collaboration of all the seedlings, and it was to take place at the forest grounds outside of Eldwoods. For those who knew what was coming, there were mixed opinions about it. Some were eagerly leaving the breakfast feast early for the forest. Others were not so enthusiastic and took their time. It was here that Simon first noticed a difference between Rachel and Fortis.

"I wonder what it's going to be like," said Fortis covetously. "Ami told me it's his favorite part of the week. To wrangle."

Rachel scowled. "I just don't understand why we should be catching animals when we can just study the ones professionals have caught. It's not like *all* of us are going to go out there to catch creatures."

"It's important. There were times when Eldwoods had to deploy wranglers from all around the world to revert an outbreak. Besides, it's mandatory, since everybody is required to wrangle at wrangling season."

"Studying them first in a controlled environment will prepare us better than throwing us out there to catch animals."

"Either way, it looks like we're going out," Simon interrupted, annoyed that they were speaking over him as he was consuming his pie. "So wranglers catch magical creatures. You know what kind?"

Rachel finished her juice and said, "There are about a two thousand species that inherit magical properties naturally. Most aren't visible to Devolvers, but they still require some kind of animal control to keep them away from the Devolver population. Don't want unexplained accidents."

"Are they big?" asked Simon nervously. He had seen creatures the size of cars in Nocville, before, and he could hardly imagine himself hunting them without a sword or an axe.

Fortis shook his head. "No, not the big ones. We'll start with something small. I'll probably sit at the sideline. I can't even catch a fly."

"I really don't get it why we aren't told about these things beforehand," said Rachel crossly. "It just makes more sense that way."

"*Quarter before your session, sir.*" Chrone the pocket watch shouted out from the inside pocket.

"Thanks," said Fortis, getting his cane. "Let's go. It won't be a short walk."

The three of them strode out of the main entrance. It was a hot, sunny day, even though they were in the midst of mountains and high altitude. At the south entrance to the forest, seedlings were already huddled in one big circle. Along the path, Simon heard excited chatters from the Aro and Uro Clearmen.

"I bet they'll give us something big," said Uro, almost shouting. "Like a *knuckle boar* or an *imp*."

"Like they'd give us that from the start," retorted Aro as she shook her head. "Probably something small and weak, like *elwets*."

"What's that?" asked Simon.

Brendon Oathrun, who was dallying from behind, shuddered as he spoke anxiously, "Elwets are dangerous. They have steel beaks that can pierce doors and even pots. My uncle tried to get rid of one when it came near his house. Pecked through the door and nearly got his eye . . ."

"They're *chicken*, Brendon. Chicken! All you have to do is grab them by the neck," said Uro, laughing.

"It's not funny!" said Brendon desperately, shocked that none of them were concerned. "They can really get you! My grandfather —"

"Gather up, lads!" The captain of the Explorer, who was towering over all the seedlings, boomed across the woodlands. "It's about to begin! Shake a leg, all of you over there!"

Since Fortis was not so agile due to newer environments, the trio made it to the sight last. On the perimeter of the forest, Simon spotted a few wardens stationed outside. Their eyes glinted as their cloaks did not even ripple. Simon hardly welcomed them. The rest of the seedlings appeared to share his discomfort, apart from Magnus and the Bloods; they seemed hardly bothered by their presence.

"Don't mind the wardens. They're just there drifting about in case there's trouble, but you won't have to worry about that today. Now, cutting to the chase," the captain rubbed his hands together. "How many of your parents are wranglers?"

About one third of the class raised their hands. Simon and Fortis kept their arms down. Magnus seemed to think he was not obliged to answer any questions.

"Good, good, more than I expected!" barked the captain, waving merrily. "Well, you know why you're here, but I'll be telling you again. I'm the captain of the Explorer, Captain Shark, and wrangling is what you're here for. Not all of you will be going about the world. You'll diverge into more sophisticated majors, like scholars, engineers, remedists, monstrologists, physicians, whatever you have in mind. But wrangling is the basics. It's a lot of sweat and blood, but there's nothing like it. You got to experience it. You got to learn. Wrangling will always be your prime objective, so you'd better learn it good."

The seedlings shuffled their feet eagerly. Many of them already shared the same excitement Ami had talked about. The Clearmen siblings and Jamey Downriver were exceptionally restless. Rachel, Brendon, and Claire Sharpcliff were amongst the few that showed opposite opinions.

"But instead of solemn, boring lectures," roared Captain Shark merrily, "you lot will be wrangling *wolpertingers* today!" He moved his foot off of a small cage that he had concealed with a cloth. He pulled the concealment off and revealed the animal within. "These little rascals are squirrels, but not your usual kinds you see at home."

Simon could see what he meant. The wolpertinger, twice as big as any normal squirrel, had tiny horns that were big as Simon's thumb and feathered wings. It scuttled in its cage, frantically scrutinizing the crowd in alarm.

"Now these folks can give you a nasty punch if you don't watch for their horns, but you can't miss it if you have your eyes on them. Their natural ground dwellers, like marmots. But they can climb trees, and they're one hell of a glider. Your best chances are to make a team and drive it to an ambush. You can try to sneak up on it, but it has acute hearing senses and good speed." The captain pointed at the river. "The wrangling ground is set up to be two miles in diameter, within the riverbank. It will give you plenty of space to wrangle, and enough wolpertingers have been set loose for you lot to chase around. You'll be learning how to skin some dead ones after lunch."

Disgusted faces formed at the last sentence. Evidently most of the seedlings wished not to skin a wolpertinger. Claire Sharpcliff made a revolted *"Ew . . ."* The Clearmens, whatever the captain said, seemed to worship his words with joy.

"Better get moving, lads!" said Captain Shark. "And you're not killing them, your catching them!" Then he pointed at Fortis. "You, lad, you can stay with me."

Simon looked at Fortis. Fortis grinned and yelled back, "I'll go along. I promise I won't make trouble."

"Suit yourself, mate, but don't go straggling off on your own," said the captain. "Go in, already! Wrangling session starts now!"

The seedlings rushed into the wrangling grounds, some picking up sticks and brandishing it like swords. Simon and Rachel led Fortis after them, where the shade was so thick Simon immediately stopped perspiring.

"Bet I can catch one faster than you," said Aro, teasing her brother as she dashed off.

"I bet you won't catch anything," taunted Uro, running after his sister.

Jamey Downriver looked like he was exceptionally aware on how to catch wolpertingers. Rubbing beads of small droppings between his fingers, he yelled out, "Brendon, come on! They're still warm. One's near!"

"Wait," called Brendon weakly. His eyes were bloodshot, and he kept clearing his nose in a piece of handkerchief. "I've got allergies. Wait!" He went after Jamey, but fell into a bramble as he tripped on his shoes. From there, out came a wolpertinger, frightened and alarmed from the abrupt intrusion.

"Ew!" cried Claire Sharpcliff, backing off. The rest of the seedlings, however, went after it, and Roth Mayberry cried, "GET IT!"

A horde of children chased after the poor thing. Soon there were only four people left: Simon, Rachel, Fortis, and Mary Shyhand.

"Feels nice in here," Fortis remarked pleasantly. "Would've hated staying behind in the sun."

"Yeah," said Simon, loosening the neckpiece on his Pupil's Cloak for the coolness to seep in faster. "We got to find these wolterpingers."

"Wolpertinger, Simon," Rachel corrected testily. She walked over a giant root and bristled, "Ugh, I'm not fit for any wrangling. I'd prefer —"

"Studying a captive one, yeah, I get it," Simon cut across, turning right. "Come on, we've got to get away from everyone. We'd probably scare everything away."

Mary looked lost, wondering if she should stand there or join the trio. Rachel quickly read Mary's dilemma and approached her kindly. "Mary?" she asked. "Do you want to join us? It'll be better if four of us work together."

Mary shyly looked at Rachel to Simon. Simon nodded and said, "Yeah, that's a better idea."

After a hesitant pause, Mary squeaked, "Okay."

The four of them headed west, the opposite direction from where the crowd ran off to. The forest was peaceful and vast. Simon never smelled fresher air. The thicket of leaves was impervious against light no matter where they went. Simon weirdly felt at ease. The whole scenery was giving him a nostalgic vibe. Why was that?

"Are your parents wranglers?" asked Rachel kindly.

Mary shook her head. "No. They're . . . teachers . . ." she mumbled, twiddling her fingers.

"That's nice," said Rachel encouragingly. "They must be thrilled you're going to be a wrangler."

Mary nodded. She nearly tripped on her cloak, which was a bit too long for her tiny features, and bumped into Fortis. Rachel held Fortis steady as she asked, "Are you two alright?"

"Yeah, no sweat," said Fortis, but it seemed he was having some problems with the uneven ground and obstacles. Mary quickly apologized, "I'm sorry!"

"I take my word back. Making it four hardly helps," muttered Simon. The footsteps halted, and Simon turned. Mary was looking at her feet, looking guilty and hurt. Rachel was leering at him with pointed, ruthless eyes. Fortis was almost sneering at Simon, shaking his head in sympathetic disbelief. "No, I meant — not because you were loud or anything! Just that we weren't — making any — not finding any —"

But Mary's mood, and whatever confidence she had, was shot down. Rachel mouthed, "*Boys!*" as she scuttled next to Mary. "He wasn't carping, Mary. Don't worry."

Fortis inched closer until he felt Simon's shoes with his cane. "That was horrible timing," he said, resisting the urge to laugh.

Foreseeing it would take time before the shock would wear off, Simon concluded the best way to remedy this situation was to catch a wolpertinger as quickly as possible and prove his statement wrong. "I'll go on higher ground," said Simon enthusiastically (Fortis snorted irresistibly). He found a protruding boulder and said, "There. I can get up that and see if anything's moving."

"Wait, what about us?" said Rachel, still patting Mary.

"Wait here. Don't make a sound. Just stay low until I come back."

Simon went ahead, fueled from the notion he should make amendments. At the base, Simon found small grooves. He hooked his fingers in them and started climbing. It wasn't so bad, since he always hiked to school in Nocville. He reached the top after a couple minutes of strife and he wiped his face dry as he caught his breath. He could see Rachel, Fortis, and Mary making their way to a nearby tree. Simon scanned the area. He looked for movements, or mismatching patterns. This was a game he was good at, since he was accustomed to mountains and forests. He waited, breath quenched and eyes peeled.

As he gazed further astray from his party, Simon caught movement. He got even lower against the rock and leaned to his right for a better view. In the midst of low brambles and pile of leaves, there was a wolpertinger, tail quivering as it heard Rachel's quiet words of comfort. It wasn't big as the one they were shown during the captain's lecture. It was tiny. A baby.

Simon frantically waved at Rachel. She spotted him and shut her mouth. Simon mouthed, "Wolpertinger!" and pointed. Rachel craned her neck. She barely managed to see it. The wolpertinger twitched its ears, perplexed to the sudden absence of human voice. Nothing moved. The wolpertinger took a few steps deeper into its twiggy protection before resuming its feast. Simon didn't relax, however. They spotted a wolpertinger alright, but the question was how to catch it. Climbing down would only produce sound again and scare off the animal. He couldn't shout orders to his party. Maybe magic could help, but he had learned nothing particularly useful in catching game. What a dilemma.

He looked back at the others. Rachel had her eyes fixed on the wolpertinger, but her mouth was close to Fortis, breathing inaudible words into his ears. Fortis listened very closely, face screwed in concentration. Simon was curious what kind of plan she was scheming. A sudden grin spread from Fortis's face. Fortis raised his hands and breathed the incantation. A few stones came up from the ground. Rachel whispered further instructions, guiding Fortis how far and low the stones needed placing. The young wolpertinger was busily munching leaves and grass.

Simon finally came to discern what was at plan. He waved again, catching Rachel's attention. He pointed at the wolpertinger, dragged his finger across until it indicated the trio, and then pointed at himself and made a sharp jab. "To you!" mouthed Simon. "To you, and I —!" Simon imitated a pounce. Rachel was quick with the uptake. She whispered to Fortis. Fortis nodded and rearranged the order of the stones. They were perfectly webbed, making a relatively straight path. Simon rechecked the arrangement. It was good. Simon gave a thumbs-up. Rachel mumbled. Fortis flicked his wrist. The stone just behind the wolpertinger dropped.

The wolpertinger sprinted forward; Simon began sliding down the opposite side of the boulder. Rachel gave swift commands, and the second stone dropped, and then the third, and then the fourth, leading the wolpertinger into a frantic linear sprint. Simon hit the ground and ran along the bushes, staying out of sight of the wolpertinger. It was getting close, only ten feet away from Rachel and Fortis. It was playing right into their hands. Putting all his strength in his legs, Simon jumped out to the clearing and dove at the creature. The wolpertinger, which had its wing spread during its run, managed to flap it once and lift off the ground. Simon's finger brushed the tail. He turned his body and rolled against his back, grunting a short, "Damn!" as he cursed his miscalculation. How did he forget about that? The captain specifically told them they were skilled gliders.

"Oh!"

Simon stood up. Mary, who seemed dumbfounded at her accomplishment, was holding the wolpertinger in her arms. The creature had apparently glided straight into her. The wolpertinger was deliriously kicking the air.

"Hold it, hold it!" gasped Simon, jumping over a root and joining up with the three.

"O-okay!" squeaked Mary, her hands tightening over the scruff of the animal's neck. The winged-horned-squirrel went into a calm trance.

"Whew," sighed Simon, dropping to his bottom.

"Success?" asked Fortis.

"Yeah," said Simon. "She caught it in midair."

"Well done, Mary!" praised Rachel. Clapping her hands. "See? I told you four was better than three. *You* did it, Mary! You did it!"

"I-I don't — don't —" Mary mumbled, stupidly staring at the frozen wolpertinger.

"Yep, you did it," said Simon, still shocked by turn of events. "Who would've thought —" Rachel gave a daring look, and Simon said, "— you'd — be — so good at catching stuff, eh?"

Mary blushed as she looked into innocent creature. "I did it . . ." she whispered, and she hugged the little thing tight in her arms like a stuffed doll.

"Let's get back," said Rachel, checking her watch. "It's almost time."

As it turned out, there were far more seedlings that failed in catching any wolpertingers. Jamey Downriver threw a very jealous look at the wolpertinger held in Mary's hands. Vel was the most successful; she had managed to capture two all by herself. Aemulus held his wolpertinger by the tail. Uro and Aro were also fruitful, but they were playing a rather horrible prank on their prize by tying it onto a stick and hanging it over their shoulders.

"Like it?" grunted Uro, proudly presenting his dirtied face and clothe.

"Animalistic," said Simon cheerfully. He noticed Brendon excusing himself and running off to Elder Tree. "What happened to him?"

"Remember the captain talking about getting attacked by a wolpertinger?" said Aro, consumed with disbelief. "It really did happen. Butted him right in the nose. Should've seen it. It was *marvelous*."

chapter fifteen ~~~~~~~~

Magnus's Proposal

Simon was acclimating to his new life by the third week in Eldwoods. The food was always plentiful and great. He was socializing with kids his age that, for the first time, had common goals and interest: Wrangling. Of course, most days involved learning Passion, Wisdom, Expression, and Belief, but the popular subject of all times was Introduction to Wrangling, closely followed by Belief. Captain Shark's most daring stories of past adventures were key aspects in winning the hearts of his audience. Seedlings couldn't help but spend the weekends at his ship, living the tales of capturing jackalopes, riding griffins, defeating minotaurs, and escaping from wyverns. Captain Shark's popularity pole grew to be indisputable amongst the kids.

Contrastingly, the opposite end of the pole was none other than Head Scholar Venator. His talent to discourage seedlings was a gift nobody in Eldwoods possessed. Pupils sighed when session started, and grimaced by the end of it. In Simon's session, only Magnus and Vel were spared of criticisms since they excelled on the subject beyond anybody could dare dream of. On the fifth week in Eldwoods, Magnus had produced a fine typhoon composed of tens of paper planes.

"It seems that at some cases," hissed Venator quietly, "predecessors can be much of a failure compared to his successors . . ." He shifted his attention to Mary, who was sitting right next to Simon. "And some are simply hopeless. I cannot express how relieved I am you were not designated to Expression."

Mary, who accomplished nothing in Expression over the past month, was at the verge of tears. Simon crushed his plane in his palms. He was getting tired of being compared.

"Leave us alone, would you?"

He could've been swearing in public. Planes that were levitating dropped as if they were shot down. Nervous glances shifted from Simon

to Venator. Venator did not remove his locked fingers under his extruded nose. His calm, implacable eyes narrowed.

"Leave you alone?"

"*Us* alone," said Simon loudly. Mary flushed and shrunk in size. "It's not like we're in your major. Why do you care if we suck or not?"

A few people gasped at his daring comment. Venator, in contrast, couldn't be any less surprised. He ticked a finger. "You will spend the upcoming weekend skinning wolpertingers over by the ship on the evenings. Captain Shark will be the one responsible to report your attendance. And on top of that, I expect you to fly your useless paper model a thirty yards off of the platform by next session."

"You can't do that," said Simon, outraged.

"I have all the authority to hand out punishment to pupils," said Venator dangerously. "And you are neither good nor bad; you are *problematic*. One more word of objection and you will remain here until lunch, along with two weeks' worth of skinning." Venator indicated the chair with his spidery finger and said softly, "Now, *sit*."

Simon leered at Venator with utmost distaste. When he slowly lowered himself into his chair, Venator snorted and addressed the class sharply, "Resume, or I will send *all* of you to do same."

The following Saturday, Simon was aided by Rachel and Fortis to accomplish his small feat. Nothing that they suggested seemed to click. The key, according to Rachel, was to fuse his irritation into the wind since it was the easiest emotion to portray. Fortis advised it was the *touch*, like his fingers were being magnetically repelled by an unseen force. None of these seemed to work for Simon. He was so angry he was unsure what emotions he was meddling with, and the magnetic force thing was just way too philosophical. The strangest part he couldn't get over was the absence of an incantation. Unlike *Passio*, *Sofia*, and *Fides*, nothing was said to command the wind.

"I've thought about that, too," said Fortis oddly. "Why aren't there incantations? Other majors have them."

"It's because technically, for all majors, you don't need to speak the words," Rachel explained.

"Don't need to? Then what is Passio? Were we talking gibberish this hold time?" asked Simon.

"No," sighed Rachel, shaking her head. "*Spells* exist to give the impression there are multiple ways to cast magic. The basics which are Passion, Wisdom, Expression, and Belief can be exercised without speaking the words."

"Still don't get it," muttered Simon.

"Master Dreamwalker."

Agilis intruded the unit. Simon asked, "Yes?"

"You have a guest," said Agilis. Behind him, Ami Goldstone waved into the room.

"Oh," said Rachel, beaming. "Hi, Ami! Come in!"

Ami stepped past the threshold. Agilis bowed and returned to his post.

"What's up?" asked Fortis.

"Nothing. Just wanted to check if you three were spending your time wisely," said Ami, leaning against the desk.

"Wisely, yes. Productively, no," muttered Simon miserably.

Ami laughed. "I could never get the hang of Expression. Good old Venator wouldn't even bother looking at me. Oh, and to answer your question, Simon, here's a better example. Spells are nothing more than names, really. Let's say I told you to think of an animal with a long neck. What would you think of?"

"Uh . . ." There was so many long-necked animals. "I don't know . . . a giraffe?"

"Good example, but let's say I said to think of an ostrich. Now what do you think of?"

"Ostrich," said Simon mechanically.

"There you go," said Ami. "It's just a name. *Passio* is fire, *Sofia* is water, and *Fides* is earth. Simple."

"But what about Expression?" asked Fortis curiously. "Wouldn't it work the same way?"

"*If* it had a visible characteristic," said Ami. "I can't catch or measure air, and it certainly doesn't need producing like fire. I'd say it's really a major where you have to feel things before you see it. It's only for the," Ami did a quote-and-quote gesture, "*talented* people."

"Talented?" asked Fortis strangely. "It's the first time you've come up with this."

Ami laughed very dryly. "I wouldn't want to talk about them even if it was my birthday. The pupils of Expression don't have a good relation with any of the majors. You noticed how little got into Expression at the Blood

Avowal?" The three nodded. "There you have it. They think taming the wind is the most advanced major compared to the rest. They especially look down on Belief. Think we have it easy with rocks and minerals. Easy to see and measure compared to air."

"That's absurd!" retorted Rachel, raving. "The Elds found all four to be equally valuable. People shouldn't discriminate just because their majors have delicate approaches than others!"

"Actually," said Ami, grinning rather regretfully, "It's been just like that for a long time, Rachel. Passion has always been competitive, both within and outside of their majors. Wisdom, as you'd well know, prides with knowledge and history. Expression frequently had the most skilled wranglers of all times. And Belief is . . . well, a bit queer, as you can tell from me and Fortis.

"You can't mix these people as if you're making a strawberry smoothie. Yeah, Eldwoods is a place *to be harmonious*, but that's a thin line to walk on. Look at you three already," said Ami, starting from Rachel. "You have completely different ways solving problems. Magnetic force, Fortis?" Ami laughed hard. "Talk about science fiction."

"Yeah," said Fortis, laughing along. "You have a point there."

"But Vel's not like what you say," said Rachel defensively. "She doesn't discriminate. She's nice!"

"There are some exceptions," said Ami, admitting Rachel's case. "I'll buy that. But most aren't so peaceful like you'd hope they'd be. For example," Ami grinned insightfully, "the Bloods, no?"

"Highly dislikable," agreed Fortis.

"Total d-bags," grunted Simon.

"Simon!" seethed Rachel, revolted at the choice of words.

"Can't blame him, Rachel," said Forits, spouting a hearty laugh at Simon's uncensored outburst. "They are what they are."

"Right you are," said Ami, pacing the room. "The Bloods, through most of history, have really strong beliefs that they're born great, and that's why they prefer Expression over other majors. *The path for the gifted*; that was the motto. That confidence was probably why Expression had more notable wranglers."

"So Magnus thinks he's *gifted*, huh," muttered Simon, remembering the moments when he spotted Magnus bullying Fortis. "Sure has an ego."

"Well, that might've changed," said Ami slowly. "Since you came along." He chinned at Simon.

"What?" Simon pointed at himself stupidly. "Why me?"

"Isn't it obvious, Simon?" said Rachel, hitting her forehead. "You took his fame away. He's jealous of you!"

"The mighty Bloods are always looked up to with awe and beatitude. But now they're second place of interest once a Philosopher made its return." Ami sneered. "It's a nice wakeup call for them. Their influence could be challenged."

"Challenge? Me?" said Simon doubtfully. "I don't even know how to fly a paper plane! What am I going to do, talk them to death?"

"Oh, Simon . . ." sighed Rachel, shaking her head.

"You remember the Blood Avowal?" said Ami. Simon nodded. "People were scrambling to take a good look at you. You know what I mean? You're like a dinosaur in the twenty first century. Wherever you go, they're gonna see you as the Philosopher, not Simon Dreamwalker. Everyone excluding a few," he graciously gestured the occupants of Simon's unit. "It hasn't happened yet, but a lot of people are going to start approaching you. Spare the seedlings and sproutlings; they're too young to see it. But from bloomings and up, you'll be a subject of fame. Everybody's going to want you. Everybody."

It was a surreal truth to accept, and a shocking point of perspective. Did he really take the spotlight from the Bloods to himself? If that was the case, he wasn't entirely certain if he wanted to keep it to himself. Existing to be liked; he could care less of how desirable he was. He came to Eldwoods to find a life free of past inflictions, and he was off to a good start with Rachel and Fortis by his side. No one was going to play him into their silly show.

"I'm off," said Simon, throwing the paper plane through his window. "Captain Shark's probably setting up dead wolpertingers."

Fortis grimaced. "You'd probably do better in skinning, wouldn't you, Rachel? Since your parents are doctors and all . . ."

"Oh, haha," said Rachel sarcastically, fuming in disgust as well. "Skinning doesn't have to do anything with doctors. And my parents aren't surgeons."

When Simon got out to the forest, he marched straight to the ship resting on the west side, where the mountain supported it nicely from tipping. Next to the anchor, Simon spotted the captain presenting a long, ancient bench with rows of dead wolpertingers. The wings were clipped off, and — thankfully — they were all gutted. The sailors from the Explorer were bagging dead remains of wolpertingers, muttering under their breaths as they examined each one to see if their conditions were valid for skinning.

"You there!" roared the captain, waving his giant arms. "You here for work?"

"Yes, captain!" yelled Simon, running to greet Captain Shark. Whatever punishment he was being forced to do, the captain's presence lightened his mood a little. "I'm here because —"

"You disrespected Head Scholar Venator, I heard," said Captain Shark, contorting his face and looming over Simon. When Simon cowered, the captain split a rowdy laugh and ruffled Simon's hair. "You're good, lad. It's natural for kids to be a bit rebellious!"

Simon smiled weakly and asked, "You're letting me go, sir?"

"No, lad," said Captain Shark fairly. "Punishment is punishment. You're skinning them lot. It's good work, too. On top of everything, you're a wrangler. You'll have to learn this stuff sooner or later." He stalked to the bench and tapped the surface. "Shake a leg, lad. There are plenty to skin."

And so, standing next to the captain, Simon went away skinning wolpertinger after wolpertinger. He followed the captain's lead by cutting a small part below the neck, putting a finger into the groove, and then tugging downwards in one powerful stroke. It wasn't so horrible. The skins peeled off pretty smoothly. Simon thought it came close to removing a sweaty rubber glove. But the hide dangling in his hand was not the most pleasant thing to look and be exhilarated about. He quickly chucked them onto the table.

"Simon, was it?" asked the captain.

"Yes, sir," said Simon, putting his knife down to flex his fingers.

"So you're the Philosopher everybody's been riled up about," said the captain. He winked. "How are you finding the place?"

"Alright," said Simon, picking up the next wolpertinger. "Didn't know there was a place like this. Where are we exactly?"

"Deep in the Great Cascades, disguised. Devolvers would never find it. Not unless they awaken."

"Did you awaken, too, sir?" asked Simon. "Did it hurt?"

"Awaken, yes," said the captain. "Hurt? No. You're talking about paroxysm, aren't you, lad? Doesn't happen too often. Dangerous happening. Normal awakenings are small, like bending forks or splashing water. Very minor things." He looked at Simon and asked, "How bad, mate?" Simon shook his head. "Hurt yourself?" asked the captain softly. Simon nodded this time. "Sorry to hear that. It's a one in a million chance, paroxysm."

"Yeah," said Simon gloomily, looking at his hands. Not a scar showed what pain he went through that night.

"Chin up, lad," said the captain, doing a perfect peel and laying down the hide. "It means you have great potential. One that would never come to see in a life time. Several lifetimes. Heck, not even Bloods get a backlash. You just need to know how to control that beast inside of you, now." Captain Shark pointed at Simon's chest. "You're going to be a wrangler nobody's ever seen before. I guarantee you."

That was quite a boost in moral. Simon thanked the captain. "Thank you, sir."

Captain Shark winked and perfectly skinned another wolpertinger. The sun dipped into the mountain ranges, painting the sky red. A flock of geese formed a sharp V-formation as they continued their migration south. Was it already reaching that time of year? Simon finished skinning the last wolpertinger and placed the knife on the table. When he checked behind, however, there were still ten of them sprawled on the ground, and they were in terrible shape. The sailors were still examining them, filling a third bag of dead wolpertingers.

"What're those?" asked Simon, pointing at the carcasses. "How come they're all ripped apart?"

"That's what we're trying to investigate, lad," said Captain Shark, stooping over the dead creatures. "Something's hunting them down. And the funny part its, only their hearts are missing. Those few that you skinned, they're the lucky ones."

"Lucky?" Simon asked quietly.

"Well, spared from a savage death," Captain Shark explained.

"What did this?" asked Simon.

"Not a clue, lad. Wolpertingers are natural prey, but eating only the heart . . . That's something I'll have to look through some records." The captain leered into the forest. "Something's out there. Something bad." He grimaced darkly. Simon stood there, wondering if he should just stand there next to the captain. When Captain Shark recollected himself and spotted Simon lingering, he hitched away the scowl and grinned broadly. "Don't worry yourself, mate. You go on in, now. Good work!"

Simon grinned. "Okay. Bye, captain!" But once he turned away and headed to Eldwoods, his smile faded as he glanced into the forest. Now that the captain mentioned it, he wasn't feeling the refreshing pleasantry he usually received. It felt like . . . something had intruded the peace of Eldwoods.

"Simon?"

Simon whipped about. Mary was standing by a tree, her Pupil's Cloak dirtied around the hems. Her hair was untidy as well, either windswept or discorded from branches.

"Oh," said Simon. "Hi, Mary."

"Hello," she said in a tiny voice. "Where are you going?"

"Back inside," said Simon. "Finished skinning for tonight."

Mary blushed and dropped her head. She mumbled as she twiddled her fingers. "Thank you, for standing up for me on Thursday . . ." She looked Simon in the eye. "N-nobody's stood up for me like that."

"No sweat," said Simon, grinning back. "Hey, if you need help, you can ask, okay?" With an afterthought, he added, "Can't tell how much help I can be in Expression, though."

Mary made a restrained giggle. "Thank you." She scuttled past Simon, head bowed as she did everything possible to conceal her blushes.

Simon sighed. Maybe he was just imagining things. There was no possible way danger could be roaming the forest. They had wardens — despite their unsettling presence — safe guarding the place. The captain was on the watch, too. Even if there was danger, the Governors were present. Cybele was present. Wasn't the Tale of Elds full of their undisputed power?

Simon snorted and turned. Out in the distance, he spotted Head Warden staring into the thicket of woods. He appeared to be conversing with his wardens, since there were shadowed movements behind the trees. The Head Warden nodded and looked about, and then his eyes found Simon. They stared for a second, and then Head Warden stalked away into the woods. Yes, he was an unpleasant man, but he sure looked like he could scare off anything. And yes, his wardens looked equally unbreakable. And yes, Simon was convinced his mind was just playing a silly game on him. Maybe a hot bath before sleep would ease his mind.

"Dreamboy."

That was by far the least favorable voice he wanted to hear right now. Magnus was cutting through the woods with his followers, Lent the pudgy, Vass the tall, Latus the odd, and Celsis the accented. They walked with their usual proud, dignified demeanor. When they came, Magnus halted.

"Enjoying your time?" seethed Magnus gleefully.

"What do you want?" muttered Simon ungratefully.

Magnus smirked and chinned away from Eldwoods. "Your time. How about a chat?"

"Not interested," said Simon, striding rightwards.

"Hey, now," said Magnus pleasantly. Vass and Celsis stepped before Simon and blocked his path. "Temper, temper. I'm striking a deal with you. A *pro-po-si-tion*. You won't regret it." Magnus spread his arms as a sign of peace. "What say you? Care to hear me out?"

Simon wasn't really in the mood. But, he was also curious why Magnus was being so persistent to speak with him. What was this proposition? What could he possibly offer to bargain with Simon?

"Say it here," said Simon, not really inclined to go into the forest after a couple of hours of skinning wolpertingers.

"Take a chance, would you?" said Magnus, strolling into the forest blissfully. "This way."

Simon really preferred to return to his unit, but Vass and Celsis looked quite stubborn to take him along. Hoping it would be brief, Simon followed Magnus.

There were obviously some varying factors to the forest compared to the wrangling grounds. The grass was untidy and wild, and treading straight was never an option. It was obvious the wrangling ground was tended for the pupil's convenience. Simon couldn't imagine how he would wrangle in this kind of environment. He abruptly thought that it was dangerous to be alone in the forest. What if a tiger came out? Well, tiger's didn't live in the cascades. Bears, perhaps? What would he do then?

"Hey." Magnus was facing him. Simon was so absorbed to his surrounding he briefly forgot he was not alone. The trees that towered like sky scrapers, the dim illumination, the giant roots; something felt very nostalgic right now. "Dreamboy." Magnus snapped his fingers. "Wake up."

"What is it, just spit it out," said Simon irritably, still intrigued to the forest.

Magnus snorted. Vass, Latus, and Celsis stationed themselves in a circle and set up a perimeter. Lent went to Magnus's side, his pudgy face sweating already from the walk. Taking no particular notice of Lent, Magnus paced from tree to tree.

"You know, the Tale of Eldwoods is pretty fun, don't you think?" said Magnus softly. "There were times when I asked, what *really* happened? I mean, let's face it. The Philosophers *made* the Runes. They waged war against the Governors prior to Eldwoods, and it was they who dove into Hollow to save that *Lady* Cybele."

His words were loaded with distrust and animus. This was odd. Simon would've thought his pride and confidence came from the notion his ancestors were the ones that saved the world from collapsing. Instead, he sounded like he had the short end of the stick.

"The Philosophers were *powerful*. They knew and did stuff nobody could even imagine. Everything we have, we do, and it all came from the Philosophers. And what did the others do? Make a giant tree? Take the Runes to govern? And what about in The Plight? It was the Philosophers that got rid of Hollow. It wasn't the all-powerful Governors, the celestial Primals. It was the Philosophers."

Simon couldn't tell where this conversation was going to. Lents, Vass, and Celsis were nodding in solemn unison. Latus had a very hard look between his eyes. What did all of them have in mind?

"If that's all you have to say, I'm going," said Simon.

Magnus's eyes glinted as he ceased and turned to Simon. "Do you really believe it? That after all they accomplished, the Philosophers would just *die* and never come back? You know what I think?" Magnus pointed at the Elder Tree. "*They feared them.* The Primals, Governors; they knew the Philosophers were better off, more powerful than any Eld. It makes perfect sense that they'd let the Philosophers go on a suicide mission." Magnus stomped on a dry branch and crushed it rather ferociously. "They needed to get rid of competition. You see? Without the Philosophers, the Primals could brainwash the Governors to worship them, since they could *heal* the lands. But the Philosophers? No, they were stronger. If the Philosophers realized how things were going to run, nobody would have been able to stop them."

Magnus pointed at Simon. "And that's what they're doing to you. You really want to become their little pet? Once they're done with you, you'll be doing everything they say." He shook his head and sneered. "But not the Bloods; no, we're different. We know they're just trying to tame us. And they have righteous tasks like contain the creatures, protect the Devolvers. Let me tell this: the Devolvers, they *chose* to turn away from magic. All this power, all this knowledge, they ran away from it. Why do we have to protect *them*?

"The Bloods know there could be a future without restrictions. A *better* future. We're related by blood, you and I. Distant cousins. Did you know?" Simon didn't say anything, and Magnus took that sign as a yes. "The Bloods have plans. They know what the future should be like." He pushed his cloak open and offered a hand. "Join us. You have a place in the Bloods. Not with those lesser families you hang out with. Those Fairburns, or *Blindstone*."

Magnus made a nasty sneer. "Or that *Mutt*, Velox Windly. No, she's definitely someone to avoid. Don't waste your time with them. Join the Blood. You're one of us."

Simon wasn't buying this. It was so full of hate and distaste. Why was Magnus telling him this so freely? Did he really think he'd take this kind of rant at heart?

"Sorry, but I don't want to be a part of your *future*," said Simon shortly, leaving the hand hanging. "Go on building your pretty future. I like who I hang out with. So stop spying on me, would you?"

Magnus's face went furious after that last statement. The Celsis clicked his tongue. Vass seemed to be grinding his knuckles into his palm. Lent edged closer to Magnus and began whispering into his ears frantically. Latus watched Simon, not possibly believing the offer was rejected.

"I'm leaving," said Simon, and he turned away from Magnus.

"I smelllllllllll . . ."

Simon stopped. He stared at Celsis. Then at Vass. Both had their mouths shut, intercepting him, but in no mood to talk. He could hear Lent still talking away under his breath, but that was not the voice he had just heard. Latus was mute and unresponsive.

"The blood . . . So puuuuuurrrrrreeeeeee . . ."

"Better think through about this, Dreamboy," said Magnus quietly, his voice thin as a whistle. "You're throwing aside a great opportunity."

Simon ignored that comment and strained his ears. That voice, crippling and blood chilling, was carried by the wind ever so lightly. It wasn't odd that Magnus or any of the Bloods were hearing what Simon was.

"So pure . . . for my baby . . . for my baby . . ."

"Told you, Mag," growled Vass, looming over Simon. "He'll never be a true Philosopher."

"Expected, isn't it?" said Celsis, brushing off a leaf from his shoulder delicately. "You can see it already that he's sided with that loser of a Primal."

"*Shh*," said Simon, looking past Vass.

Vass looked like he was ready to swing a fist. "What did you say?"

"Ease off, Vass," said Celsis casually. "Won't want to show the newbie something so unsightly." He pointed at Latus, who didn't appear too concerned about what actions might be taken. "Our fathers don't know we're doing this. Leave a mark, and it'll show we disobeyed them."

Magnus seemed to have subdued his anger, and his eyes reverted back to their usual state, misty and impenetrable. He still had the malicious mask on, however. Magnus moved closer and pulled Simon around. "You'll come to regret this moment. No use crawling back to us once the Bloods get their glory back."

"I don't care about your glory," snarled Simon, still searching. "Just shut up for a moment."

"What did you —?"

"Come to me . . ."

Everyone froze. It was much closer. Maybe too close, enough for everyone to hear. Simon got a very bad vibe about this. That ominous suspicion about the forest came back.

Scrape. Scrape. Scrape.

"What's that sound?" said Lent, gradually inching between Magnus and Simon for protection. "What is it? Is something out there?"

"You have dung for brains!" whispered Celsis, looking around in alarm. "Of course, there's something!"

"It can't be anything dangerous," said Vass loudly, but his domineering frown was long gone, and he was taking tiny steps backwards.

Magnus was also moving away from trees. With the visibility so low now, that confident face was hidden beneath a fresh layer of shaky anxiety. "Anyone there!" he yelled, his voice slightly trembling.

"The blood . . . I need it . . . my precious blood . . ."

Scrape. Scrape.

"If you're a warden, come out!" Magnus took a giant step back. "My father's Ladon Trueblood! You're messing with the wrong people!"

"You're giving us away," breathed Latus, looking about.

"He gave us away a long time ago," muttered Simon.

"*Blood . . .*" The voice underwent a savage transition. Simon could literally feel his blood curdle. "*Blood . . . for Bloods . . . Blood for Bloods . . .*" It went silent for a moment. "*But no . . .*" Scrape. Simon whipped to his left. Scrape. To the right. Scrape. Dead ahead. "*My blood . . . the blood of an Eld . . .*"

"Show yourself!" yelled Magnus, mustering false courage out of his trepidation. "Who's there! I'm a Blood, I'm —"

Simon spotted something. Just a few yards up ahead, there was a shadow that was darker than the ones casted by the trees. It wasn't corresponding to the environment. Simon squinted. One of the roots shifted ever slightly. It was definitely a separate, living extension, most likely a tail of some reptilian nature. Up behind the trunk, a sickening yellow eye unveiled itself. It pointed directly at Simon, and the voice returned speaking, "*Young blood . . . Eld blood . . .*"

"Run," whispered Simon, echoing what first came to thought.

"What?"

"My blood . . . MY BLOOOOOOOOOOOOOOD!!!!!!"

"RUN!" yelled Simon.

They bolted, Simon barely glimpsing at a huge serpentine body uncoil itself from the tree. Magnus pushed Celsis aside and took first place in the escape. Simon beat down branches and brambles as he heard the earsplitting cry of, "BLOOD! ELD'S BLOOD! COME TO MEEEEE!" Simon cut his eye as he hit a lower branch. He jumped through a two trees rooted tightly together, and he felt a claw slash at his cloak. A good chunk of it got torn off.

"ARGH!" screamed the monster as it failed to worm through the tight crease.

Go, go, go, go! Simon urged himself desperately. Whatever that was, Simon didn't dare ask why at the moment. "Captain!" he yelled. "*Captain!*"

Simon heard a thud a few feet ahead. He broke through a wall of leaves and found Lent on his belly, sweating and huffing as if he was already dying. "M-Magnus!" he squealed. "Come back! Don't leave me here!"

Simon skidded to a halt and groped Lent's arm. "Get up!" He pulled Lent with all his might. "Up!"

Lent wheezed as he teetered. He looked in no shape to run. "I don't want to die. I don't want to die!"

"Shut up," snarled Simon, supporting Lent. Why was this boy so absurdly heavy? He must've been hogging on cows a few minutes ago. "Shut up and run. We have to get to the captain." He yelled, "Captain! Captain Shark!"

The horrible scream came from behind. Simon looked back. All he saw was a giant hand stretching out for his face. During that brief moment of terror, Simon made out the dirtied claws that were mostly broken. Skin was pale blue, and it looked more dead than alive.

"MIIIIINNNNNNEEEEEE!!!!!!"

Simon summoned the nerves to jump back, pulling his head downwards as much as possible. The claws ripped through his cloak and sliced a deep gash into his right shoulder. The monster of deadly intent crash-landed, lashing its serpentine tail. Simon got the brunt of the force after throwing Lent out of the way. The tail sent him flying into the air until he hit a tree. His head ached horribly. None of his body parts seemed to understand his command.

"My food..." A pair of irresistibly deranged eyes leered at him. The monster was slithering its way towards Simon, hands ready to gauge holes into him. "*My baby's food. Come here, little thing. You will be a special additive to my heart!*"

The monster lunged forward. Simon raised his arms to brace for impact, though knowing all too well it was the end of everything.

"AAAAAAAAAAHHHHHHHHH!"

Agonized scream stabbed Simon's eardrums, and the monster rampaged past him as it cleaved the ground with its scaly tail. Simon saw a fiery cataclysm blast across the woods, gracefully managing to avoid Simon by an inch. When it died, Simon saw a tiny streak skid next to him.

"Boy!"

Simon could've cried his relief. Ignis crouched by his side, facing the heinous monster with serrated claws and razor-sharp fangs.

"Ignis," mumbled Simon hoarsely.

Ignis spitted viciously. The monster was shrieking in outrage. Its tail had angry burn marks, and some places were still melting down to the inner flesh.

"No! My food! I must have it! Out of the way!"

It dove again. Something sharp whistled past Simon's ears. He looked around and found Terram scrambling towards them. She rattled her back, and another shower of thick, knifelike thorns sniped forward.

"Away, snake!" Terram screamed, and Simon ducked. The thorns pierced through the scaly tail. Blood painted the ground red.

"NO! NOOOOOO! MY BLOOD!"

The monster rampaged into the dim forest, splatters of blood soaking the dirt, grass, and trees. Simon went loose and dropped his head onto the ground. He puked, but what came out was a stinging pool of stomach acid.

"Boy," growled Ignis urgently. "Are you hurt? Let me see!"

"I'm . . . fine . . ." Simon feebly spat excess goo out of his mouth. An unexplainable numbing sensation was engulfing him. His teeth clattered as foam expelled. "I'm — m — m —!" What was happening? The already dark forest was swimming into a deeper abyss.

"SIIIIIMMMMMMOOOOOOONNNNNN!!!!!!" Ventus came shooting from the sky. She had Aqua clutched in her talons in a dangerously odd angle. "What happened, Simon? What happened?!"

"Stop your fit and go inform Lady Cybele!" shouted Ignis immediately. "The boy needs the Remedial Master —!"

That was the end of it. Simon let slip his consciousness, drowning himself to the world unknown.

chapter sixteen ~~~~~~
Third Colloquy

She left. He stared at the door. How many years was it since her reappearance. She was always so mysterious, concealing her work no matter what. She was the most beautiful, but also terrifying.

"She came back, sir."

He nodded.

"Yes, for a minute."

"Did she say anything?"

He turned away from the door.

"His *heart* . . . endures till this day."

chapter seventeen ~~~~~~
Gorgon

Simon's eyes flickered. With immense strife, he pulled his lids open. Blinding light made him fume. He felt extremely rusty, like an old car that was having its first test run in decades. Something was pressing his forearm. Simon managed to crane his neck above his chest. Rachel's head was resting upon the blanket, snoozing in peace. Simon spotted a dark patches stretching below her eyes.

"Oh, you've finally awoke." A woman loomed over them. Her hair was shoulder length and nicely combed. She had an intellectual look on her, and her glasses were framed and square. "It's a safe recovery, but you should rest more."

Simon knew the woman. She was once a neighbor.

"Mrs. Fairburn?"

Mrs. Remei Fairburn beamed back at him as she finished jotting down a few lines on her clipboard. "Hello, Simon. It's our first time meeting *properly*, isn't it?"

Simon wasn't finding the *proper* words to express his bewilderment. He let Mrs. Fairburn check his pulse and feel his forehead, and all that came out from his lips were, "How long was I out?"

Mrs. Fairburn undid the buttons and took a look at Simon's shoulder. The injury was covered in bandages. By the smell of bitter ginseng, Simon knew it had to be the same kind remedial bandages he used to have back in Nocville, the night of his awakening.

"Three weeks and five days," said Mrs. Fairburn, undoing the bandages and examining the wound.

Three weeks and five days?! Simon couldn't believe it. "Seriously?" he croaked hoarsely.

Mrs. Fairburn offered him a glass of water as she continued to look into the gash. "Quite serious," she muttered. "We were lucky you were strong. Gorgon venom is . . . challenging to remedy. But don't worry yourself now," she said, smiling kindly. "An antidote was prescribed."

Rachel jerked awake. She rubbed her eyes haggardly and mumbled, "Mom?"

"Yes," said Mrs. Fairburn. "You'll be surprised whose up and awake."

Rachel turned to Simon, and then gasped so hard her hands did a weird flip. "*Simon!*" she squealed, and then she lunged herself on top of him before giving a neck-breaking hug. "Simon, oh, Simon!"

"R-Rachel," gagged Simon feebly, fearing he might fade out again. "Can't — can't breathe —!"

"Oh, oh," Rachel whimpered, realizing she was embracing him to his death. She wiped her tears, but immediately broke into a horrible sob and covered her face. "I thought you were going to — to —" She doubled up and then cried, "I thought you were going to die!" She hit her face into the bed, and Simon felt his elbow get crushed. Rachel's mental breakdown was evidently dangerous to any bystanders.

"I'm okay," said Simon through gritted teeth, doing his utmost best to smile over the pain. He heavily removed a hand from the blanket and patted her disfigured ponytail. "Be happy more, would you? I'm not in a deathbed."

"I'll fetch some potions from my cabinet," said Mrs. Fairburn. "Try not to injure the patient, Rachel."

Rachel lifted her head, but she was hiccupping on every heartbeat. She frantically dried her eyes and pressed them to ease the swelling. She barely managed to say, "O-o-o-ok-ay!"

Mrs. Fairburn closed the door. Simon liked how the ward became much more private, now. He asked, "How are you? And Fortis?"

"H-he's fine," gagged Rachel, managing to pull away her hands. "He went to his s-s-session. He'll be back after."

"Great," said Simon.

"No, it's not great!" Rachel said in a more collected voice. "A *gorgon* in Eldwoods, that's absurd! Simon, what happened exactly?"

"Gorgon?" asked Simon hoarsely, getting dried throat again.

"The thing that attacked you." Rachel was looking extremely grave and frightened. "They're dangerous monsters; classified wrangling subjects. They're not supposed to be here. The grounds are protected by Primal magic!"

"Not helping," said Simon, only remembering a serpent's tail, broken claws, and a pair of inhuman, putrid eyes that glinted in the dark. "Is it even something we catch? How would anybody face that without getting killed?"

"You're right," said Rachel. "They're not something wranglers catch. They're . . ." Rachel looked uncomfortable to express the truth. "*killed*. They use black magic; they maim you, and it's a risky procedure to reverse the effects. So they're usually avoided at most cases. Capturing one would be out of the question."

"Feel better already," muttered already, looking at his gash.

"But you're clean. Mom found an antidote just in time," said Rachel hastily. "They've been around for a long time, so remedists were able to study their curses. I've read about them in a couple of books. They're not exactly natural-born."

"You lost me again," said Simon.

"They're from Hollow," Rachel explained grimly. "Gorgons weren't always heinous, though. Before they became what they are, they were gifted with godlike beauty. Oh, but terrible, all the same. They used black magic to defile all the lands."

"And one of those things is in Eldwoods," grumbled Simon, rubbing his forehead. "Can't imagine that being good."

"Of course it isn't good, Simon!" snapped Rachel exasperatedly. "You almost died!"

"Yeah," said Simon. He heard the dreadful voice echo in his head again. "Blood for Bloods . . . Blood of Elds . . . Heart . . . Baby . . ." Simon muttered under his breath. "Blood for Bloods . . ."

"What?" asked Rachel, barely catching that last bit.

"No," said Simon, shaking his head. "Just something that thing said. It kept repeating stuff, like it was a song." The door opened. Simon said quickly, "We'll talk about it later."

Mrs. Fairburn came in with a cup of lime potion and an acupuncture needle.

"Drink this," she said, handing the cup over.

Simon took a first sip, and then frowned as his eyes watered. It was extremely sour. "What is it?" he asked.

"Saps from the plant *eatless*, distilled with sleeping agents," said Mrs. Fairburn. She added after noticing Simon's doubtful look by the name, "Don't let the name fool you. It helps the blood circulate and counteracts most poisons."

Simon finished the contents with three massive gulps that made his throat contract. He was immediately feeling the drowsy effects take control. He saw Mrs. Fairburn roll up his sleeve to place the needle. "An' waz zat?" said Simon, each second dragging him into a blurry haze.

"A needle from mandrake," said Mrs. Fairburn. Her voice already seemed distant. "It'll stimulate your immune system as —"

The rest of the words drowned until Simon no longer heard anything.

chapter eighteen ~~~~~~
Scholar Sciens

It turned out Simon was told to stay in the medical bay for another three weeks. Mrs. Fairburn wished to examine his condition, despite Simon's protest, to affirm he was fit for a normal life again. Simon found this very annoying. Being stuck in a closed ward with nothing to do was driving him nuts. Heck, he was pacing most of the times. He even thought about jumping out of the window for freedom, although he grimly acknowledged that was a crazy idea.

Hence, he spent his time reading books about gorgons. Rachel was kind enough to stop by every night and join his boring session of reading. However, the curfew had been moved to eight due to the gorgon incident, thus her company was limited.

"The study of eternal youth has always been a subject of interest. The most famous practice of this subject was exercised by gorgons of Hollow. Gorgons were once beings of unnatural beauty, and their obsession to groom their offspring more glamorous than others was well known. But their most well-known feature divulged consuming blood of their victims, a ritualistic tradition of their race in belief they will stay beautiful and young for eternity. It was later discovered by Scholar Sciens, however, that youth was not obtained through any type of blood consumption. The only accountable youth that remained eternal were the Elds.

"Due to their reptilian features, gorgons are partially cold-blooded and go into hibernation over late autumn and winter seasons. Gorgons perform a unique habit of shedding their skin before hibernation by coiling —

"Really," groaned Simon, throwing down the book and rumpling his hair. "I don't need biology lessons."

"You know, if you just studied like that in Nocville," she said, crouching on his bed as she slowly flipped through pages, "you would've gotten perfect grades." She seemed to think good of Simon's enthusiasm for reading, and she often encouraged him to continue this habit. Simon, on

the contrary, only read as long there was the word 'gorgon' written in the book, and he was fond to detach himself from any other books.

"I don't have memory banks like you, Rachel," said Simon, yawning spectacularly. "I hate books."

"You seem to enjoy them, now," she said.

"Not by a long shot," said Simon, leaning back. "It's a time killer, really."

Knock, knock.

Fortis stood at the entrance with his sentry, Vigil, levitating behind him. "I'm back," said Fortis, holding a notebook under his cloak. "That's all, Vigil."

"I will await your return —"

"No," said Fortis stubbornly. "I'm staying here until nighttime. Don't wait for me."

Vigil looked ready to speak some objections, but in the end he bowed and flew off. Fortis grinned and took a seat by the bed. "Follows me all the time after that curfew. He thinks there might be a gorgon around every corner."

"It's their duty to keep us safe," said Rachel. "Of course they'd care."

"You're handling it well, though," said Simon, sitting up. "Has he gotten *ruthless*, yet?"

"The last three weeks, he's tried," said Fortis. "But I brushed him off. Like a pile of dusts." He and Simon laughed.

"So, did you get it?" asked Rachel eagerly.

Fortis passed the notebook to Simon, who was in equally enthusiastic to take a peak on this. "Yeah, Ami got everything about bloods. It took him a couple of recommendations, but he managed to look it up at the *Athenaeum*. But . . ." Fortis added as Simon opened the pages. "He didn't find much."

"Hmm . . ." Rachel rubbed her forehead. "Blood of Elds . . . highly sacred . . . uncertain stimulants . . . yes, yes, I know about these stuff already," she muttered as she got went to the rest of the pages and scanned with her fingers. "Wyvern blood, no . . . Kraken blood, ugh, god no . . . Heart of a Primal, no . . . no . . . no . . ." She abruptly stopped and raised the notebook. "Hey, now this is interesting."

"Found something good?" asked Fortis.

"What's it say?" Simon scooted next to her.

Rachel pointed out a paragraph and started reading, "During the Plight, gorgons were accounted to raid Governors' lands, mostly to consume blood of magical creatures. But at one point, they were successful in killing a weakened Governor and drink its blood. As a result, they were cursed; serpentine tail, and the rest deformed into the most heinous creature alive.

Their obsession eventually brought forth their own fate." Rachel then flipped forward and read a different paragraph. "Now look at this. "The blood of Elds was highly compatible to substitute one another. There were multiple accounts when, after a conflict, Governors drank the blood of Philosophers to replenish themselves. However," Rachel tapped each word as she spelled them out, **"any being less than an Eld cannot make practical usage of the blood of Elds.** Small dosages, however, may be processed to induce an unnaturally deep coma known as Deathwish. During this state, natural time does not apply to the victim, and they are preserved until the effects are treated by an antitoxin."

Rachel looked at Simon, fascinated. Simon knew what that look was and said, "Don't give me that. I'm not available for laceration."

"I don't know what to think about you," said Fortis, tapping his cane. "That Deathwish part . . . scary or fascinating, can't tell which one to pick."

"I'd prefer neither," said Simon. "I'm not about to prick my finger and start feeding people."

"Toxic blood . . . toxic blood . . ." muttered Rachel, still unsatisfied with something.

"Stop saying that," snapped Simon. "I'm not toxic."

"But it just doesn't fit!" Rachel burst out, flapping pages after pages. "Why would a gorgon want blood that wouldn't work on anything less than an Eld? It's counter intuitive. They suffered the consequences to know the effects."

"Rachel, we're not solving this problem," said Fortis. "The Governors, wardens, and wranglers are the ones who're going to find the gorgon."

"Yeah," said Simon, relieved Fortis was so kind to remind them. "I'm not looking forward for another death encounter."

"Oh, for crying out loud!" retorted Rachel, throwing down the note. "You really think it's going to be *that* optimistic? The gorgon already made it to Eldwoods with wardens and wranglers on constant patrol. What makes you think it won't be able to slip past them again?"

"If it *does* get through, it's Simon that's going to need worrying the most." Fortis thought for a second and added, "Or the Bloods, too."

"Yeah," Simon said quickly. "It said *blood for Bloods*. It sounded distracted for a moment when it heard Magnus."

"Argh," said Rachel impatiently, untying her ponytail in frustration. "All of this still isn't helping me. There's got to be a reason that we're not seeing." She shut the notebook and tucked it into her cloak. "It's not fair how pupils aren't allowed in the Athenaeum. I want to look at the Scholar's records. You can learn so much in there!"

"Yeah, courtesy of Head Scholar Frao," said Fortis. "He gave Ami access to the Athenaeum. But not the Scholar's section. That would've caused trouble."

The rest of the evening was spent with more books Rachel had sacked from the Pupil's Archive. When the sun set, however, Simon couldn't go on anymore. His eyes stung and drooped.

"Ten before eight," said Chrone's dreary voice from Fortis's pocket.

"Ugh, you guys go back," said Simon, going into his blanket. "It's curfew."

Rachel looked equally fatigued, eyes red and skin pale. But her mental concentration was unparalleled, and she tucked the books for further reading. Fortis, who was unable to read normal books, was dozing next to the bed.

"Fortis!" yelled Rachel, shaking Fortis. "We got to go."

Fortis grunted and collected his cane. "What time is it?" he asked, yawning.

"Ten before eight," said Simon sleepily.

Rachel held Fortis's hand and led him out of the ward. Fortis said dreamily, "Night, Simon."

"See ya."

He was back in the forest, again. He found the entrance to the cave. He hopped down. He wasn't alone. There was someone else. But it was different. Different from the last time. It was huge, chained, and slightly gaunt. It raised its head. "Mommy?" it called.

Simon spoke back. "No."

It asked, "Who are you?"

Simon asked back, "Who are you?"

It spoke, "Grendel!"

Simon replied, "I'm Simon."

Grendel looked around. "Where are you?"

"I'm here."

"Where?"

"Here. I'm right —"

It was a mystery how he slipped out of his dream, but Simon woke. He opened his eyes. Something had disturbed his sleep. He couldn't tell what. Sitting up, he rubbed his eyes as the vines from the ceiling gradually pulsed and provided illumination. What was this feeling? He had a queerest notion that there was someone else in his ward.

Hmm . . .

Simon poked his head under his bed. There was nothing there. Was he imagining things? Doubting his suspicions, he cuddled back into his blanket and welcomed the lights to diminish. He closed his eyes and waited to drop back into slumber. It was quiet. Quite. But he got up again. His nerves kept yelling to look around.

"Hello?"

No answer. Of course, there couldn't be. This was absurd. He went back into his blanket. And then for the third time, he jumped up again. He was finding himself to be ridiculous at this point. But he called out anyways.

"Is anybody here?"

Right as he said that, he noticed someone standing next to his nightstand. Simon stared. He had a clean face, short hair, and a hooked nose.

"Who are you?" asked Simon.

The man pushed his right sleeve back. "Scholar Sciens," he said, placing a scarred hand on the table. "You *are* Philosopher."

That wasn't a question. At least, it didn't sound like it. Simon watched Scholar Sciens remove a single ring, black as ink, with an eye staring back. Nothing about it really stood it, other than that it was a bit ugly.

"Scholar Sciens . . ." Simon muttered. It was easy to remember; sound liked *science*. "I know you," he said. "You studied gorgon. I read it in Ami's notes."

Sciens was not heeding much attention to Simon. Instead, he said quietly, "This is yours by right."

"Mine?" Simon pointed at the ring. "This thing?" It looked unimportant.

"*Ring of Thieves*," said Sciens, nodded. "It is yours, now."

Simon picked it up and examined it. He put it on. Nothing happened. "What does it do?" Sciens was already at the door. "Wha — excuse me! What is this?"

Sciens turned at the door. He said curtly, "The debt has been repaid." He grabbed the knob. "Do not speak of our meeting. Do not mention me. Do not find me." He went out as he finished with, "We won't meet again. Farewell."

The door closed, and Simon was left stunned, staring at the door stupidly as he tried to comprehend what was going on.

chapter nineteen ~~~~~~~
Chipper the Fat Wolpertinger

November passed like it was never there. Winds were cold and sharp to the skin, and they cut through deep into the bones. Snow poured every too often, and the grounds were becoming difficult to access. Introduction to Wrangling was becoming a new hell for everybody, since they had to now wrangle while their feet sunk a foot deep into the freezing white. Good thing was they were provided with boots.

"Wolpertinger fur!" Captain Shark held boot up easily protected from the knee down. "Great insulators. Won't feel a thing as long as you keep them on." Seedlings were torn between being horribly shocked, or bemused about the transformation of a creature so weak and innocent. Mary was looking absolutely terrified to try one on. "Go on, put them on! Won't last ten minutes without them," said Captain Shark, forcing the boot on as Mary watched with bulging eyes. When Simon squeezed his legs into the warm, plush footwear, the captain passed by and muttered, "Great work, lad. Would've liked mentioning you, but since it was punishment . . ."

"No sweat," said Simon, tightening the leather straps.

They were wrangling *kobaloi* today, and by the looks of them, Simon hardly thought them affectionate at all.

Captain Shark held a cage with a gnome-like creature, really sharp ears, skin pale as chalk, and a great deal of mischief imbued in their face.

"These lots, you need to be a bit tactful," said the captain as the kobaloi jumped about. "They can fool you into traps you'd easily overlook. Chase them without a plan, and you'll get yourself into a tight pinch. One way to counteract that," Captain Shark held up a sack of potatoes, "is with garden vegetables. Goes absolute bonkers with a few of these. Or," another closed sack was retrieved, but it squirmed rather ominously, "you could try using roaches."

Screams from the girls erupted, making the kobaloi to rattle the bars as it laughed dementedly. Claire was the representative of the girl community as she spat out a horrified, "*YUK!*" Rachel was equally revolted,

and she stepped behind Simon, which looked odd with her being slightly taller than him.

"Works better most cases," said the captain, as if he was immune to these kinds of reactions. "Can't really find out why, but what works, works. Pick what favors you. Roaches won't bite, and with the cold they'll be slow if not stagnant. Anyway, take a knife, rope, and a few of the roaches or potatoes."

"Why the knife?" asked Brendon nervously.

"Oh, you'll see," said the captain, grinning mysteriously. "It'll come in handy."

At the end of the lecture, many shifted to specific individuals who had actively proven themselves to be skilled in wrangling. The most popular pole so far was Vel, and then Simon. Apparently, the two of them were consistently bringing back their game without fail, and therefore always amongst the ones to leave early without extra work for the rest of the morning. Rachel was always excused as well, since Simon was always inclined to catch her load as well.

And, there was a secret to his success, all thanks to Rachel's discovery of a useful spell a few weeks prior. It turned out, he was *excellent* at it.

"Simon, want to work together?"

"Could you help me with mine?"

"Or just show us how you do it."

"I can't run."

"Show us the *Stasis*, Simon. Show us!"

"Look," said Simon, getting a bit weary he was getting these love calls. "I'll catch as many as I can. Just . . . just try your best while you're alone, okay?" Simon muttered to Rachel, "Who would've thought, eh?"

"You're great at it, though," said Rachel. "I've never seen anyone do it at their first try."

Most of the pupils went for the potatoes, taking three or four and putting them in a rucksack. Uro and Aro, as usual, were the few who found disgusting things to be equally fascinating as beautiful things. Uro held a roach by the backside. It was *huge*. It could've easily been the size of his palm.

"Awesome!" he cried, sacking five and hoisting it around his back.

"Are they special breeds from Eldwoods?" asked Aro, taking seven.

"*Lake roaches*," said the captain, nodding. "Will have to ask a monstrologist to find the details."

"Come on, Aro!" yelled Uro from ahead. "Jamey, Brendon, let's go! The first to catch one gets to decide on the trip!"

Brendon yelled back as he picked up a few potatoes, "But my mom hasn't said yes, yet!"

Simon spotted Magnus scoot away from the sack of roaches, scowling like he was tasting bugs inside his mouth. "Catching kobaloi," he hissed disapprovingly. "We're *nobility*. What a joke." Simon snorted, remembering how all of them seemed to disperse in the face of danger. What *nobility* was that?

"Oh, Aemulus," Rachel said quietly, frowning at the distance.

Aemulus Ashblood picked up three roaches and put it in a rucksack, quite indifferent to their appearance. Rachel said quietly, "Didn't think he'd be so bold." Fortis abruptly spat a muffled laugh. "What?"

Fortis grinned rather teasingly and said, "Don't tell me you're falling for him?"

"Wha —" Rachel went slightly red, but she said loudly, "No! I didn't mean it like that!"

"*Bold*," muttered Simon. "Or *charming*? *Brave*? Lovely context."

Vel was also one of the few to be impassive to gross things. She was less receptive to requests, however. She took one Lake Roach and went off into the woods, a school of children still following her to witness the glorious catch. Simon, foreseeing this won't be an easy hunt, saw the need to take roaches for bait, and he stuffed his sack with fifteen of them. Rachel was not so pleased.

"Can't help it," said Simon, shrugging. "The others will ask for help, remember?"

With Fortis having no choice but to sit out on this subject, Simon and Rachel went into the woods together. The snow really was hindering their movements. Simon couldn't have thought of a better variety show. Young kinds, wearing wolpertinger boots, hunting for little gnomes that would pull tricks on them in the dead of winter; he knew it would be a perfect mix of excitement and sympathy for the audience.

"Right, let's —"

Simon cut off as he felt an almighty jolt from his ankle. He dropped his sack (which was thankfully tied) and went straight up into the air. He grunted as he stared at the snow, feeling the blood rush to his head.

"Simon!" Rachel looked shocked as she bent low to match eye level. "Are you okay?"

"Ugh," said Simon, looking at the thick vine that suspended him. "Great. So *this* was why we need a knife." He pulled out his knife and began sawing. But, when there was hardly any progress, he became irritated and snarled, "For crying out —! *Passio!*" His hand lit on fire, and he viciously grabbed the vine and sawed even harder. With combined effort of fire and blade, the vine cut like butter, and Simon fell to the plush snow.

"I didn't think they'd be this smart," said Rachel, taking steps extra carefully. "There's not even a mark."

"Well," said Simon, brushing off the snow and retrieving his rucksack, "it just means they're nearby. Come on. Help me with this."

"No!" Rachel looked positively disgusted. "I *won't* use cockroaches. I can't believe you're even holding them."

"Fine," said Simon irritably. "Then give me your potatoes."

Rachel's potatoes, after cooking it for a few minutes, were soon displayed on a hummock where trees were least occupied. Simon found a nice hiding place underneath a root and waited. After ten minutes (their boots and cloaks doing a perfect job keeping them warm), a kobaloi came trotting up, eyes fixed and mouth drooling. It was explained then how they weren't leaving any marks on the snow. When Simon watched closely, the feet never sunk in. It was basically treading the surface like a weightless feather.

"Wow," whispered Simon, watching it eat away the steaming potatoes. "We're supposed to catch that? It would run off in a heartbeat."

"Well, that's why you learned that spell," said Rachel. "Ready?"

"Yeah," said Simon, flexing his fingers to keep them warm and nimble. "Here I go."

He jumped into the open and ran after the kobaloi, although it was more like hopping than running. The kobaloi flinched as he was initially alarmed. But when It watched Simon sluggishly pounce up the hummock, it cracked a hearty laugh and started spanking its bottom. That was no concern of Simon. Just as the kobaloi pulled a funny face, cross-eyed and tongue extended, Simon pointed his palm at it before making a tight fist and yelled, "*Stasis!*"

The kobaloi froze in motion, retaining that awful face. Simon got to it after a dozen leaps and tackled the creature. The spell wore off in a few seconds, and the kobaloi thrashed in Simon's arms, smacking Simon's face with its twiggy hands.

"Rachel!" Simon yelled as the kobaloi stuck its fingers into his nostrils.

Rachel was still a good five feet away, and she yelled, "*Stasis!*" Now both Simon and the kobaloi were immobile. Rachel yelled, "*Fides!*" and took a careful aim before shooting a rock straight at the temple. The kobaloi went sagging, motionless once more. "Sorry," muttered Rachel at the kobaloi apologetically.

"Sorry at *that*?" grunted Simon he was lifted from Rachel's spell.

"Well, it was the only way," said Rachel, shrugging. "But really, Simon, I didn't think you'd be so good at spells!"

"Why's that?" asked Simon, tying the kobaloi with a rope.

"Because," started Rachel, helping Simon, "spells are from the majors. Passion, Wisdom, Expression, and Belief; different combinations and measurements is what leads to a perfect spell. You're doing it brilliantly!" She had that fascinated look on her face again. "Maybe it's because you're a Philosopher. You weren't assigned to a specific major, remember? You have infinite possibilities, Simon!"

"Yeah, yeah, I get it," said Simon. "Stop staring at me like that. Looks like you're about to cut me open and start a surgery."

Once they captured the second kobaloi (using one of Simon's roaches), they went on a quest to aid others. It was almost a routine to find Mary hesitating from wrangling anything, thus Simon did the honor of helping her first. "Here," said Simon, offering the tied kobaloi. "Don't lose it." Mary beamed widely. Afterwards, it was helping whoever he came across first. It was a miracle how Brendon had caught one. He had run into a similar trap, and the kobaloi came running out to tease him, only to get squashed by Brendon when he managed to cut through the ropes and fall. Uro, as it turned out, was a tactician, snaring a kobaloi from an identical trap he set up with sluggish roaches. Aro was lucky; she chased her own kobaloi, lost sight of it, and then ran into another one that Roth Mayberry had been chasing. The Bloods seemed to handle their tasks, though they kept flinching when they heard unexpected noises. Aemulus was, to Simon's unexplainable displeasure, successful as well. Vel was everybody's heroin again, catching at least ten kobalois, although it seemed like she was just finding way to kill time.

"Jamey!" yelled Uro, who was so inclined repeat his ritual by tying the kobaloi onto a stick. "You're last! Hurry up!"

"Stop yelling!" hissed Jamey, apparently furious Brendon had beat him in the contest. "You're going to scare them away!"

"Not quite," said Simon, pointing at a rather stupid looking kobaloi that wandered to the last Lake Roach he had to dispose of. It bit off a chunk before Simon yelled, "*Stasis!*"

The kobaloi froze open mouthed, and the contents dropped out and spoiled the snow.

"*Oh, yuk!*" said Rachel as Simon fastened the ropes.

Simon dunked the kobaloi's head into the snow a few times until the filth was wiped off. "Easy clean," he said, passing the rope to Jamey. "There you go."

"Thanks!" said Jamey, cradling the kobaloi as if it was his dearly beloved. "Hey, Simon, it's wrangling season and all, so we're going on a month trip to Hawaii with our parents. There's a Hawaiian branch there where wranglers are deployed to wrangle, too, so it's going to be a lot of fun. You want to come?"

Wrangling season utilized all wranglers in a massive operation that required a clean sweep of the continents to ensure dangerous creatures were far from human habitat. One of the hotspots for regular infestation was, to Simon's surprise, Diablo Lake, just five miles off of Nocville. Therefore, during the winter season, it was a month break for all pupils except the ripelings, who were obligated for hands-on experience that was not in a controlled environment.

"What do you say?" asked Jamey.

"Uh . . ." This was unexpected. Simon had never thought about going on trips. He was technically financially broke. "I . . . Thanks, but I'm fine. Don't have the money to go."

"We can pay for your plane ticket," said Jamey excitedly. "Uro's and Aro's family won a lottery, so it's all covered. No sweat."

It was surely a thankful proposition. But, it didn't feel right for Simon. It was a very sudden decision to make, and he had already thought about going back to Nocville. He felt dutiful to visit Ms. Bluebell. He owed her that much.

"I'm fine," said Simon, grinning and shaking his head. "Maybe next time. Hey, you guys have fun, okay?"

Simon and Rachel slowly went back, their kobaloi still unconscious.

"Why didn't you say yes?" asked Rachel curiously. "It would've been nice for you. You've never traveled at all."

"I did," said Simon, untangling his kobaloi as it rolled into a bush. "We *technically* did travel to here. I'm having a blast."

"That doesn't count," said Rachel disapprovingly. "We're here to study. Not — oh!"

Simon, who had managed to pull his kobaloi free, stepped into another suspending trap and was dangling upside down. Simon cursed as he extracted his knife. "Seriously?" he growled. "*Passio!*" It was much thicker than the last one, and he ferociously hacked at the vine as it crinkled under the heat.

"You're going to hurt yourself!" yelled Rachel, looking at the blade nervously. "Here, let me — oh, hello, Mary."

Simon looked down (or up, in his case). Mary had emerged, and next to her was Vel. They were watching Simon undo the link.

"Hi, Rachel," said Mary, looking a bit breathless. "How are you?"

"As you can see," said Rachel, pointing at Simon, "wonderful."

"Why're you still here?" asked Simon, wiping the sweat off his face. Mary's cloak seemed to be bulging in odd spots. "Hey, I thought I caught you one? Don't tell me you're still holding onto it."

"Oh," said Mary, smiling uncertainly. "Well . . . now that you mention it . . . I thought about asking you, too . . ."

"What?" asked Simon, stopping for a moment.

Mary added importantly, "But you can't tell anyone, okay? Promise you won't tell!"

Simon and Rachel exchanged looks, and then Rachel quickly put on a smile and said kindly, "We won't tell anyone. We swear."

Mary hesitated for a brief moment, and then opened her cloak. In her arms, something fat, much like a small wombat, hung with its pudgy fat pushing up to its face. There was no telling what it was, until Simon saw a pair of horns and wings sticking out just barely. Simon gaped.

"What, on sweat earth, is *that*?" he exclaimed, not believing his eyes.

"Is that . . . a wolpertinger?" asked Rachel, sounding extremely unsure.

"It's Chipper," said Mary, hugging the wolpertinger.

"That's *not* the one that we caught during summer," said Simon, choosing not to believe. "It's — it's a freaking dog!"

"He got bigger," said Mary, putting Chipper down. The poor thing could hardly move without teetering. "When I heard they skin them, I — I couldn't let them get to him! So I made a small hole in the wrangling grounds to hide him."

Rachel looked perplexed on how to take this in. She looked at Vel, who was shrugging mutely. Mary held Rachel's hand and said, "But my family wants me to come over so they could see me! Chipper needs someone to give him food during the winter. And — and I couldn't think of anyone but you three and Vel!" She collected Rachel's other hand and gathered them like she was ready to pray. "Please, please, look after Chipper. Maybe a few minutes at lunch and dinner, that's all! Or else he might die!"

This was the most ludicrous request Simon had ever encountered. An overweight wolpertinger and an obsessively caring girl; he imagined Fortis just exploding with laughter.

"Mary, it's *wildlife*. It — Chipper can take care of itself!"

"No, he can't!" squealed Mary, looking down at her precious Chipper. "Chipper didn't collect any nuts. I read that squirrels collect nuts to last the winter, but Chipper didn't collect any whenever I came over!"

"You've been feeding him," said Vel quietly, staring at the massive wolpertinger as if it was an entirely new species. "Of course, he wouldn't learn how to feed."

Mary was looking desperate now. She held Rachel even tighter as she pleaded, "Please, help me. He'll die!"

Simon made eye contact with Vel. Their relationship had not been resolved, but at this moment he could tell Vel was in agreement with him. This was not going to happen.

"Mary —"

"Okay," said Rachel. Simon and Vel looked at her as if she had triggered a death bomb. Rachel smiled at Mary and announced, "Okay, we'll take care of Chipper until you come back."

"Really?!" Mary looked at Simon and Vel very hopefully. From the depth of his upside down stomach Simon wanted to regurgitate objections after objections to reason with Mary, but she was already flushed with happy tears coming out of her glens. The words never left his mouth. An unexpected lump clogged his throat, and Simon did an involuntary nod to rid of it. Mary cheered in joy as she ran to Simon and hugged him.

"Thank you, Simon! Thank you!"

Simon gaped, half infuriated that Rachel had spoken him into this ridiculous treaty. Out from the corner of his eyes, he saw Vel shake her head and turn away. Out of stupefaction, desperation, and the sudden need to vent, Simon developed the urge to cling onto something and said blankly, "You're helping, too, right?"

Vel looked about, her shock wiping her face stolid. Mary gasped and turned to Vel. She squeaked in a trembling voice, "Would you, Vel? Would you, really? You said you were staying. Oh please, help."

Vel evidently did not want any part of this nonsense. But, at the same time, the look on Mary was so expectant, her throat seemed to clamp up, just like Simon's. And, just like Simon, she was drawn aboard by Rachel's fair words. "Yes, she'll help. All of us will."

Mary squealed and hugged Vel. Simon could see her falling into a maelstrom of numbing apathy. "Thank you, thank you!" Mary picked up Chipper and buried her face into his fat and fur. "You'll be alright, Chipper! They'll take good care of you! So don't be sad when I don't show up for a while, okay?"

Chipper the fat wolpertinger seemed to have dozed off during its lovey-dovey hugging moment. Mary skipped off with Chipper swinging like a towel in her arms. "I'll show you where he lives after lunch!" she yelled as she vanished into the woods.

The three of them looked at one another. Simon was the first to speak. "Really?" he said, glaring at Rachel. "You had to include me in this?"

"It's only for the wrangling season," said Rachel, sounding generous and guilty at the same time. "We can do her a favor."

"I was going to visit Nocville," grunted Simon furiously. "Way to cancel the flight. Now I can't leave because Mary will see me board the Explorer if I do. *Feeding a wolpertinger?*" Simon smacked his forehead, and it rung like a gong. He had forgotten he was hanging upside down all this time and the blood in his head was starting to accumulate rather profusely. "Jeez, its whole purpose is to survive the wilderness."

"You're the one to complain?"

Vel was looking daggers at Simon. She looked like she was ready to pull Simon's hair out and scrub his bald head with sand paper until his skin turned raw red.

"I . . ." he really couldn't think of anything to say. He had tried to make amendments (although deep down inside he was still not convinced he was at fault for anything), but this dilemma . . . was probably going to set that back.

"Come on, Vel, it will only be a few weeks," said Rachel soothingly. She could've just dropped ice into a boiling pot of oil. It was she who gave admission without Vel's consent.

Simon heard a *snap* and fell to the ground. The fire had apparently wilted the vine. Simon disentangled from his cloak and put a hand on the trunk to support himself. The blood required some time to circulate. The bark dug into his skin, and he recoiled irritably. *What the heck?* Tip searched if there were thorns in his palm.

"I'm not doing it," said Vel disapprovingly. "You're not supposed to feed a wild, magical creature. It's as good as dead if it's that fat. It'll only hurt Mary more when she finds it eaten one day."

"We can reason with her as time goes by," said Rachel, still persistent in persuading her. "You don't have to do it every day. Maybe three times a week —"

"I know why you're doing this," said Vel passionlessly. "You want me to make up with him." She pointed at Simon, who was at the time not looking. "I don't care if he feels sorry or not, okay? I'm over it."

"Guys," said Simon ghostly, staring at the tree that just pricked him.

"Oh, Vel, for goodness sake," said Rachel rankly. "Of course, *you're not!* You always fume when you see Simon during lunch time! You have to talk —"

"Guys!"

Rachel and Vel turned. "What?" asked Rachel.

Simon was still staring at the tree. The trunk was completely sabotaged, like rows of giant, jagged teeth had decided to gnaw at it over and over again. The pealed surface spiraled up the tree, and the grooves were one directional. Rachel came closer to examine the scars as well.

"This isn't from a kobaloi," said Simon slowly.

"It's not from *anything* we've wrangled, Simon," whispered Rachel, rubbing her hand against the shaven surface.

"Look." Vel was pointing at other trees showing identical inflictions. There were at least half a dozen.

Rachel gasped and looked at Simon. Her face couldn't be any paler than now. "Simon," she whispered in horror, "the book. It said before winter, gorgons shed their skin!"

Something fluttered just above Rachel. It looked like a plastic bag. Simon reached up and pulled it off of the trunk. It was rough, pattered, and moderately flexible. It gave off an unnatural, soapy rainbow color. It was shed skin.

"*Hibernation*," breathed Simon, looking into Rachel's aghast and Vel's alert faces. "It's in hibernation. *It's still here.*"

chapter twenty ~~~~~~~
I'm Grendel

Many pupils went off home for the wrangling season, and Simon couldn't believe how empty the place looked like with most of the wranglers gone. Pupils, as well, had departed, and Simon watched the Explorer sail away bitterly. He was really looking forward to visit Ms. Bluebell. "Summer . . ." he muttered. "In summer . . ."

Feeding Chipper was just as dull as reading books. As it turned it, Chipper had a glutinous appetite, and he finished a bowl of nuts, a cherry pie, and a slice of pudding the first day before he finally settled down and dropped into a slumber in his cozy den. Simon was sure if they did this for another week, Chipper would die of a heart attack.

"Let's try to cut down on the food," said Rachel, jotting down a few notes. "Like nuts and beans, only things that Chipper would find in the wilderness. He doesn't need the pie or pudding."

"Couldn't be any plainer," said Forits, squeezing Chipper's belly. He couldn't wipe his amused grin off for a second. "I still can't believe this is a wolpertinger. It's like I'm touching a pillow."

"Yeah, tell me about it," muttered Simon as Chippers burped. "Imagine skinning that thing. It's just gonna peel right off like whip cream."

"Simon!" hissed Rachel in disgust.

"What, it can't understand a word what I'm saying," said Simon indifferently.

As they returned the cozy tree-hive, Rachel jotted a few more notes down and said, "We'll have to exercise him, too. Simon, you're best at that, so why don't you ask Vel to come with you and help."

"No can do," said Simon flatly. "That thing won't budge even if I poked it with a nail. And ask Vel?" Simon snorted at Rachel. "You've obviously made our relationship worse. What makes you think she'll listen to a word I say?"

"Look, just try, okay?" said Rachel tetchily. "It's not like it'll kill you."

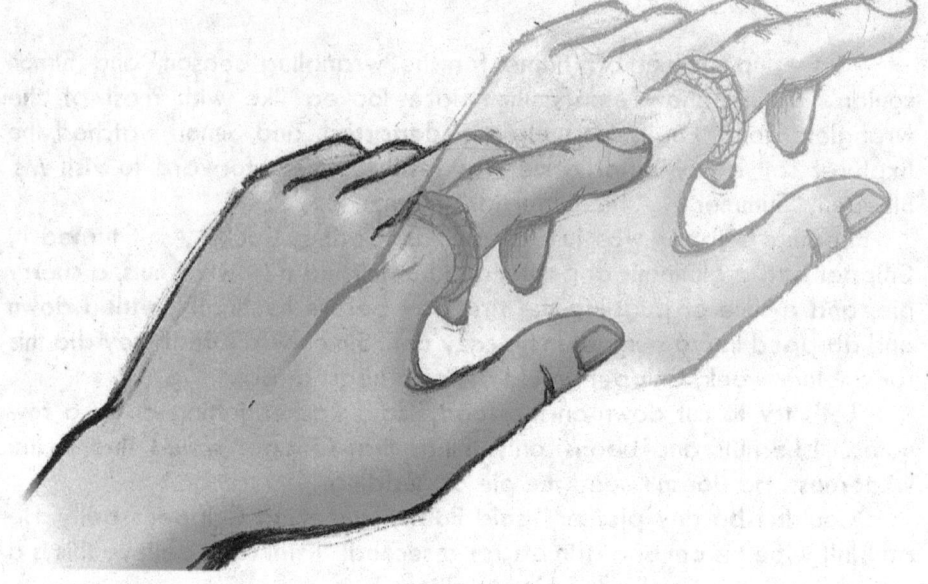

"It'll kill their relationship, though." said Fortis under his breath.

The notion that the gorgon was still in Eldwoods was a fear factor. The three of them were constantly visiting the Pupil's Archive, hoping they'd find any hint about the gorgon's hibernation process. But, as expected, there were even less about gorgons than Ami's notes.

"This is so unfair!" Rachel exploded, undoing her ponytail furiously. "The Athenaeum probably has ten times more information than here! Twenty times more!"

"Hate to break it to you," said Fortis, who was reading braille. "Before Ami left, he said he can't get in the Athenaeum again. It was like a onetime favor from Frao."

Simon sighed. "We can't go off of books. We've got to go out there."

"Are you *crazy?*" hissed Rachel. "You know how it's like to get attacked by that thing! Now you want to go looking for it?"

"It's in hibernation, Rachel," said Fortis, thinking hard. "It won't come out during the winter. And plus, it's not like the wardens are gone."

"Yeah, I see them go in and out of the forest all the time," said Simon.

"Then leave it to them, okay?" Rachel slammed her book angrily. "Our job is to find out what the gorgon is after, and if we manage to before the wranglers do, let them know what we found. We're *not* skipping out there like it's a picnic. People could die from this. And plus, do you think the wardens won't catch us wandering in the forest? They're trained experts; we wouldn't even last ten minutes."

"With me, maybe ten seconds," said Fortis, and Simon laughed rather depressingly.

Simon watched the forest from his unit. The moon seemed exceptionally brighter, today, and thanks to that he could barely make out the wardens emerging from the woods once in a while. They probably knew it wasn't over long before Simon did, and that was probably why the curfew was still up. Would they eventually find the gorgon? Rachel had a point; their duty was the safeguard Eldwoods. If it was going to someone to unveil the mystery, it was definitely not going to be a few kids with theories based off of books and records. Simon conjured up an image of Captain Shark wielding a mighty club as he stepped upon the fallen monster, suffering from horrendous scars but triumphant from the heated battle. Yes, that appealed Simon more than anything else.

Simon took out the Ring of Thieves and tossed it rather carelessly. He never really had the opportunity to inspect the trinket. Was it worth millions of dollars? Simon scoffed as he thought, *Yeah, right* . . . If it was from a scholar, Simon doubted it would be an object familiar to the normal world. What did it do? More than once he had put on the ring, and he even wore it on purpose while he was accompanied with Rachel and Fortis. But nothing happened. Therefore, it had uselessly sat in his pocket for all these months.

He slipped it on again and observed. It was ugly, really. The surface wasn't smooth, and the eye almost looked genuinely alive. Someone with butterfingers must've made it in a hurry. He took it back off and put it in his pocket.

"Master Dreamwalker."

Agilis was hovering before the door. Simon turned and asked, "Yeah?"

"You have a guest," said Agilis.

Rachel or Fortis, perhaps. "Let them come in."

Agilis shifted aside. Vel stepped over the threshold. This was an unexpected guest. "Oh," said Simon, thoroughly taken aback. "Uh . . . Hi."

Vel nodded. "Can I speak with you?"

"Sure," said Simon quickly, drawing up a chair. "Thanks, Agilis."

Agilis bowed and went back up to his post. Vel softly shut the door. Rather than taking the lone chair, she stood in the middle of the room. There was an awkward pause.

"About that day," said Vel, cutting right to the chase. "I'm sorry." Simon was so relieved the topic had come up from Vel. He was at a predicament how to absolve the grudge ever since the day they met Chippers. "I heard you had some rough times yourself. I shouldn't have judged you."

"Nah, you're fine," said Simon quickly, getting butterflies in his stomach from the fact that they were finally establishing harmony. "You always looked forward to coming here, right? And you even saved me back then. I owe you, still."

Another pause, a little inelegant. Again, Simon wasn't smart enough to start a conversation. He tapped the windowsill awkwardly. Vel, who was contrastingly much braver than him, strode to the window and said, "I'm sorry I didn't come. Is — Chipper, right? — Is Chipper fine?"

"Better than any of us," said Simon, moving next to Vel. "With that bulk, he'd last a year."

"I can come along," said Vel, staring at the wrangling ground. "Tomorrow, if you guys want me."

"Yeah," said Simon, stepping on Vel's shadow. "Yeah, you should come. Rachel's scheming a diet for Chipper, though. She wants us to be his personal coach."

Vel raised her eyebrows. "I don't think it would matter once Mary comes back." She turned back to the door. "We'll have to train *her* before training Chipper."

"Right," said Simon. Vel opened the door. "Vel?" She looked back. "Thanks . . . for coming."

Vel nodded. "Sure."

Back in the dream world. Simon found the cave much easier. The same hulking being greeted him.

"Hi, I'm Grendel."

"Hi."

"Are you Simon?"

"Yeah."

"But I can't see you."

That was odd. Why couldn't Grendel see him? Simon sat down directly in front of Grendel.

"I can see you," he said.

"But I want to play!" said Grendel, flailing his arms. They were chained. Simon found that very odd.

"Why are you chained?" asked Simon.

"Mommy told me it's because I'm special," said Grendel.

"Mommy?" asked Simon. "Where's your mom?"

"She's sleeping," replied Grendel. "She said she'd bring me something special when its spring."

"What kind of special?" asked Simon.

"Something reeaallyy special," said Grendel happily. But then he said sadly, "But she won't play with me . . . even though I'm more special . . ."

Simon thought for a moment. "Don't you have any friends? Why are you alone?"

"Because mommy told me I'm special," repeated Grendel. "Nobody knows this place because it's special. Nobody remembers it anymore. Because it's special. Nobody outside is special anymore. But mommy's special. I'm special! So we know! We know where this place is!"

"That's not really a reason to be alone," replied Simon.

"But mommy said special kids don't play with other kids! They have to be special, like me!" He then asked, "Are you special, too, Simon? You found this place. You're special, aren't you?"

Simon thought for another moment. "Yeah . . ." he said slowly. "I am kind of special . . ."

"Then we can be friends!" yelled Grendel his voice ringing off of the walls. "We're special! So we can be special friends!"

"Uh. . ." It sounded impolite to refuse. Simon said, "Yeah, okay. Let's be friends."

Grendel yelled, "Yay!"

"Greeendeeeellll?" Someone was calling from behind. "What did mommy tell youuu? You have to be quiet, okay, Grendel-bell?"

"Uh-oh," whispered Grendel. "Mommy's awake! She doesn't like strangers! Go, go!"

Simon woke up the next morning, not entirely sure what dream he'd just had.

chapter twenty~one ~~~~
The Chamber of Primals

Wrangling season came to a close faster than Simon could expect it to, and the Explorer was home, again. Pupils were sprightlier than when they left. Uro and Aro, Jamey, and Brendon were completely tanned. Aro had done a magnificent job of leaving parts of her bodies pale in flower patterns. Uro, living up to his expectations, returned with the most fashionable combination of clothes: a Christmas hat, voluminous lei, a life vest, a coconut, and swim trunks. Uro presented himself before the public (despite the pouring flakes), and he bowed as roars of laughter and applause greeted him.

"Can't go wrong with Hawaii," said Uro happily. "You should've come, Simon! The lay-deeeeeeeez! They seriously wanted to take me with them!"

"Yes, I'm sure they did," said Aro, taking off her sunglasses. "Give you the clothes to launder that you drooled all over." She added, "But visiting the Hawaiian branch was fun. There were a lot more wranglers than we thought."

"Here, Simon!" said Brendon, his tanned profile making it hard to recognize him. "We got you presents!"

Uro threw an enormous straw hat over Simon. Jamey gave him a huge picture of the Waikiki beach with ladies dressed in grass skirts, and Brendon gave a small tiki figure that made a horrible, painful cry that echoed throughout the foyer when Simon pressed its head. Aro, who was the most thoughtful out of the four, gave him a set of pajamas. "Heard it was your birthday," she said, beaming. "Didn't know what to get you, but a fancy pajama always works, right? I bought it extra big so you'd be able to grow into them."

"Wow," said Simon. It was rare to receive gifts in his life from anybody other than Rachel. "Thanks, guys!"

"Yeah, why did you bottle it up?" said Uro loudly. "You really didn't think we'd just let it slip by, did you?"

"How'd you guys know?" asked Simon, bewildered.

"Rachel," said Aro.

Rachel and Fortis, who were next to him, beamed and gave him a parcel. "Happy birthday. Sorry we forgot the celebration," said Fortis. It was a fresh batch of linen bandages with healing wax imbued in them. "Since you're always getting hurt, thought this might help," said Rachel. Fortis added, "Mind you, that's hand made from us. Thought about getting it from Rachel's mom, but she said it would be nice if we actually made one."

Mary showed her appreciation of taking care of Chipper by giving them basket full of sweets for Simon, Rachel, Fortis, and Vel. "Thank you so much!" she said happily. She turned to the forest. "I've got to see Chipper. See you later!" And she ran off. Vel quietly followed her to give a Do-Not-Feed-Magical-Creatures lesson.

Sessions were resumed, and as expected, most pupils were clumsy for the first week. Simon, who hadn't bothered to practice his fundamentals at all, was having trouble sustaining his fire without burning his hair again. Mrs. White appeared to have predicted his drop of concentration, but that didn't spare the pupils from her stern remark.

"I hope you all regain your touches by next week," said Mrs. White curtly. "If you do not, you will remain in this session until lunch time, and attend the afternoon session as well."

Upon her warning, seedlings were snapping their fingers double time. The only one that seemed to have remembered to keep their senses sharp was Aemulus. He was now igniting both hands. When Simon continued to make failed combustions, Aemulus shook his head in disbelief and scoffed. Simon glared at him.

"I thought I told you it's none of your business what I do?"

"I never I cared," said Aemulus coolly, exercising his exceeding achievement. "Just thought you're really clumsy for a Philosopher."

"Yeah?" retorted Simon viciously. "And you're really showing that awful side of your Blood traits, you know that? Why don't you just join the others to Expression?"

Aemulus shot a dangerous look and snarled, "Don't you dare talk like you know me."

"I already do," said Simon nastily. "I'm keeping my mouth shut about you and Magnus because that's your problem. I'm doing you a favor, okay? Maybe a little gratitude would be nice."

"Oh, a favor, is it?" retorted Aemulus, his red brows looking extra sharp. "I know all about you being funded by our family's foundation. Looks like we've been doing you a life time favor, doesn't it?"

"Aemulus, Simon," said Mrs. White as she passed. "I'd advise you two to focus on your own work. Simon, please make improvements until next session."

Aemulus looked away with his chin high, but Simon was furious that he was dealt an extra penalty. It was their first time talking since the first day in Eldwoods, and their natural depreciative algorithm couldn't be more discreet.

Wisdom and Belief were not much of trouble, but Expression was hell again. The only thing that spared Simon was Vel's mute advices. As a matter of fact, her guidance was much more effective than Rachel's or Fortis's. "Blow, into your hand," she muttered from the corner of her mouth, "and then think *up*." It really worked. Simon's plane floated a foot off his hand, but barely. Venator, however, saw right through their cooperation and leered upon Simon. "If you are receiving aid, *Philosopher*," he said softly, "I will expect you to make *drastic* enhancements by the end of spring. Don't," he added menacingly, "disappoint me." Simon found that pointed nose remarkably appealing for a good twisting and hammering.

Wrangling, was for the first time, dull as they were faced with the most unexpected creature throughout the year. When the captain presented them the cage, there were "*Ew!*"s coming from all the girls. Claire was the most shocked, and she cried a disgusted, "*EEK!*"

"*Ravagers!*" yelled Captain Shark. It was a giant caterpillar, munching away on some wooden bark. Its eyes were huge, and there were thick fur protruding from the green skin. "These lots are a pain if you leave them alone. Glutinous eaters, really. They'll eat through trees in an hour. Horrible for the ecosystem."

The captain pointed at a solid chrysalis lying next to the cage. "These little deforesters will go into hibernation during the winter season. Around the end of March, they'll start coming out again to eat trees. Their transformation to *coral jackets* takes place on their fifth year, and trust me, you'd rather get rid of them when they're still crawling." He handed out knives and said, "You'll be fine working alone on this one! Two chrysalises for each pupil! No more, no less."

Fortis was able to join Simon and Rachel on this quest, but was more like keeping company for the both of them. He laughed heartily as he heard Rachel scream.

"Ew, yuk!" Rachel jumped back as slimy goo came out from a crack and started splattering Rachel's cloak. "Oh, gosh, so gross!"

"Rachel. Just. Cut. It!" grunted Simon, who was on top of an eight feet branch sawing on his own chrysalis. When the thing finally snapped, it landed on a serrated rock. When Simon jumped down to see if it ruptured, the chrysalis was fine as new. "Wow," said Simon, tying Rachel's chrysalis since she was so revolted to even touch the thing. "Imagine something like this dropping on your head."

"Forget coma," said Fortis, knocking on the chrysalis. "It's instant kill. Depressing if that happened, though. It rather get killed by a coconut than this."

As March came and went, the sun slowly conquered the bed of snow, showing bare ground and slushy earth. Vel, who was usually quiet and reserved, was becoming slightly more proactive. She was going out with Mary and Rachel more to the wrangling ground. Simon speculated it was to help Mary develop a sense of responsibility to slowly groom Chipper to take care of himself. It was working, somewhat. When Simon was feeling rather good with the sun outstretching its powerful rays, he and Fortis joined the girls to visit Chipper. He was leaning out, and Chipper now showed remarkable dislike for sweets and human food.

"What on earth did you do?" asked Simon, watching Chippers rummage through leaves to collect nuts that Mary had planted.

"Vel!" said Mary happily, patting Chipper when he successfully dug up the seventh nut. "She's been making Chipper exercise, and chipper is on a strict diet, now!"

"Was it hard?" asked Fortis, surprised after he felt Chippers leaner belly.

"No," said Vel quietly.

"It's all thanks to you!" said Mary, and she held Vel's hand as if she was her twin sister. Vel blankly watched Mary bounce up and down, not quite appealed to the idea to join in the girlish skittering.

Simon wasn't so merry mind like most, however. Spring meant warmth, and warmth meant one thing: hibernation was at an end. The gorgon was definitely coming back from its deep slumber, whether it was far from here, or right under their nose. His fears were the same with Rachel and Fortis. But, Rachel's most excellent brain for detective work was stalled as she kept repeating the paragraphs Ami's notebook said.

"Consume blood of magical creatures . . . The blood of Elds . . . Governors drank the blood of Philosophers to replenish themselves . . . Deathwish . . ."

"Man," groaned Simon, yawning as he covered his face with Ami's notebook. "Talk about stalemate . . ."

Fortis laughed, reading a braille version of the notebook that Simon and Rachel helped make over the wrangling season. "Yeah, it's hard to actually fit the puzzles."

Simon made himself comfortable in his bed and groaned.

"A visitor, Master Dreamwalker," said Agilis.

Ami was at the door, grinning just like his little brother. "Still haven't found what you were looking for?"

"Nope," said Simon, getting up. "Can't connect any dots."

"Gorgon's are special classed wrangling subjects," said Ami. "I doubted from the beginning the Athenaeum would carry any valuable information regarding them."

"Well," said Fortis, shutting his own notebook, "we're out of luck, then."

"Take it easy," said Ami, patting Fortis. "I know you guys are into your little detective work, but it's about time you give it up. It's the job for the wrangler's, not pupils."

"*Ugh*," said Rachel, rocking her head. "There's something that I'm not seeing! I know I can solve this. There's something I'm overlooking."

Ami laughed. "You were always persistent when you were a kid. Glad to see it stayed with you all this time."

The eight o'clock signal came as Chrone croaked, "Ten before eight."

"Night," said Simon.

"Night," said Rachel and Fortis.

He was walking. Why was he? Oh, because it was a tunnel. Tunnels were meant for exploration. Simon went deeper into the abyss. It was a miracle how he was navigating through this dim labyrinth. Why was he here again? Oh, because it was a tunnel. And tunnels were meant for exploration.

"Mommy . . ." That was Grendel. Simon neared a chamber. In the corner where, sheltered from view, Grendel spoke, "Mommy, why can't I go out? Why can't I?"

A pair of grossly yellow eyes glided across the chamber. "Don't touch it, my baby. You can't leave, yet. We need more food. More food for our precious heart."

Grendel went into a wild tantrum.

"I WANT TO GO OUT! I WANT TO GO OUT!"

"SILENCE!"

Grendel subsided, whimpering his miserable woe. For a moment they were both breathless.

"Baby, my sweat one," she said in a mock baby voice. "You can't go out, or other babies will start teasing you and make fun of how you look. Do you want that? Do you want other babies to hit you with sticks and throw rocks?"

Grendel whimpered. "N-no!"

"Then wait," said mommy. Her eyes averted back to the tunnel. "Mommy must find more food. And when we feed, we will be perfect. Everyone will love us."

Grendel said hopefully, "When I'm p-perfect, I c-can go out-t?"

"Yes, baby, just you wait," said mommy, and she violently drawled up the tunnel and to the exit. "I will bring the blood it needs. The blood of Elds. And then, I will rid of this curse. AND THEN, WE WILL BE —!"

Simon jerked awake, sweating as if he just finished a marathon. Dawn was approaching, the thin ray of morning shine barely making it over the mountain range. He got up and wiped the sweat off of his chin. He was cold, yet hot. He wrapped himself in his blanket. For an unknown reason, he felt exhausted. His body shook as if it was having a convulsion.

He got up to the window and pulled it open, allowing some cold air to get to his lungs. Most of the snow were long gone. It was really spring. That made him feel better. His stomach eased. Simon observed the dawning forest to help the process. But what he saw, a mere ten yards away from the base of Elder Tree, made his inside churn as a whole.

A writhing, sliding, and whipping tail faintly glistened rainbow. Even from three hundred feet away, Simon spotted a pair of yellow pupils, glowing brighter than diamonds. His skin shriveled as the gorgon seemed to gorge into a limp carcass flailing in its hand. It braced itself to full height, and then dove into the darker parts of the forest.

Reacting as if it was his duty, Simon threw off his blanket and ran to the door. It was back. Someone had to follow that. And right now, it was only he who saw it. Any chance of tracking that thing was with him.

When he burst out of his unit, he heard Agilis wake with a familiar *crack*. He swooped down.

"Master Dreamwalker."

"Agilis!" Simon ducked out of the way. "I gotta go! It's important!"

"It's twenty minutes before seven," said Agilis, gazing at Simon. "Curfew is still in effect."

"I know," said Simon breathlessly, "but the gorgon! It's back! Someone has to follow it, now!"

Simon ran off, twisting and turning down the corridor as fast as he could. Truth be told, Simon was uncertain if he was even going the right way. All that came to thought was just run.

"You're headed the wrong way."

Simon felt something pull him up by the shoulders. His feet dangling, Simon tried to discover what the cause of his aviation was. It was Agilis. With stunning strength for a creature so small, he soared to a window and flew out of the Elder Tree, Simon all the while horrorstruck he was hovering three hundred feet from his death.

"Where, Master Dreamwalker?" said Agilis quietly.

"Over there!" shouted Simon, pointing at the entrance. Agilis bolted earthward. Simon's eyes watered as he cut through wind like a missile. Reaching the ground in four seconds, Simon spotted blood and said, "Stop, stop!"

Agilis made a mighty flap and slowed. Floating above the trees, Simon stared at a dead carcass of a deer. It was . . . horribly mangled. Simon couldn't bear to see the open ribcages.

"A deed of no men . . ." muttered Agilis gravely.

"It went that way," said Simon, pointing left. "Go, go!"

Agilis circled the Elder Tree, which Simon suspected was the most probable area to chase. The gorgon wanted *his* blood, after all.

"Do you see anything?" asked Simon.

"No, Master Dreamwalker," said Agilis. "I'm afraid we might be too late."

"No way!" hissed Simon. "Keep going! If it's inside, we got to warn —" "*You!*"

A rope lashed out of nowhere and wrapped around Simon's ankle. Agilis's grips failed as he was ripped off and pulled to the ground. Simon landed square on his back, the wind completely knocked out of him. He was being dragged. Simon writhed as an iron grip caught his throat and brought him to his feet. Through watery eyes, Simon saw Head Warden glaring down at him. Simon gagged as the grips tightened.

"Sneaking about, are we?" hissed Head Warden dangerously. He looked up at Agilis. "And *Agilis* . . . Now, what wonder . . ."

"Master Dreamwalker has spotted the gorgon," said Agilis, descending quickly. "We were on pursuit."

"Pursuit, is it?" Head Warden shook Simon, who was really suffering suffocation. "Your job would naturally require keeping him indoors. You are overstepping your boundaries once more. It would please me no more," he added maliciously, "than to see you chained in your little den. The Council will judge you for this."

"I speak the truth," said Agilis, his eyes fixed on the strained grip. "Let go of my master."

"*Lies!*" seethed Head Warden. "You will accompany me to the —"

With all the might he could muster, Simon punted the Head Warden's mask. The hand released, and Simon dropped. Through a swollen throat and numb lips, Simon snarl, "We're not lying! I saw it!"

Head Warden recovered. From his hand a ghostly rope formed. "You little runt," he snarled, brandishing his magical tool. "I will have you hung upside down for this!"

"Under whose authority?"

Everybody looked about. Terram came crawling out from the woods, her edged splints dancing as the sun finally breached the mountain tips. She placed herself right between Simon and Head Warden. "Head Warden, I asked you a question," she asked rather pointedly.

Head Warden rescinded his spell-rope. "Governess Terram, this pupil has broken curfew, and his sentry —"

"The child said he *saw* the gorgon." Terram cut across coldly. This was most uncharacteristic. She was usually so kind. "And you repay him with, what was it, '*hung upside down*'?"

Head Warden sounded as if he was speaking through gritted teeth. "I meant no harm, Governess."

"You were *choking* him," said Terram, fury slowly boiling in her voice. "I ask again, under whose authority do you have the right to hurt a pupil?" When Head Warden hesitated, Terram snapped loudly, "*Answer!*"

Head Warden bowed and followed with, "Forgive me, Governess Terram. I misjudged . . ."

Terram bristled. "Return to your post. I will take him back to his quarters." She turned away. "Come, child." She looked at Agilis and added, "You're dismissed."

Agilis bowed and soared away. Simon walked up the steps to the Elder Tree, leaving Head Warden stiff and sulking. Kind of fearing the ropes might come again, Simon ran the last couple of steps into the Elder Tree.

"Are you alright, child?" Simon nodded. Terram grumbled, "Head Warden has been relentless in the past, but this is the first time I've seen him harm a pupil." She shook her back heatedly. "Violence against a *seedling* . . . How preposterous!"

Simon rubbed his throat. It was strange to see Terram angry. Heated temper was usually Ignis's fort. "I'm fine," said Simon. "Thanks for saving me. I can find my way back from here."

"No, child, we are not going to your quarters."

"Where, then?" asked Simon blankly.

"It's come to our mind," said Terram, her soft sides finally surfacing, "that maybe both of us deserve a briefing."

They climbed the grand steps and into the foyer. There was no one, obviously. At the north end, where another file of steps taxed them, they stood before the beautiful fluorescent throne that was occupied by Cybele during the Blood Avowal. Upon approach, however, the vines slithered and shifted until it reconstructed itself from a throne to a dazzling corridor.

"In here," said Terram.

Simon goggled as he entered. The entrance tossed and turned until it was sealed.

"Was this around all the time?" asked Simon curiously.

"Yes," said Terram. "This is a strictly regulated access point to the Chamber of Primals. Admittance is granted by Lady Cybele, but for an Eld that is not required."

They climbed the glistening corridor, the magical vines almost making it look like the staircases to heaven. At the end of their heavenly ascension they met a small gate. Simon saw drawings of animals. The first, to the top left, was a fiery cat, but he couldn't tell if it looked closer to a lynx or a tiger. A giant sea turtle was just to that right, but it had an elongated neck that curved up, and a snout as well. Bottom left, there was a falconish bird with feathers sticking out form the back of its head. Bottom right was the most eccentric out of them all; it was a ground animal with claws that were long as its paws, and skewers sprouted from its back like a forest of deadly blades. A center piece that completed the picture was a single dial with a star that pronged four ways.

Upon their arrival, the star glowed white, and then the dial cricked and did a one full revolution. The gate made a loud *clunk* and split open.

"Lady Cybele," said Terram as she passed the gate. "I've brought the child."

The chamber was much brighter than the tunnel, and also spectacularly colorful. Not just vines, but gems big as cars were implanted within the walls, sparkling like colored water on a summer's day. Parts of the floor were submerged, and pale flowers bedded them as their feelers extended and danced. Following through the forest of flowers, Cybele sat in a hollow groove at the end of the chamber. A lone, bronze gargoyle was stationed above her, larger and more majestic than any of the sentries Simon had ever seen. Ignis, Aqua, and Ventus were at peace next to her. Ignis awoke from his slumber and turned his head. "Another failed trip?" he inquired.

"I can't say," said Terram, scuttling towards them. "The child saw it just this morning."

"Then it's still a failed trip," growled Ignis. He looked at Simon. "Boy."

"Hi," said Simon.

"Hello . . . young . . . one . . ." croaked Aqua.

Ventus screeched, "Simon! Hello, Simon!"

Cybele descended from the cavity and veered to the right. Her godly voice spoke out, "Welcome."

"Hi." After thinking twice, Simon added, "Uh . . . I mean, hello, Lady Cybele."

"I would prefer if you would address me as *Cybele*," said Cybele, looking back. "No formalities. No courtesies. With or without company. I will be Cybele to you, and you will be Simon to me. Do you accept?"

Simon nodded. He was never really the curtseying type. "Yeah, sounds good." He looked around. "What is this place, anyways?"

"The Chamber of Primals," said Cybele. The feelers from the flowers extended after her, as if dearly longing to kiss her flawless skin. "The place where Primal Atta and Madrem bound the treaty of peace between the Elds." She looked at Simon through her lucent hair. "Walk with me."

Simon followed. The chamber was big enough for a thoughtful stroll. Simon saw fishes gliding with perfect ease. Ignis crouched and observe the marine animals, his tail twitching rather irresistibly.

"We haven't spoken since your awakening, have we?" asked Cybele, stretching a hand and letting the feelers wrap around her wrist. "How is your life in Eldwoods?"

"Good," said Simon, watching Ventus nip at Ignis's tail before flying off from furious slashes.

"Any particular things that interest you?" Cybele asked.

"Hmm." Simon thought for a moment. "Everything."

"Quite an interest," said Cybele encouragingly. "I feel much promise."

"I'm not great, though," said Simon quickly. "Rachel and Fortis helps me a lot. Oh, and Vel, too."

"And so I've heard," said Cybele, now moving on again. "A fine choice of friends. I couldn't ask for a better companion. But speaking of the contrary, it seems you've also developed rough relations with others?"

Simon gawked. "How'd you know?"

Cybele smiled. "It's fine that there are some you are in discord. This is a place for harmony, but you cannot establish that without experiencing conflict. That is what being young is all about."

"You make it sound like you're really old or something," said Simon.

Cybele made a hearty laugh. "I can't deny that."

"Don't kid," said Simon, taking his turn to laugh. She might be smarter, but she couldn't be possibly older than him. Six? Seven, at most.

"Your mistake is your keen observation," said Ignis. He leaped onto Simon's shoulder, and Simon winced for a moment if the claws were going to come. But surprisingly, Ignis was mellow this morning. "Her appearance is because the Runes have gone missing. Her true form will make you kneel and shed tears of admiration."

Simon raised a brow. " . . . How old are you?"

Cybele made a thoughtful pause before saying, "Exact count has slipped my mind a long time ago, but I would proximate somewhere around forty thousand."

Simon choked, "Forty thousand years old?"

Aqua emerged from the bed of water. He was looking livelier than on land. "Lady Cybele . . . has lived . . . for a very . . . long time . . ."

Cybele smiled as she touched another garden of feelers. "Do you think me old, Aqua?"

"Old . . . compared to . . . the young one . . . My Lady . . ."

Simon continued to gape. Cybele scratched Ventus's beak and said mildly, "The Head Warden has lived longer than I, and Altum still more, and the Governors here the oldest of us all."

The oldest? Something came to thought. Simon asked, "But what about the other Primals? Didn't you say Primal Atta and Primal Madrem made this place?"

Cybele made a sad smile as she slid away from the feelers. "Their lives were taken during The Plight." She held her arms close. "I'm the last living Primal, and their legacy runs in my veins."

Simon stared. " . . . They were your parents?"

"Yes," said Cybele. She turned to Simon and said, "I suppose nobody told you the details of my becoming?" Simon shook his head. Cybele sat down, dipping her feet into the cool water. She patted her side, and Simon joined her. A couple of fishes, the size of carps, came gliding and started lipping their feet. It tickled.

"My birth," Cybele began, "was not a Primal's birth. When land and life is most prosperous, a single tree sprouts from the ground and fructifies for seven days. That is the Birth Tree. If there is no hindrance in prosperity, the fruit that has ripened falls and plants its seed into the earth, and from that seed a Primal is born." Cybele caressed one of the fishes with her toe. "That is how it's supposed to be. But I, who was destined to be the one ruler, was born here in this very chamber."

Simon looked around. It wasn't really a place suited for a tree to grow, or a seed to be planted. "How?" Cybele touched her stomach, and Simon took a few seconds until he understood. "Oh."

"It was the first ever and last to fructify a Primal that way," said Cybele. "It could've gone wrong, or *horribly* wrong. But by some miracle, it prevailed. During their pregnancy, I was imbued with the power of the Runes, and since the Runes were already fused with the Governors, my connection to the Runes and the Governors was spiritual, infrangible. And because of this, my powers expand beyond the abilities of Primals. I have the power to nurture life, but also to extinguish it. That made me far superior and valuable than any sentient being alive."

Cybele stared into the water. "But, The Plight came. Myriads of dark creatures and magic came pouring into the beautiful earth, and one by one, Governors fell from their mighty strife. The Primals were never beings of violence and numbers, thus they were captured and killed rather effortlessly. And the Philosophers, as talented and brilliant minded as they were, slowly dwindled.

"And, in those frail moments, the Rune Snatcher assassinated the last genuine Primals."

Simon looked down at his hands, finding no words worth the soothing Cybele deserved. "Sorry . . ."

"I never had the blessing to know them," said Cybele cheerfully. "It's been forty millennia, on top of that. Past souls are not meant for weeping. Everything comes from earth, and returns to earth (well, spare Hollow). You can only kiss your beloved farewell as they drift into serenity . . . from whence they came."

Simon was mute. He hit a wall that obstructed him from sharing a common insight. At the tiniest part in his heart, he was never able to fully detach his feelings from his own loss. His mother still lived in him, as a reminder why he chose Eldwoods. Cutting that part out would be like forgetting who he was.

"Following their death was my capture, along with the Runes."

Silly turned. He faintly remembered Magnus saying something similar. Saving Cybele.

"You . . . were captured?" he asked.

Cybele nodded. "That is the one piece of history that is not mentioned. I was snatched, when I was barely an infant. Speculations conclude information about the powers of the Runes and my connection to them were leaked, thus Hollow would have me unspoiled until they figured how to sever the link. Simply killing me was not an answer, you see. If I die, the Runes perish, too."

So that was why Magnus sounded so angry at the time; he felt like Cybele owed the Philosophers her life, her throne, her *everything*. Was that how every Blood family felt? Was that why Simon was being hated? Because he was siding with the wrong side?

"Thereafter, it is the story you were told at the Blood Avowal. The Philosophers ventured into Hollow, and I was safely returned, still an infant, with the Governors who have also regained their strengths." Cybele sighed. "But then that isn't the entirety of our history, is it? I'm sure you've already presumed the tension between me and the Luminaries?" Simon nodded. "They are descendants of the Philosophers. By right, we treat them as equals, but internal conflicts have sparked more often than one might think. It's a pity . . . Our ancestors fought and died for the world we live in today, and yet here we squabble, arguing who shall ascend to the throne . . ."

It was a solemn story before, but now it was downright depressing. Simon mutely watched the carps bat their tails against his feet. Ignis was curled next to Cybele, drowned in another silent slumber. Ventus, for the first time in Simon's memories, was noiseless. At the other side of the chamber, Aqua was swimming as Terram rode on his shell. They seemed to share an inaudible conversation.

"It is breakfast time," said Cybele peacefully. "It would help you fill your stomach. Unless you have other queries?"

Simon was about to push up, but then he sat back down and said slowly, "Yeah, I do."

"What is it?"

Simon looked at Cybele very strangely. "You knew the gorgon was still around."

"I did."

Simon asked, "Couldn't you get rid of it?"

Cybele tapped her thumb. "It's been a challenging task." Her voice was very serious. "The gorgon has been appearing and disappearing rather subtly. It's method of disguise is almost perplexing. At one time it's there, the next second we're chasing a ghost. Our greatest relief is that the gorgon is not keen to wander beneath the sun. That is why the curfew was established. But I was rather astounded you, above all people, would be the one to spot it in the open. *Twice.*"

"So now what?" asked Simon.

Aqua and Terram came swimming towards them. Terram spoke, "There are other gorgons that exist. They aren't in good relations with us, but we are initiating to see if there is a chance asking for help. The most numerous, and recent, interaction was with *Medusa*, and she has shown signs that she finds interest in this matter."

"Another gorgon?" Simon didn't like the sound of that. A gorgon to help find another gorgon in Eldwoods . . . The prospects was already looking grave. "Does it really have to be like that?"

"For six months, the creature has prowled our lands," growled Ignis, waking. "The best way to rid of it is to ask its brethren the patterns and methods."

"So that's it, then?" said Simon. "We're going to see another gorgon in Eldwoods?"

Cybele smiled painfully. "Its drastic measures, but with my and the Governors' powers lost, it is the only way. Our departure is scheduled in a few hours. Me, the Governors, and the Head Scholars as well. Sincerity must show to obtain her aid. Please," she said caringly, "be careful during our absence."

Ventus came swooping down, making a ruckus after a long while of silence. "Time to eat! Time to eat, Simon!"

"Yes," said Cybele, pulling her feet out of the water. "It's best if you go, now."

Simon got up as well and headed to the gate. Cybele and the Governors escorted him until he passed the gate and proceeded into the tunnel. But after a few steps, Simon stopped. He asked quietly, "Cybele?"

Cybele inclined her head. "Yes?"

Simon hesitated. "Why does it want the blood of Elds? Isn't it incompatible with a gorgon?"

Cybele and the Governors looked pleasantly surprised. Ventus made a girlish chortle. Simon stared at her. It was the most feminine side he had ever heard from Ventus. She sounded like she was enjoying the moment. In a faintly crooked way, though. "Did his homework, I see . . ." She said. She sounded a bit . . . *wicked*.

"There are many postulations," replied Cybele, her eyes drifting astray for a moment. "But our best guess . . . is that the gorgon possesses something of an Eld, and tends to use it for ungrateful deeds."

"Like what?" asked Simon.

Cybele shook her head. "I cannot say. It's still too soon."

That was the end of the subject. It was either they really didn't know, or it was top secret information that they'd rather keep away from Simon. Either way, it didn't look pretty.

Simon felt abruptly tired. He had woken earlier than usual, and his stomach was growling. It was time to really leave. He waved at them.

"Bye."

Cybele smiled back at him. "Good bye, Simon."

chapter twenty-two ~~~
Snatched

"So the gorgon tried to kill you," said Fortis slowly, "because it has something of an Eld it's trying to use?"

"That about sums it up," said Simon, wiping his mouth clean.

"No, that doesn't," said Rachel sharply, pointing her knife. "You said that Lady Cybele's trying to communicate with another gorgon, right?"

"She might've left already," said Simon, pushing his empty tray aside. "Though, I don't like that idea."

"Seconded," said Fortis, beating his cane against his hand. "Gorgons have done horrible things. I'd hate to walk around with that thing on my tail."

Rachel looked at them pitifully. Simon frowned and said defensively, "What? There's nothing good about them!"

"Is she scowling at us again?" asked Fortis, grinning.

"Kind of," said Simon.

"Right," said Fortis, leaning forward. "Let's hear it. What's the deal?"

Rachel sighed. "You two obviously don't see how crucial this matter is."

"We know it's important," said Simon crossly.

"No, you don't," snapped Rachel, neutralizing Simon's scowl. "Seriously, you guys. Remember what they said about the Elds? They're powerful, and very, very old. They know a hundred, maybe a thousand, times more than what we could possible learn. What would you think if a Governor or a Primal, who's lived far longer than anything, comes up to you and says, Oh, I can't figure this out, would you help me?"

Simon's automatic response was, "We'd give up."

"Yes, we'd lose hope, so they're trying to find a solution without demoralizing all of us," said Rachel, stabbing her knife into a sausage. "You already mentioned the gorgon might have something of an Eld, and it requires blood of an Eld to use it, right? Well, think of it this way: if, with Lady Cybele and the Governors powerless at the moment, the gorgon *does* manage to get its hands on the blood of Elds and stimulates her weapon,

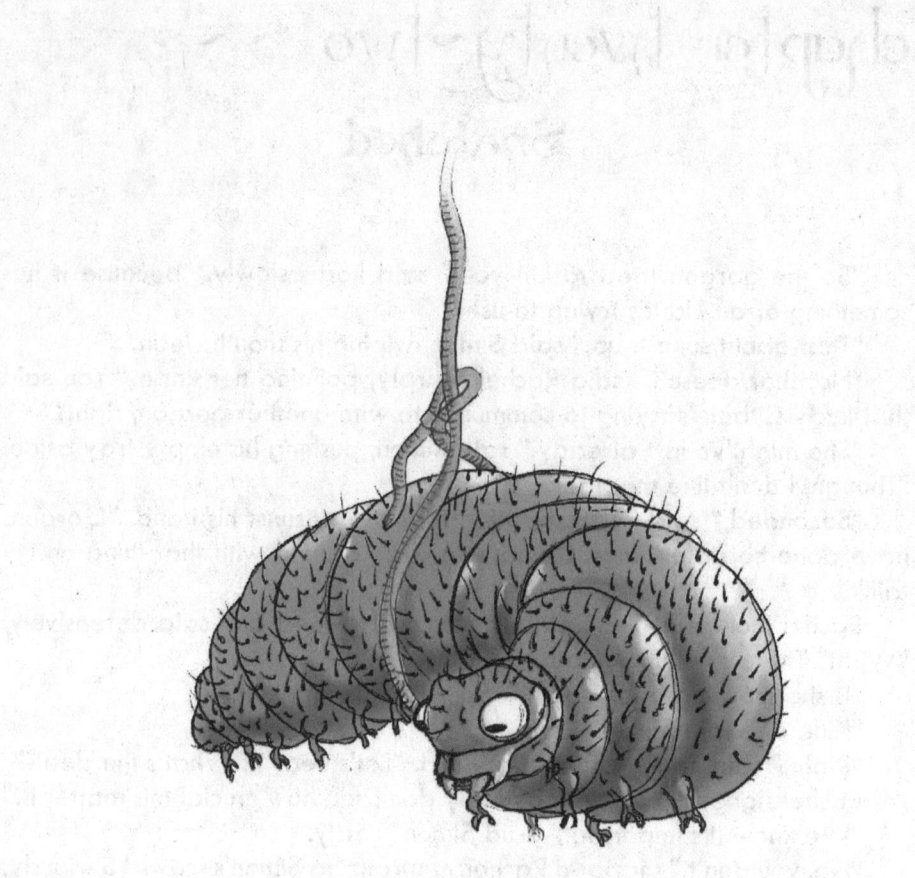

there'll probably be nothing left of Eldwoods. Worse comes to worst," she added grimly, "it could be a second Plight. Get it? It's not a simple matter of liking or not liking. They've run out of options."

"So for that to not happen, you're saying it's okay for another gorgon to roam the grounds?" asked Fortis.

"It's the wisest move," said Rachel, who took no pleasure in saying this. "It's dangerous, but the only way. They're not brutes; gorgon's can be reasoned with. If the meeting goes well, who knows, maybe it'll do more help than bad."

Fortis shook his head disapprovingly. "Still don't like the idea. They're known to kill people regularly. It's a wonder how they're keeping it quiet. If I could see," Fortis squeezed his cane, "I'd hunt them down and make them pay."

"Well," said Simon, thinking the matter in a different perspective, "We are doing that. We're hunting down a gorgon, it's just that we're using another gorgon to do the job. Ironic, eh?"

"It's ironic how you're agreeing to this," said Fortis, grinning in disbelief. "You almost got killed by one, you know?"

Rachel flipped through Ami's notes and muttered, "Something of an Eld . . . something of an Eld . . ."

"There she goes again," said Simon. "Hurry up. We have Wrangling."

But Rachel, after getting up, said, "You two go ahead. I'm stopping by mom's place."

"Sure, but why?" asked Fortis curiously.

"I'm going to look up a few things." She was already walking away. She yelled, "Didn't think about searching there! There could be something useful!"

"Nice thinking," said Fortis as he placed a hand on Simon's shoulder. "There might be remedial records that could help."

But, Rachel did not return for wrangling. Simon searched the Elder Tree as session started. He had seen her absent from school before, but not unless she could help it. This was most uncharacteristic.

"Think she might've tripped?" asked Fortis. "Sprained an ankle or something?"

"Not a chance," said Simon as Captain Shark gathered attention. "Even if she did, her mom's a remedist. She'd know how to patch herself up."

"From today and until the upcoming summer wrangling season," shouted Captain Shark, "we will be reviewing what you've learned so far. You've covered wolpertingers, kobaloi, and ravagers, yeah?" Seedlings nodded. "So, you'll be catching them as a whole for evaluation for the

The Rune Snatcher and the Primal Heart

remaining four weeks!" The beaming face of Captain Shark was a misinterpretation of how this news sounded to the pupils. Most of the pupils groaned as their shoes dipped into the slushy mud, hardly portraying any mobility. Even Simon, who was always looking forward for some wrangling, couldn't quite appreciate the conditions they were competing in.

"Don't worry, lads!" barked the captain happily. "You'll have all morning, and some of the afternoon to finish this. Plenty of time to wrangle." This beckoned more groans. Magnus and the Bloods shuffled their feet sourly, showing obvious signs they wished not to waste time on, what they considered, small game. "Your job is to wrangle two wolpertingers, two kobaloi, and three ravagers. No need to bring them back. We'll know if you caught them or not. You have your ropes, knives, boots, and baits here." Captain Shark pointed at the pile of accessories next to him. "Get to work, lads! Snap to it!"

Simon fastened his boots as Captain Shark encouraged Uro and Aro for their enthusiasm. He neared Simon next and said, "Ready to *throw a noose*, Simon?"

"Say what?" asked Simon.

"An old expression wranglers use, mate," said Captain Shark, thumping Simons' back (Simon thought his eyes might've popped out). "You're really making yourself stand out, lad. I knew you had the skills in you."

"What about Vel?" said Simon, smiling, but still not entirely comforted from the idea of running on soaked grounds. "She usually wrangles better than me."

"Yes, she's a natural," said Captain Shark, his beard rising as he grinned. "Can't help it, though. Her brother's Theseus. The bloke is a damn good rover."

"She has a brother?" asked Simon.

"Oh yeah," said Captain Shark, puffing his chest proudly. "Trained him myself, you know. One of the best that I've educated. Bides his time more than necessary, but he gets the job done clean. It's too soon to give this away," he leaned closer, "but you two are probably the only ones I've seen that show equal promise."

Simon tried to hide it, but he couldn't prevent his pride from creeping up his face. "Thanks, captain."

Captain Shark winked.

Without Rachel and Fortis, Simon was now officially alone in the wrangling competition. Uro and Aro were showing their outstanding exhilaration by taking off their cloaks and camouflaging themselves by rubbing mud onto their bodies. Vel who was always the solemn hunter vanished into the woods without the waterproof, warm boots. Simon collected his gears, two lake roaches, and directed himself away from everybody else.

The first he managed to catch were two ravagers, which required little to no effort since all they did was just eat. The wolpertinger was much trickier, since it required Simon to layout the stones himself and scare it to dash towards him. It took an unexpected turn at the last second, but Simon was able to launch himself and catch it in its flight. The last ravager was seen by the end of the morning hours.

"Nice sequential catch," said Fortis, as sandwiches were brought to them at lunch time. "Just need to focus on tackling the difficult ones, now."

"Yup," said Simon, biting off a chunk and swallowing it whole. "Getting there." He was still down a kobaloi than Vel.

After replenishing his strength, Simon managed to catch the kobalois in succession. Simon presumed without the snow the disadvantage would be canceled out, but it appeared it was just as mobile on wet ground. The last wolpertinger brought forth great effort and devotion to wrangle, since it was preyed upon by Vass as well. Simon managed to exploit his skills and experience in the mountain terrains and snatch it right beneath Vass's chin.

"Hand it over," growled Vass as Simon held his prize by the scruff.

"Get your own," panted Simon. "I already caught it. It's mine."

Vass contorted his face, but the rules were unbreakable. A sailor neared them from the woods, and he made a mark on his clipboard and said, "Simon Dreamwalker. Task complete. You may return."

Simon handed over the wolpertinger and stalked away, leaving Vass shaking his arm in fury. Simon got back to the clearing, and Captain Shark clapped his hands very loudly. Fortis, predicting from the captains exuberant laudation, clapped along.

"As I've expected, lad!" said Captain Shark as Simon pulled off his boots. "More than expected! You are first in place!"

"What?" said Simon, shocked at the unexpected upshot.

"You're first!" yelled the captain, thumping Simon as if to break his shoulder. "Closely followed by Vel and Magnus! I saw you right, lad! I saw you right! I knew you had it in you!"

"Congratulations," said Fortis, smiling proudly. "Better tell Rachel. She'll go fruity."

"But what happened?" asked Simon in disbelief. "Vel only had a ravager and a kobaloi left! She could've caught them in less than an hour."

"Luck plays its parts," said Fortis, patting Simon's arm. "Besides, being first all the time makes it lame. Fun to mix it up once in a while, don't you think?"

"Doozie!" said Captain Shark, his booming laughter still echoing. "Down right brilliant! Oh, here comes our second," said the captain, his grin spreading even wider. "You two tickle my beard. I can't stress how —"

Captain Shark broke off. It wasn't Vel. Nor was it Magnus. Not even Aemulus, Uro, or Aro. Mary emerged, with a moderately fat wolpertinger in her arms. Her face was clean and expressionless, and her eyes lost focus as she walked spiritlessly. Simon gaped. "Mary?"

"Well, if this isn't a surprise!" said Captain Shark, both stupefied and amused. "You managed to wrangle the remaining five? Now that's what I call a feat!"

But Simon knew that couldn't be it. Mary's face was blanched with shock. She was squeezing Chipper tight as she could, and she was limping. The moment she came into the clearing, Simon rushed forward as she dropped to her knees. She was shaking like a leaf. Captain Shark immediately marched over and knelt next to Simon.

"What is it, missy? You hurt?"

Her eyes were unfocused. Simon shook her slightly and yelled, "Mary!" Mary jumped and found Simon. Her eyes grew even larger. "Mary," Simon said loudly, "what happened? What is it?"

Mary opened her mouth, but gagged for a few seconds. The captain grabbed her as he said, "Up you get, missy. Remedists can patch up that ankle. You'll be good as new once they're done."

But Mary suddenly dropped Chipper and grabbed Simon's arms. Her grip was taut and resolute. "Simon!" she whispered, tears abruptly pouring.

"What?" breathed Simon. "What? What's wrong?"

Mary shook her head furiously. "I — I —" Her lungs took in a mighty drag. "Chipper — he came running — from — from the — the —"

Simon's guts flipped as he immediately imagined yellow eyes, broken claws, and a tail so big and long, it could crush a cow like a toothpick.

"Is it out?" whispered Simon. "Did the gorgon show? In daylight?"

Mary nodded frantically, her tears flying off. The Captain rose to his feet and barked at the sailors near him, "Call in the seedlings! Alert the wardens surrounding the wrangling ground to tighten security! Send word to Head Warden we need every unit he could spare!"

But Simon knew she wasn't done. Mary was now showing signs of fainting from uncontrollable stress. Simon clapped his hand over her cheeks and said, "What then? What?"

"Ah —! Ahg —!" She barely pushed down a tremulous cry and said, "And then Vel c-came a — ah-n — ahg — and — she — she pushed me out — out of —!"

Simon's head went absolutely white. Disbelief, stupefaction, and most of all fear. Mary finally gave out and expelled a heart-aching wail. "IT TOOK HER! IT TOOK HER! IT TOOK VEL!"

chapter twenty-three~~~
Unto Darkness

Simon remained still, covering his eyes and leaning against his knee. Fortis sat next to him, gripping his cane as if to shatter it. "Don't give up," said Fortis strongly, but his face was somber. "Everybody's working on finding her. She's strong. She'll be alive."

"Last time I got scratched, I almost died in a minute," said Simon quietly, hating himself that he recalled that part of his memory. "She can't survive that."

"Mary said it *took* her, not hurt her," said Fortis. He was forcing his voice to sound confident and assured. "She's alive. Don't lose hope."

Simon pushed his eyeballs deep into his skull, imagining Vel alive. Crushed within the coils of the monster, limbs torn just like the deer, blood spilling like a fountain; that was the *least* dreadful thought he could muster. He hated himself for that.

"Cybele's gone," said Simon gravely, "Ignis, Aqua, Ventus, and Terram's gone. Head Scholars are gone. Nobody's here."

"We have Head Warden, still," said Fortis.

"Like he'd risk his life for kids like us," growled Simon, clenching his hair. "He'll wait for Cybele to come back. By that time, Vel will be dead."

"You don't know that," said Fortis.

"*I know*," said Simon harshly, his fingers cracking. "He won't help us. He'll let Vel die." Simon cursed out loud. "I know how he thinks of us. He doesn't care about seedlings. He nearly *choked* me this morning. . ."

Silence took over. It was thirty before five. Simon couldn't pray harder for time to cease, prolong Vel's life, and spare her mercy. It wasn't fair. It was Simon who should've been caught. It was after him. If only he fell into the gorgon's hands that day, innocent people wouldn't have been involved. He wished he could revert time and uphold that fate, so Vel could be still in the wrangling ground, arise as first in the evaluation. And yet, here he was, taking both her places in wrangling and life. Why did it come to this? Why . . .

"Master Dreamwalker," said Agilis. "You have a visitor."

"I don't want to see anyone," said Simon gloomily.

The door crashed open, and Rachel marched in with Ami's notebook and a huge book. Simon got up at once and said, "How's Mary?"

"She's fine," said Rachel, her expression chalked, but sane. "Mom gave her sleeping agents. She . . . she couldn't stop blaming herself."

Simon understood that. He couldn't forgive himself as well.

"But you've got to see this," said Rachel, slamming down the book on the desk.

"It doesn't matter," said Simon, his knuckles bloodless. "It was supposed to get me, but I let Vel get captured instead. It's all my fault. I should've let it take me last time."

"Don't say that," said Fortis gratingly, almost sounding like he was punishing Simon. "Nobody's life is worth giving away. You lived. That's what counts."

Rachel found the page she was searching for before slapping the notebook down this time. She flipped through the notes and pointed. *"Blood of Elds, compatible to substitute one another."* She nearly ripped the page off as she proceeded to the next one. *"Heart of a Primal, can remain alive under dormancy while being fed the blood of animals, can be reawakened by the blood of Elds."*
She then threw the notebook aside and jabbed her finger on the giant book. "A Primal Heart, also known as the Seed of Life, is known for its unfathomable life force that could ail desolated lands. The heart of Primal Madrem is said to have removed the inflictions from The Plight and restored nature to an inhabitable domain. The Primal Heart is also known for its absolute power to cure any curse or wound. But, a Primal Heart unwillingly taken dwindles, or stoops into dormancy. By offering the blood at a regular basis prevents the heart from failing, but it cannot be reawakened unless a blood of an Eld is contributed. The only known successful applications of Primal Hearts are bequeathed by Primal Madrem and Primal Tristis."

Rachel slammed her palm down and weakly, "I can't believe I missed this part. I was so focused on how she was going to weaponize the blood, it didn't occur to me that its goal was to lift its curse. I was so stupid!" She slapped her forehead so hard, Fortis raised his eyebrows in concern. "It was right there! I should've paid attention."

The fact that it took Vel for keeping the heart alive gave Simon new hope, but not enough to make him stay and wait. He saw Vel suffering in pain as the gorgon slowly poured her blood on top of a beating heart. There was no way he was going to let that happen.

"We have to stop it," he breathed. "We have to go after it and save Vel."

Rachel looked like a she just got shot. Fortis got up and said, "Calm down, Simon —"

"Calm down?!" yelled Simon, turning at him. "This is calm as it's going to get! Vel's kidnapped, and nobody's going to do anything until Cybele gets back, and by that time Vel won't have a drop of blood left in her! You want to hope for a miracle, fine go ahead. But I'm not going to sit around and pray when Vel's out there waiting to die." Simon threw down his cloak. "I'm going, and you two aren't going to stop me."

Simon glowered at them as if to dare to challenge him. Rachel was paler than before, and she kept squeezing each of her fingers. Fortis was solemn and contemplative. But no objections aroused. Simon's nostrils flared.

"Good," he said, stalking to his desk and opening the drawers. Fortis stood there as he slowly tapped his cane. Simon collected the animal repellent received from Claire, the tiki figure from Brendon, and the linen bandage imbued with healing wax that Rachel and Fortis made by hand. The knife he hadn't returned from wrangling was placed under his belt.

"Alright, I get it . . ."

Simon turned. Fortis had an odd crease upon his brows. Fortis mumbled, "I'll come along."

What on sweet earth could have instigated that reaction? Simon immediately said, "No. I'm going alone. Vel's —"

"Vel put herself in danger because she knew it could save a life," said Rachel piously, also displaying a sense of duty. "It's better three than one."

Simon gaped at her. "I thought you didn't like wrangling?"

"Oh," said Rachel, laughing nervously, "it's all about getting used to it, isn't it?"

Simon turned to Fortis. In truth, it was a worrisome prospect. Fortis couldn't see, which made him prone to injuries.

"Don't even think about it," said Fortis, reading Simon's worries. "You heard me this morning. I'd hunt them down and make them pay."

"But Simon," said Rachel uncertainly, "how are you going to find it? Nobody's been able to —"

Simon already knew that answer. The dreams he was having . . .there was already an answer. "The reason they couldn't find it," said Simon, retracing his dreams, "is because it's underground. Grendel said it's a forgotten place. A cave, and then tunnels. And," Simon closed his eyes and revisited the cave entrance, "I know where it is."

"Are you sure?" asked Rachel anxiously. "How do you know all this? Who's Grendel? Did Lady Cybele tell you?"

"No," said Simon. "She doesn't know. Nobody knows. For a reason." He asked for the last time, "You two really are coming? I won't be able to keep you safe, you know?"

Rachel gulped and nodded. Fortis laughed dryly and said, "You're hot headed sometimes. You need people like me to pull your leash and keep your head cool."

Simon pocketed the bandage and animal repellent.

"Agilis!" Agilis came swooping in. Simon asked, "You heard everything?"

Agilis nodded. "I will assist you in whatever way necessary."

Simon said bluntly, "Then there's something I want you to do . . ."

The way out of the Elder Tree was heavily guarded by patrolling wardens. It took considerable effort on Simon to sneak up to their shadows and cast rocks to distract their attention while Rachel quickly guided Fortis to the next cover. Rachel whispered, "You know, for a *warden*, they're surprisingly dense, aren't they?"

"Yeah," said Simon, searching up ahead. "Let's hope it stays like that."

They swiftly made it to the foyer, and praying they wouldn't get spotted, they hurried down the grand stairs (Fortis with some difficulty). The entrance was guarded. Seeing those wardens in a single file, glaring into the forest, seemed almost foolish to try to penetrate.

Just as they hid to the right within a small corridor, Agilis glided to their side from the top windows. "How does it look?" asked Simon.

"Most wardens are stationed within Elder Tree, Master Dreamwalker."

Simon took deep breaths. He handed over the tiki figure and said, "I'll meet you outside."

Agilis took off. Simon glanced at the wardens. They seemed rather reluctant to budge. Would they fall for it? If not, he was going to have to knock them out with a stick or something, and he preferred not to.

Minutes passed. Did Agilis find a suitable spot? Just as Simon was getting worried, a painful, reverberating cry came from somewhere above. The wardens turned to the grand stairs. "What was that?" One shouted.

The second tiki scream rattled the air, and the tallest warden roared, "It got through! Rally everyone!"

The wardens dashed up the steps. Thanking his plan worked, Simon ran towards the entrance and out into the forest, Rachel and Fortis hot on his heels. The three of them moved away as fast as possible.

"Where is it, exactly?" asked Fortis.

"It's somewhere close." Simon traipsed near the Elder Tree, looking for gaps between the roots. "I dreamt about it," said Simon quietly, beginning to climb a bit. "I walked from the forest, and then there was a cave. It was up on the roots. Or inside of the roots. It was open the first time, but it closed up. I could still get in, though. I was like . . . like a ghost or something."

"You know," said Fortis, lingering at the bottom while Rachel followed Simon clumsily, "you really sound a bit . . . nuts."

"I've been nuts all my life, remember?" said Simon, wrenching at a channel of vines that broke and threw him off balance. "I'm getting quite used to it, now."

"But Simon," panted Rachel, her feet slipping, "haven't you ever thought relying on dreams could be farfetched?"

"Not since I came to Eldwoods, nope," said Simon, hopping down a few feet. "Magic, remember? Anything could happen."

"Yes, but not this!" grunted Rachel as she leveled with Simon. "These aren't visions, Simon. You said you were seeing things that were actually occurring. Clairvoyance is made up stuff. There isn't magic like that."

"Well, that's a first," said Simon, digging through dirt. "Something that even you don't know. Maybe you can write an essay about it."

"Simon!" hissed Rachel, irritated.

Agilis loomed over them, making Rachel jump and almost fall. Simon caught her as he said, "How long till they find out?"

"At most, two minutes, Master Dreamwalker," said Agilis. "And your other request . . ."

"Yeah?" said Simon eagerly.

"There is a location fitting your descriptions." Agilis pointed. "It faces the east."

"Show me," said Simon, helping Rachel back down to the forest ground.

They headed east, keeping close to the roots. Fortis yanked Simon back when a wrangler stuck his head out the lower windows, but they managed to travel undetected. When the setting sun was completely masked by the Elder Tree, Agilis lifted Fortis and took him up the roots. "This way, Master Dreamwalker."

Simon climbed the roots, turning back once in a while to confirm Rachel was following. It was not that far up. Simon reached where Fortis stood and pulled Rachel up. Rachel's lack of athleticism was showing; sweat dripped from her chin as they streamed beneath her hair.

"You sure you're up for this?" asked Simon doubtfully.

"I'll be fine," said Rachel, wiping her chin dry. "So, where is it?"

It was exactly as Simon remembered it. In the midst of abnormally tall trees, where light barely made it through the coats of branches and (newly formed) leaves, he stood before a gaping fissure between two roots the size of school buses. Vines and lesser roots were entangled within the gap like a net. Simon stepped on something. He looked down. It was a shed skin, dry and decaying.

"Who would've thought," he whispered, picking the shed skin up. "Everybody was so obsessed it was out there. It only did appear in the woods, so people naturally suspected there had to be a nest further out, somewhere dark and unsearched." He then looked at the vines. "Nobody could've even thought about it. Not even Cybele." Simon knelt and lowered his hand. "That the gorgon was right under Elder Tree."

The roots and vines abruptly uncoiled, and the familiar gaping hole presented itself to them. Deep. Ominous. Rachel gawked at it. Simon knew there was little to no light down there. He held up his index finger and said, "*Passio!*" It lit like a candle.

"Now that's what you meant," said Fortis, waving his cane and confirming the cave's existence. "This is probably the worst handicap for us. I'm okay without light, but you two are really going in blind."

"*Passio!*" said Rachel, lighting her finger, too. "We have Agilis. Gargoyles can see in the darkness."

"Yes, Miss Fairburn," said Agilis. "I am quite capable."

"No wasting time," said Simon, and he jumped down first. His feet hit wet earth. The place was a lot damper than the outside, but breathing was the same. "It's good. Come on."

Agilis carried Fortis down as Rachel received help from Simon. At that precise moment, the cover draped the entrance once more, cutting all light and sound from the outer world. Simon's and Rachel's feeble flames kept their faces from being eaten by the darkness.

"Oh, for goodness sake," said Rachel irritably. She produced a bigger flame, igniting her entire hand.

The tunnel brightened. Simon could see a good six feet ahead. "I'd do that, but then I can't hold it past thirty seconds without singing my hair."

"Really, Simon, you're good with spells, but you can't do the basics," said Rachel, shaking her head. "You really surprise me sometimes. Agilis?" She turned to the pair of white, glowing eyes. "Would you mind staying ahead of us? You can see everything well, can't you?"

"I will make sure you will not come to harm," said Agilis, "as long as I live and breathe."

"Let's move it," said Fortis, putting a hand on Simon.

They ventured inwards, sloping down slightly. The walls became damper and stickier as they progressed. Footing was definitely unpredictable, and Fortis eventually folded his cane and abandoned all effort in trying to map the ground in his head. Agilis was doing a great job guiding them. His white hair also stood out from the contrastingly darker surroundings. But there was something that even Agilis couldn't cover.

"Master Dreamwalker," said Agilis, halting in midair. "We've met a fork."

Two paths lied before them, equally dark and ominous. Simon stared from one, to another. What now?

"A fork?" said Fortis.

"Yeah," said Simon uneasily. "How far can you see, Agilis?"

"Until darkness subdues my sight," said Agilis, shaking his head.

"Not a problem," said Fortis. He picked up two rocks from the damp soil. "Tell me where they are." Simon directed Fortis to the left tunnel. Fortis shot a rock in that direction. "Next." He shot another rock into the right passage. Fortis put his hands behind his ears and listened very intently. The sound of the stones hitting the ground echoed.

"What are you doing?" asked Simon.

Agilis immediately responded, "He is judging the depth by sound, Master Dreamwalker."

Fortis grinned and pointed to the right path. "There's more ring to that one. The left path's blocked."

"I couldn't hear the difference," said Simon, tilting his head.

"Fortis has been blind for a long time, Simon," said Rachel. "He most likely developed sharper senses than us."

"Especially hearing and sensing," said Fortis as they walked into the right tunnel. "Wait." Fortis knelt and marked an arrow pointing towards the right. "Helps us keep track."

"Agreed," said Rachel approvingly.

Fortis's hearing paid off greatly. Every fork, or three way, they met, Fortis threw stones and guided them to the deeper parts of the tunnels.

Occasional drops made them uneasy, however. It seemed like they were at least a mile down the earth.

"Eek!"

Simon quickly looked back. "What? What?"

Rachel was pointing at the ground. Bones were scattered rather unceremoniously; different parts, sizes, and skulls that Simon couldn't make out if it was really an animal or not. "Oh, gosh," grumbled Rachel, covering her mouth as she kicked a square looking skull out of the way.

"Bones?" asked Fortis

"Yup," said Simon.

"Might be from animals that came in accidentally. Got lost and starved to death," said Fortis mildly.

"Yeah," breathed Simon, grunting as he hit the ground from a four feet drop. "But that's the least of our concern. This place is a maze!"

"Yes," said Rachel, fuming as she broke a skull during descent. She redid her ponytail to push back the few strands of hair that stuck to her drenched face. "But it's not a masterpiece. Fortis can always tell what direction's blocked. If I really had to speak my mind," she added as Fortis descended with Agilis, "I don't think it's the gorgon who made this place."

"What then?" asked Fortis.

Rachel looped her finger. "The way we've been going is a constant funnel. We're going down in a spiral. The other tunnels seem to just be a distraction. But I mean, talk about confusion, it's too simple. If they're so easily detectable, why build them in the first place? Unless the gorgon dug them to add in the flavor."

Now that Rachel mentioned it, Simon abruptly recalled a little piece of his dream the other night. Grendel mentioned this place was forgotten, that nobody outside remembered. "Maybe," he said quietly, "this place is really old. You know, before the gorgon and all."

"It's a theory," said Rachel, being careful not to make hasty conclusions. "But if it is. . .it's probably really, really ancient, with really, really old magic hidden somewhere."

"You have a point," said Fortis. "And plus," he added as he touched the walls, "you'd think you can find tunnels anywhere, but even minors need support shafts to hold the ceiling from crashing down. But there aren't any, are there?"

"No, Sir Goldstone," said Agilis from up front.

"See?" said Fortis. "This place is holding up like it's nobody's business. Only bones," Fortis tapped a ribcage with his cane when he ran into it, "that don't even help. There had to be some magical work done to prevent the routes from caving in."

They met a four way, and Simon rolled his eyes. "Well, with bones or not, this is getting really annoying."

"You're not the one doing the work," said Fortis, grinning. "*Fides!*" Four stones came to his service. "Let's see . . ." He shot one down the furthest left. "Nope." Another flew into the second path. "Hmm . . ." Fortis frowned. "Maybe, but just to make sure." He shot the last two into the remaining paths. His frown got tighter. "Let's see." He stroked his chin for a moment, and then shot two more stones down the second path, and the last. "I think," he said, lowering his hand, "it's that one." He pointed at the fourth tunnel.

"You sounded uncertain for a moment," said Simon as Agilis and Rachel shifted in that direction.

"Well, they both sounded deep," said Fortis getting closer to the second hole. "But . . . I don't know . . . this was . . . it sounded like my rock got caught or something. Didn't even bounce the second time."

"Let's go," said Simon, grabbing Fortis's hand.

"Ye —"

A large pincer stabbed out of the darkness and caught Fortis by the waist. In a flash, Fortis was jerked away from Simon.

"FORTIS!" yelled Simon, and he dashed after him. He could hear Fortis's cane whacking upon something hard, but whatever caught him was scuttling away too fast. "Fortis! Where are you?" yelled Simon. Something caught him by the ankle, and he fell facedown. He muttered, "*Passio!*" and increased his fire, taking a look at what was holding him.

It couldn't be something that nature possibly created. A lizard, skin so pale that Simon could see the veins running through it, seethed as its tongue extended out of its mouth and squeezed over Simons ankle. Eyes were milky, and it's thick, slimy vibrissa quivered as it crawled nearer to Simon.

Simon extracted his knife and stabbed it into the fleshy tongue. Purple goo spilled and spattered his hands. Simon grunted as the monster hissed angrily and threw him aside. Simon scrambled back as the lizard approached again, its tongue going right for the neck.

"Simon!" yelled Rachel.

Agilis came rocketing, putting Rachel down with nimble grace as he sunk his fingers into the lizard's tail. The lizard thrashed as Agilis pulled it away from Simon. "Leave it to me, Master Dreamwalker," said Agilis. Simon got back up and chased deeper into the tunnel. Fortis's grunts resurfaced, but the cane wasn't hitting anything.

"Fortis!" Simon waved his lit hand.

At the end of the tunnel, Fortis was being held by a giant scorpion, just as pale as the lizard and equally sized. Its tail was quivering, ready to deliver the deathblow. *No!* Simon leaped and dove at the grotesque creature, grabbing ahold of the poisonous tail. The scorpion rocked. With blinding dexterity, Simon gripped his knife in his blazing hand, setting the hilt and blade on flames, and cut through the hard shell and severed the tail clean off.

"Fortis, run!" Simon shouted as the scorpion released Fortis in pain. The monster turned to Simon (teetering slightly) and snapped its pincers. Simon ducked the first onslaught, jumped over the second, and landed on top of the scorpion. The pincers reached backwards, but they were just shy from tearing Simon's face off. Simon held on tightly as the scorpion galloped about. He dropped his knife as his hand hit the shell. "Damn!" grunted Simon, punting the scorpion. His knuckles burned in serious pain.

"Fides!"

Simon looked up. Fortis was holding his ribs, but a huge rock, the size of a watermelon, floated before his other outstretched hand. His face was contorted in concentration. "Tell me where," said Fortis in a strained growl.

"To the right!" yelled Simon, doing his best to hold on. "No, a little bit more! Down! There, right there!"

Fortis grunted as he sent the rock bulleting. It hit the scorpion square on the head, and a nasty *crack* told them the shell caved in. The scorpion dithered, its pincers still trying to reach for Simon, and then dropped onto its belly, lifeless.

Simon hopped off of the dead beast and rushed to Fortis's side. "Fortis!"

There was blood, but not a lot. Simon carefully lifted the shirt and saw a small cut. Fortis grunted.

"I won't bleed to death," said Fortis jokingly. "But . . . I think it got one or two ribs."

"Do you think you can walk?" asked Simon, cautiously putting an arm over his shoulder.

"I can manage that," said Fortis, grunting as Simon pulled him to his feet. "Right, this wasn't the right way after all."

Simon collected his knife, and they headed back. The fight against the lizard seemed to be victorious, since Simon spotted Rachel's kindled hand and Agilis's glowing eyes. When they neared, however, Simon saw Rachel was in absolute shock. Drops of purple blood decorated her face, and blood covered her hands and shirt as she looked down at the dead lizard. Its severed tail was stuck through its chest.

"Rachel!" said Simon, lowering Fortis next to Agilis. "She did that?" he asked to Agilis.

"Yes, Master Dreamwalker," said Agilis.

Rachel stared blankly into her drenched palms. Simon quickly took off his sweater. "Here," he said as he dried her blood-coated hands. "Look, it's fine. You did what you needed to do."

"Y-yes," stuttered Rachel, still failing to pull herself together. "I-I'm fine. Just — just a little rattled."

Simon patted her shoulder. "It's okay. You're fine. Here, take a look at Fortis, would you? He's hurt. His bones might be broken."

Rachel shook her head furiously and slapped herself back to sanity. She took two giant breaths and crawled over to Fortis. "Let me see." She lifted the shirt up and examined the flesh wound first. "It won't be a problem. It's shallow." Simon held his lit hand closer as Rachel now proceeded to poke a few areas around the gash. Fortis scowled a couple of times.

"Right," said Rachel seriously. "One of his ribs is broken, and I think the one below it is fractured. It's not life threatening, but if the broken rib shifts, it might take a stab at the wrong place." Rachel looked at Simon and shook her head. "He can't go on like this."

Fortis grinned painfully. "I guess I'm staying behind."

Simon thought very hard, and then said resolutely, "No, you're going back." He turned to Agilis. "Agilis, take Fortis back to the surface, and see if Cybele's back. She needs to know about this place."

"Nuh-uh," said Fortis reluctantly. "You'll be going in blind. You need Agilis."

"And you'll die," said Simon. "Agilis can come back. We marked the paths we took, so he won't have trouble finding us." He looked at Rachel. "We can manage ourselves."

"He's right," said Rachel, nodding resolutely. She took the bandages from Simon and started wrapping it around the wound. "First aid's not enough. You need medical attention."

"Master Dreamwalker," said Agilis.

Simon pushed away the censure. "Agilis, you *have* to take Fortis back. I swear to god I'll change sentries if you don't."

Agilis contemplated agonizingly, but he eventually bowed and said, "I will return to your side with utmost haste."

"Yeah," said Simon.

Rachel pulled off Fortis's cloak and managed to make a loose crib. Agilis held it up with Fortis resting peacefully within. The four of them went back to the four-way. Fortis turned his head in Simon's and Rachel's direction. "If you face something more dangerous, head back that instant, you got me?"

"I hear you," said Simon. "Safe flight."

"Master Dreamwalker."

With that, Agilis and Fortis soared out of sight. Simon and Rachel now faced the fourth tunnel. Simon took out the animal repellent and uncorked it. "I was right bringing this along." He poured half of the content into one of Rachel's hand, and then rubbed the rest onto his own neck. The odor was sharp, and Simon gagged for a few seconds. "Ugh," said Simon, shivering. "That's strong."

"It's harsher on animals," said Rachel, who seemed to handle the scent more gracefully than Simon. "There are eatless leaves in here. The buds are what give the sap, but the leaves have a really strong aroma to it."

"Courtesy to Claire's aunt," said Simon. "Let's go."

They pressed on, marking the ground with an arrow beforehand. It was difficult without the aid of their two navigators. Listening to rocks called forth acute attention, and twice they took the wrong turn. Thankfully, there were no monsters creeping about, either because there weren't any, or the animal repellent was doing a fine job.

Just as they took their sixth turn, Simon noticed the light didn't illuminate further ground. "Rachel!" hissed Simon, and he grabbed her before she fell straight off the cliff.

"Oh!" Rachel backed away. They both stared.

"A ticket to the underworld," said Simon, increasing his flames again and holding it up.

"Look," said Rachel, pointing. "A bridge!"

Simon thought Rachel was just implying a log or a pile of rocks that provided a platform to cross over, but it turned it there was really a genuine stone bridge, ancient, but still holding. Simon gaped. "You're right," he whispered. "This place must be . . . *really, really old.*"

"Do you think it's safe?" asked Rachel.

"Only one way to find out," said Simon. He joined his back against the wall and carefully inched towards the bridge. "Up you get," he said as he helped Rachel board the crossover.

"Oh, I hate heights," muttered Rachel.

"Well, you can't really tell since you can't see the bottom," said Simon.

"And that's supposed to help me?" snapped Rachel, getting more tetchy each step. "You're so dense when it comes to comforting people. *Girls,* especially."

They advanced. At about twenty feet, Simon knew they had reached the center since the bridge dipped back downwards.

"Do you hear that?" asked Rachel acutely.

"What?" said Simon.

They halted.

Bzzzz . . .

"It's just a bug," said Simon, looking about. Rachel looked at him like he was dumber than a brick. "What?"

"*It's a bug,*" said Rachel, putting the oh-my-gosh face on. "Here. Underground, probably more than a mile from light. With *wings*. Bugs that live underground don't fly. They crawl."

Simon looked about. *Bzzzz . . .* "Maybe they just evolved that way."

"Oh, please, Simon," said Rachel, rolling her eyes and bending over the bridge. "It's coming from below. And if that sound can reach us . . .." She froze.

"What?" asked Simon.

Rachel's face was stricken with horror. She slowly reached down, and retrieved something large as her torso. Simon went chalky as well. It was a chrysalis of a ravager.

"Don't even —"

BZZZZ!

Rachel jumped back as a bee shot up from the darkness. It had grassy-green stripes and a menacing sting the size of Simon's thumb. Its outer shell was crinkled, hinting it hadn't eaten regularly. Saliva was dripping from its mouth, soaking its pincers that made an uncomfortable scissor sound when they shut.

"*Coral jackets!*" yelled Rachel.

Five more rushed up and joined the first, and they swooped in for the killing blow. Simon grabbed Rachel and pulled her to the ground, missing the first strike by a hair's width. "*Stasis!*" The first one froze, but a second coral jacket came diving and jabbed where Simon stood a split second ago.

"They're attracted to the light!" yelled Rachel, extinguishing her hand as she rolled. "Simon, turn off your fire!"

Simon put out the flames. Everything went dark. Simon could hear the coral jackets zooming over their heads. He kept absolutely still. He heard, one by one, the coral jackets land on the bridge. That didn't bode well. Without light, he couldn't land a single spell on them, not unless they happened to touch each other, and Simon was sure if that happened he wouldn't manage to deliver the first strike.

Something touched him, and Simon reflexively whipped his hand away. A sharp hiss followed. That was a coral jacket. "Rachel?" said Simon.

"*Shh!*" Rachel's hand miraculously found target and slapped over Simon's mouth. "Just listen, okay? We don't have a lot of time."

More buzzing, and it seemed to slowly converge on them. Rachel brought herself as close as possible to Simon and put her lips against his ears. "They probably lived off of the monsters we saw back then, but they're underfed, and their colors aren't right, meaning thy might be deformed in some way," breathed Rachel hastily. "Coral jackets are bees, and bees detect things by vibration. Even me talking right now will eventually give us away. But, all bugs act the same when there's light and heat." The buzzing drew closer. "They're hungry, so they'll just dive to attack. Avoid it, and burn their wings." Simon could tell the coral jacket was just a few feet away. "When I say so, we split, okay?" hissed Rachel, and since there was no time to argue, Simon nodded. "One. Two. *Three!*"

Both of them lit their hands and dove opposite directions. The bees took flight again, and Simon kicked the closest one out of the way as it went airborne. Three coral jackets were on him. *Piece of cake!* Simon thought to himself, spreading his legs and lowering his weight. The one from the left jetted at him, brandishing its sting. Simon stood his ground until the last second, and when the poisonous needle was inches from his neck, he pulled back his body leftwards — his back almost cracking from the strain — and reached out for the wings; they easily caught on fire. As the wing burned like tissue the coral jacket spun and swerved until it fell below the bridge.

"One down!" yelled Simon, getting back up. "Bring it!"

The second coral jacket shot forward. Simon sidestepped and smacked the wings. It went up first, and then down into the pit like a rock. Simon spun around and eyed the third coral jacket, expecting it to dive. But, this particular one tentatively circled Simon. Simon shook his hand, but it didn't buy.

"Careful, eh?" said Simon, confidence boiling.

The coral jacket flew upwards, into the veil of lightlessness. Simon slowly rotated, continuing to ring his hand. "Come on," he whispered. "Come get me." Simon heard the other coral jackets continuing to bombard Rachel. He really wanted to go help her. Why couldn't this stupid bee just charge at him any sooner?

. . . zzzZZZ!

Simon heard it from behind, and he instinctively pulled out his knife and turned his shoulders. The coral jacket's sting went straight for his liver, but it halted a few inches shy as the blade sunk into its thorax. Simon lost his grip over the hilt as the coral jacket pulled back in agony. It bobbed up and down as the cold steel eventually drained the insect's life. Down the coral jacket went, just like the past two.

"Rachel!" shouted Simon, hurrying towards the other side of the bridge. "Rachel!" His heart sunk when he saw her. Two of the coral jackets were subdued as the flames went past their wings and engulfed their entire body. The remaining one was still lively, preying upon Rachel. Rachel was on the floor, one of her arms limp on her side. She was still sustaining her fire, but her face was strained in excruciating pain. Simon urged his already screaming legs. "Hey!" he spat out. "Hey, bug-face!"

The coral jacket faltered, addled. Simon skidded next to Rachel and waved his ignited hand. "Over here!" The coral jacket fixed his attention on Simon, and it did a full circle before lunging its abdomen. Simon twisted his body, barely avoiding collision, and lashed his hand like a whip, setting the wings on fire. His insect-foe, spinning as it lost balance, went under the bridge, joining its fallen brethren.

Simon knelt and said in a trembling voice, "Rachel! Where're you hurt?" Simon looked at her arm. It was a light scratch, but the wound was unpleasantly swollen. "What do I need to do? Tell me!"

Rachel kept her eyes closed as she said quietly, "Can I have your knife?"

Simon went for the belt, and then realized the blade was down with the blasted coral jackets. "I lost it!" he said weakly.

Rachel sighed painfully. "Then could you get me that?" She pointed at the dead insect's mandibles.

"This?" said Simon doubtfully, grabbing the sharp pincers.

"Yes," said Rachel, a tear finally escaping her lashes. "Hurry."

Simon immediately ripped off the mandible and brought it to her. Rachel took it in her kindling hand. Simon watched anxiously. And then, quite suddenly, Rachel drew a very large breath, raised the mandible, and stabbed it into her swollen arm. An agonizing cry filled the closed space, and Simon gasped.

"Rachel, what —?"

Rachel threw the mandible aside. Blood seeped; it was grotesquely dark and thick for the first three seconds. After that, it was moderately red and unpolluted.

"I need some healing wax," said Rachel feebly.

Simon retrieved his bandages from his pocket and carried out the duty of patching her up right away. He then ripped a part of Rachel's cloak off and tied it over the bandages. After that, Simon ripped another part of Rachel's cloak and made a sling.

"Is it really okay, now? Will you be fine?"

Rachel nodded. "I disinfected the pincer, and most of the poison I got out." She cradled her arm. "But I can't move my arm. It's numbed." She contorted her face, the pain apparently still lingering at some point. Simon held her. She couldn't go on. She was bound to get killed at first sight.

"You have to go back," said Simon.

Rachel opened her eyes. She seemed to foresee this conclusion coming. "Simon . . ."

"Go back. You can still walk, right? Go back, and meet up with Agilis. He's probably on his way. Tell him that I ordered him to get you back safe. And check up on Fortis for me." Rachel's eyes watered, out of pain, but also out of misery. Simon helped her to her feet. "And don't feel sorry for me, alright? You don't have a choice."

Rachel, finally hiccupping and leaking some of her woe, hugged Simon. "I'm sorry, Simon." she said quietly. "I'm sorry. I'm sorry . . ."

"It's fine, Rachel," said Simon. "Told you it's fine. Living's what counts, remember?"

Rachel squeezed even tighter. Simon patted her back gently. Rachel said in a watery voice, "Don't you die on me, okay? You have to come back with Vel." She relinquished him. "I'll bring help. I promise."

Simon nodded. "You'd better get back fast, then. Who knows, maybe Fortis already got some."

Rachel laughed through a fit of hiccups. "Yes . . . maybe . . ."

Simon patted her. "Go on. Hurry."

She looked reluctant to the last second, but Rachel slowly turned and walked back down the bridge. Halting at the tunnel, she looked back, tearing up again. How long had they known each other? Their entire life, rounding up the years. It was weird, Simon admitted, staring like this. It could have been any other day, seeing her walk away, to home, to class, to anywhere else, and he would just wave back without much thought. But tonight, the contexts were very unforgiving. He surely hoped this wasn't going to be the last time. That'd be terrible.

Simon nodded, trying to give a little nudge of confidence to Rachel and himself. Rachel nodded back, but took great strife turning her back. She went through. Simon watched the flickering light slowly fade, and then turned the opposite direction.

"Right," said Simon, breathing calmly. "Here I go."

He marched forward. It was true his concentration and physical stamina was really starting to wane, but there was no time. Vel needed rescuing, and he was the closest person to her. And so Simon went through a new tunnel. He expected there to be more divisions to confuse him, but for some reason it ceased to split. Simon went deeper. And deeper. And yet, deeper.

After what felt like thirty minutes, Simon halted. There was light. A separate, wonderfully peaceful light. Simon extinguished his hand. He couldn't be more thankful. The toll that was taking him to maintain the spell was unbelievably arduous. Now acting like an insect himself, Simon walked towards the glimmer. It was so beautiful.

"Vel?" croaked Simon, reaching out. "Vel!"

Simon walked into a chamber. A ball of light, formless and mysterious, was emanating from the center. Simon was captivated. He dragged his feet and came closer. Squinting, Simon made out a thin cord with green leaves coiling around the light. Simon shielded his eyes when he was mere feet away. It was so warm, and so celestial.

"This . . ." Simon was inches from it. "This is . . ."

THWACK!

Simon felt ringing pain from the backside of his head. He fell, and then lights were out.

chapter twenty-four ~~~
Lamia

"Mommy, I got the food. I got —"

"Oh yes, good boy! Good, Grendel! Yes, mommy can make you perfect, now. Mommy can make you perfect."

"I'll be perfect, mommy?"

"Yes, my sweet thing. You will be."

Something sharp and uneven stroked his cheeks.

"Ah, yesssssss. This is the one. This is the blood of Elds!" It took a long, drafty sniff. "Oh, I can smell that accursed blood running through his veins."

Simon felt warm breath wash over him, and he opened his eyes. Repulsive yellow-green eyes leered upon him. There were only two gaping holes for nostrils. Pair of fangs on both top and bottom rows of teeth shined as the long, slimy tongue licked them. The grey, dirtied hair was wild and feral, obnoxiously matching the dark-green skin tone.

"My heart will be complete," said the gorgon, making an ugly smile.

Simon tried to move, but his hands and feet were tied. He was suspended six feet off the ground, and below him was the kite-patterned tail slithering restlessly.

"Feed him to the heart, mommy. Feed him, mommy."

Simon looked around. Where was that voice coming from? It almost sounded like it was moaning.

"Yes, Grendel, yes. Yes, my baby," said the gorgon. She tasted Simon with her long, unattractive tongue from chin to cheek. "But we must be patient. His blood is the key."

Grendel?

She moved away, and Simon finally saw Grendel for the first time in the flesh. He was huge, four feet just by being crouched, another four feet if he perhaps stood up. His skin looked they were burned a minute ago, and a few parts looked like they were ready to be peeled off like rotten barks. Its face was long, thin, and hairless. One eye was disfigured by a

huge wart sprouting from above. Its ears were large as Simon's head. Huge chains restrained him from approaching either Simon or the heart.

"Let mommy do her work. It needs to be perfect . . ."

The gorgon faced away, whispering and muttering over the radiant heart. Simon writhed to free himself, but instead he hit something on his left. He looked over, and then gasped. Vel was next to him, unconscious and rather limp. Simon said hastily, "Vel!"

"Quiet, Eld," said the gorgon dangerously. "Or I will kill you first."

Simon dropped his voice and whispered, "Vel! *Vel!*" She didn't respond. Simon rocked right and left. He hit her with his hip, but in vain. She was still as a plant, suspended in the same fashion as Simon.

"Vel?" Simon turned. Grendel was staring at them. "Is that called . . . Vel?" He crawled their direction, curiosity showing in his eye. Simon stared at Grendel. He knew it. He had seen him in his dreams. Vaguely, but definitely the same contour.

"Grendel," whispered Simon. "Grendel, it's me! It's Simon. Do you remember?"

Grendel eyes widened. He beamed, teeth showing (some were rotten, others not so rotten). "Simon?" he said aloud. Simon nodded viciously. Grendel said happily, "Simon!" The chains strained, holding him a few feet apart. "Simon, you're special! You're my friend!"

"No, Grendel-bell!" The gorgon lashed her tail, and Grendel retreated. "You mustn't play with that thing. What did mommy tell you? They will throw rocks at you. Tease you. No, they think you're ugly, bad, stupid. But once the heart is complete, you can throw rocks at them! You will be the one they look up to. So don't play with those disgusting little humans. They won't do you any good. They will be inferior."

Grendel looked from his mother to Simon "But Simon's special," he said innocently. "He said so. He's my friend. Right, Simon?"

Simon nodded, but the gorgon hissed, "Yes, Grendel, but he's not *as* special as you. He's weaker, lower, not worth looking. You will know. Just you wait. Wait patiently, my love. You know mommy loves you, don't you?"

"Yes, mommy," said Grendel, and he retreated back into the shadows, rubbing his arm.

"Grendel!" hissed Simon, wriggling. "Grendel, help me!"

But Grendel beamed again. "Mommy said you're not as special as me. We can't be friends, Simon."

It was no use. Grendel was totally brainwashed. Simon eyed the gorgon and asked, "Grendel, is that your mom?"

Grendel nodded. "Lamia. Mommy."

Simon averted his attention to Lamia the gorgon. He asked viciously, "He's your kid. Why do you have him in chains? If he's special, why do lock him up?"

Lamia hissed viciously. "Don't listen to him, child," she whispered. "Don't listen to him." She was again occupied with the Primal Heart. Simon looked about the chamber. The details he failed to grasp when he first stepped in were revolting. Bones and decaying carcasses littered the floor. The biggest pile was by Grendel. Simon spotted skulls of unknown animals, but also humans. There were even dirtied clothes that suggested there were wranglers or wardens that had been consumed in this chamber. Simon thought he was going to puke.

"How did you survive all this time?" Simon asked bravely. "How weren't you noticed?"

Lamia was facing the Primal Heart from the opposite side of the chamber. Her eyes darted up at Simon briefly before returning to the heart. "Food is plentiful at the belly of the beast. I simply stole, and often killed, to sooth my hunger." Lamia scooped a handful of blood from a fresh carcass of a raccoon and poured it into the glowing orb. The light turned orange for a moment, and then back to its ethereal glow of white and green. "It wasn't easy, staying hidden, avoiding notice, as those wretched Governors came and went!"

Simon watched the Primal Heart pulse blue when another scoop of blood was delivered. "How did you get the heart?"

Lamia hissed rather triumphantly as she prodded the light. "Through confusion. Primals were always frail beings. Hard to find, but each and every Primal Hollow took pleasure in using them to heal countless monsters. Two my sisters killed, but we didn't know until later their hearts were of priceless value to our curse. Blast them! They wanted it for themselves, said it was our fault we turned out cursed. But when the Runes were taken, oh the chaos gave brought forth a chance. I waited until the right moment. And then I snatched the heart from the dead Primal. Oh, no one noticed. Not even the Elds. I brought the heart down here, but the blasted heart was in dormancy."

"And that's why you needed the blood of an Eld," said Simon, picturing everything Lamia had spoken so far. "But why not Cybele and the other Governors? Why didn't you attack them?"

"Imbecile," seethed Lamia. "A Governor cannot be taken by normal force. You must chip away. Little by little. Make them weak. Until they do not have the strength to fight back."

Simon felt boiling rage rise from his stomach. "So that's how you took out the Governor," he yelled. "The one that you guys drank blood from and turned into — into *that!*"

"Yes, into this grotesque form!" screamed Lamia, and her tail hit the floor and left a dent. "You cannot fathom how many years I've brooded, waited for my chance to come. To rid of this unsightly body. To be reborn. To be perfect once more."

Lamia resumed her magical preparations, pouring different kinds of blood to stimulate various colors. Simon watched as the light was slowly getting brighter and more captivating. Was it near completion?

"You'll never be perfect," said Simon, twisting his wrist to see if there was any way he could undo the ropes. "You were never even close to perfect. The heart's just going to cure that curse. You'll go back to the same you before The Plight."

Lamia laughed merrily and crooned, "Silly boy, *beauty* is perfection. All of Hollow bowed to us when it came to artistry. We were the epitome. Our charms were deadly to those heinous creatures, for they would spend days and nights starving, just looking at us until their mind could bear no more. And then their blood became our baths, our fountain, and we would continue to be beautiful."

"But you were wrong!" Simon cut across. "You eventually grew old. I read about you guys. You would grow old, so you wanted eternal youth. That's why you killed a Governor."

Lamia stiffened for a second. "Yes," she said quietly. "Yes, we were nearly perfect. But we couldn't have *lasting* perfection. So cruel. Sooooo cruellllllll!" Lamia quivered in fury. "It always were the Elds that were better off. *Them!* Who had no beauty, no fairness. They had the secret to an immortal life!" Her shriek echoed. "Curse them. They knew the way. They wanted it all for themselves. And when we Gorgons wished the same, they damned us into hideous beasts, and let us linger. And my *babies!*" Lamia expelled another screech. "Oh, my babies were all doomed to filthy creatures, unintelligent, and unhelpful! Worthless form of life!" Lamia stroked the glamorous light. "But not anymore. *Not anymore!* I will be born anew, and my dear Grendel," she added, "you will be perfect. Mommy promises."

"Yes, mommy," said Grendel cheerfully. "And I can go out, then? I can play with the children? I can play with Simon?"

"Not Simon, my sweet one," said Lamia, swooping over Grendel. "He's our food, remember? Food to make you perfect, Grendel-bell. But the other . . . you'll get to throw them, chase them, laugh at them. You can do whatever you want, Grendel, because they won't be beautiful."

Grendel giggled, but it sounded more like hiccups than anything. "Yes, mommy! Yes, mommy!"

Simon writhed in desperation, but then stopped when he noticed a strange implication. Grendel was her baby, but she mentioned just a few seconds ago . . . *babies*. In plural form.

"Wait," he said, looking at Lamia. "Grendel . . . isn't your only kid?" Lamia slithered back to Simon. She cut the rope, and then wrapped Simon in her serpentine tail. "Hey, answer me!" Simon shouted. Lamia slowly crawled towards the heart, her eyes focused and immutable. "Grendel!" Simon turned his head, barely seeing Grendel's shackles. "What happened to the others? Where're your brothers and sisters?"

Grendel tapped his feet and replied happily, "Mommy said they went out to protect the tunnels. So that Grendel and mommy can become perfect."

Simon slowly turned back at Lamia. She was whispering into the heart, and her hands were ringing like she was having a fit. The images of the giant lizard and scorpion returned. And not just the lizard and scorpion; the countless bones that littered the tunnels, too. A dreadful answer came to Simon.

"You . . . *abandoned* them," he said quietly, insides squirming from disgust. "They weren't like Grendel, who could at least talk, who could at least think. So you sent them away, let them die, because they weren't *good enough*."

"Mommy said Grendel was special," said Grendel, peeking to see the beginning of the slaughter. "So they wanted to protect Grendel, and Grendel deserved it, because he will be perfect!"

"Yes, my sweet child, yes," said Lamia, turning her claws on Simon. "Yes, your brothers and sisters couldn't be perfect, so don't you worry about them. You will be something they could never be. No need for trifling matters. See?" She stared as she caressed Simon's collarbone. "It's ready, baby. Just a few seconds, and everything will be fixed. You and mommy together."

The claws descended, slowly edging towards Simon's chest. But Simon did not resist. He was engulfed in fury and repulsion. It came deep down from his stomach, like fire ready to be belched. As if feeling the heat coming from Simon's eyes, Lamia halted. Time froze just like that. All this time, Simon couldn't imagine anything more terrible than Lamia's appearances, but he had kidded himself big time. It was a fresh wave of nausea, hatred, bitterness, and animus . . . all sorts of ungrateful feelings.

"You're a *monster*," said Simon darkly. "You're no mother. You're a sick monster."

Lamia looked like she had been stabbed right through the heart. Her hand slowly closed over Simon's throat, and she seethed, "*What did you say?*"

"Whatever the books say about you," Simon continued, no longer concerned about the consequences, "you guys never deserved children in the first place. You never loved them, did you? The only thing you wanted was your children to be better than others. And now that you see no chance in that happening, you just discard them like they're trash, so that you can erase the fact you ever had kids like them."

The hand ceased tightening. The truthful shock was numbing Lamia body and soul.

"You never loved your children," Simon repeated. The memory of his mother resurfaced. "You're anything *but* a mother. Even if she hates herself, a mom always cares for and loves their kids for who they are, not their appearances or skills." *Eternally love, my dear Simon.* That was what she wrote in her death note. Eternally love. That was what a true mom would do. "You don't have any love," Simon whispered furiously. "You don't even love Grendel. You only keep him because you think you have a chance to — to *correct* him. No, to correct *your* mistake. The books had it all wrong. You're the most ugly, shameful thing I've ever seen." He added ominously, "You're the lowest."

Simon saw Lamia's stricken face, and then closed his eyes as hot pain sliced through his shoulder. The claws that slashed across flicked blood onto his face.

"YOU —! YOU —!" Lamia screamed furiously, but words did not connect properly. "YOU DARE INSULT *ME*!" She flipped Simon and let the blood run down his arm. "I — I WILL KILL YOU! I WILL RID OF YOU IN THE MOST PAINFUL WAY YOU CAN IMAGINE! I — I — I WILL EAT YOUR HEART OUT!"

"You can't drink blood of Elds, remember?" hissed Simon, smirking. "But go ahead. Maybe you'll turn into a *real* snake this time."

Lamia howled and gripped Simon's wound. Simon cried in pain.

"Give the blood," hissed Lamia, watching more drops trickling down Simon's arm. "I won't kill you yet, you stupid little boy. Once we are cured, I will hurt you, torture you, and curse you until you beg for death. And then my baby will play with you more, and when he gets bored of you I will hurt you again. You will wish you never had said that. You missed your chance for a swift death." The blood accumulated on Simon's index finger. "Now *drop!*" Lamia screamed, pressing her fingers even tighter. "*DROP!*"

A single drop of blood finally detached. Simon watched through watery eyes as it fell in slow motion, into the Primal Heart, dispersing. Flash!

Simon was blinded as the heart expelled its brightest radiance yet. It slowly began to pulse like a beating heart.

"Yessssssss!"

Simon was thrust aside, and he crashed landed on his back. He stared up at the illuminated ceiling. It was over. He could see the light shifting, meaning Lamia was lifting the heart for a remedial bite. She will be cured, and then she will do all sorts of caustic deeds. His doom was imminent. And he couldn't even save Vel. *Sorry, Vel* . . . thought Simon, turning at Vel. *I'm sorry* . . . ? She wasn't there. The ropes were pendulous without its subject.

"Mommy?"

Simon turned to Grendel. There was an odd, blank expression drawn upon his face. Lamia, who was about to consume the blinding light, looked about and said, "Yes, what is it, Grendel-bell? What is it?"

Grendel was stiff as a rock. He croaked, "You don't . . . you don't love me, mommy?"

Lamia seemed to receive a major shock from this query. She quickly recovered herself and said, "No, Grendel, that's not what mommy thinks." Grendel was staring at the heart, now. Sensing the doubt grow, Lamia hastened to her baby's side. "Here, my sweet child." Lamia undid the shackles with a prod and transferred the heart into Grendel's hands. "Take a bite. Eat. And you will be perfect."

But Grendel sat still, staring intensely at the heart. " . . . I will be perfect?"

"Yes, Grendel," said Lamia soothingly.

Grendel looked at Lamia. "And mommy will love me?"

"Yes," said Lamia, slowly losing her patience. "Eat it, my sweat Grendel. You will be perfect, and mommy will love you forever more."

Grendel stared down at the heart, and then back at Lamia.

" . . . But you won't love me . . . if I'm not perfect?"

There was a pause. Lamia's face started to show unease. "Baby, it's perfection. You always wanted that, didn't you, Grendel? Didn't we?"

Tears slowly filled as Grendel shook his head. "I . . . I want you to love me, mommy. I want mommy to love *Grendel*." Each second, Grendel contorted his face more and more. "But mommy will — will only I-love perfect Grendel! Didn't you s-say you will a-always love me, m-mommy?"

Grendel's hands were pressing against the Primal Heart, and Lamia eyed it before grasping his wrists. "Grendel, baby, you mustn't — mustn't listen to that stupid boy. Let go of the heart, my sweet. *Let go!*"

Lamia tried to pry the hands apart, but Grendel, who was quite physically able, constricted his arms and glared at his mother.

"Mommy lied to Grendel! MOMMY LIED TO ME!" Angry tears swarmed as Grendel abruptly pressed his palms together, as if to extinguish the light with force. "MOMMY IS A LIAR! MOMMY DOESN'T LOVE ME! MOMMY DOESN'T LOVE GRENDEL! GRENDEL WASN'T SPECIAL! I HATE YOU MOMMY!"

Lamia shrieked as she did everything she could to keep the hands from crushing the heart. Her tail coiled around Grendel's leg.

"Let go, Grendel! *Let go!*"

They thrashed, rolling around the floor as mother and son conflict reached physical violence. Lamia's tail untangled and cleaved the wall with bone-crushing force. Taking this chance, Simon ducked out of the giants' qualm. He just hoped that Grendel's feet wouldn't send him flying with broken bones. "*Vel!*" He shouted. "VEL!" Simon felt his lungs and throat burn from the effort. "VEL! WHERE ARE YOU?"

Lamia, who was now snarling viciously, slashed at her son. Grendel howled as blood splashed from his chest. "MOMMY HURT ME!" But his hands squeezed even tighter around the heart, resolute to crush the one and only thing that would revert the cruse. "I HATE YOU MOMMY! I HATE YOU!"

"*Give it here, you stupid child, give it here!*" yelled Lamia, and she slashed at Grendel's arm. Grendel roared in pain and dropped the heart. Lamia flashed her deranged eyes and lunged for the taking. But the heart skidded away while a flash of blinking metal cut through her hand. Lamia recoiled in agony as she spotted her unforeseen foe: Vel.

"VEL!" yelled Simon.

"You little rat!" screamed Lamia, trashing her tail.

Vel dodged with nimble legs as she brandished her knife. But behind her was Grendel, who was howling like a rabid bear. Vel wasn't going to escape in time. She was fatigued, Simon could see it in her eyes. With the only thing that came to mind, Simon sprinted right at Grendel, cupping his disgusting gash.

"Argh!"

Simon head-butted Grendel's ankle with all his weight, and Grendel's finger brushed Vel's temple as he fell to the ground. Simon scurried up his body and shouted, "Grendel!" Grendel looked up, and at that exact moment, Simon removed his blood-filled hand, tilted it, and dripped the rosy contents into Grendel's open wound. Grendel froze. He looked like he had been struck by lightning. Simon and Grendel shared gazes, knowing what was to come next.

"I'm sorry . . ." whispered Simon, dropping his hand. "You can't have her."

Grendel trembled, meaning the blood of Elds was beginning to take effect. The wound seemed to calcify as his skin gradually turned white and hard. Grendel touched his chest and felt the white crust rub against his skin.

"M-mommy?"

Lamia's scream tore through the air. Vel pulled Simon out of the way as Lamia leaped over Grendel and propped him up in her arms. "My baby!" she breathed lovingly, kissing Grendel's cheek. "Grendel-bell! Look at mommy! Oh, look at mommy, sweety!"

The calcification continued to spread, followed by ominous cracks. Grendel's breaths thickened as his torso turned to stone. "Mommy," he whispered, grabbing Lamia's arm. "Mommy."

"Yes, my sweet, mommy's here!"

His legs were no longer mobile. Grendel gasped as white death crept up to his shoulder. "M-mommy, do you love G-G-Grendel?"

"Of course, my sweet. Mommy loves you. Mommy will always love you."

"E-even w-when I'm not-t per-f-fect?"

"Mommy loves Grendel," said Lamia, dirty, thick tears cascading from her glens. "Always."

Grendel smiled. Simon couldn't bear to watch, and he turned away. Crumble. Lamia's scream couldn't sound any more woeful. When Simon finally had the nerve to look back, Lamia was sobbing over Grendel's dust, finer than sand, and lighter than air.

"NOOOOOOOOOOOOOOOOOOO!"

Lamia's eyes found Simon, and her rage expelled as her face convoluted into an ugly knot. Her fangs showed, and foreboding liquid dripped from her claws and singed the earth.

"I WILL TEAR YOU TO SHREDS!" cried Lamia, and her claws reached for Simon. "COME HERE, YOU VILE CREATION OF LIFE! NO MERCY! NO —"

Lamia screeched. Vel's wrangling knife was digging into Lamia's back. Lamia thrashed with all her might, but Vel was holding on. Simon bolted to her. Lamia's tail pummeled Vel at full force. Vel's strength started to wane as each strike made it harder on her body.

Simon immediately jumped onto Lamia's tail. He was noticed the moment he made contact, and Lamia reached for her backside. Her strike missed, went passed Simon's head, and struck Vel. Vel gasped and let go of the knife, falling onto the ground as she writhed in burning pain. The Primal Heart fell out of her arm and rolled out of the chamber.

"VEL!"

The experience of gorgon venom was fresh in Simon's memory, and in a few minutes Vel was to be split from life. Simon jumped onto Lamia's back, clutching the knife that made her scream again. He roared and pulled the blade out with tremendous force. "Eat this!" he yelled, and he smeared his blood against the gash.

Lamia gasped in horror and stopped moving. Her body trembled, just like Grendel's before his death, but ten times worse. Simon skidded off and landed on his back. He watched Lamia twitch, gasp another time, and then start to shrink. Her arms gradually squirmed into her shoulders, her face cricked and cracked as it became smaller and pointed, the torso began to grow scales and meld with the tail. She became smaller, smaller, and tinier, tinier. . .

When the transformation stopped, Simon saw a serpent, barely two feet long, thin as his thumb, and a shade of copper. The blood of Eld had cursed her even further, into a pitiful, unintelligent, ugly snake, just like Simon had wished her to become.

"You deserved it," said Simon, his vision blurring. "You had it coming."

The degenerated, transformed Lamia hissed and oscillated, seething. Simon chucked the knife at her, grunting, "Go on, get out." Lamia skated away.

Vel was quaking. Simon grunted and crawled next to her. "Vel," he said, propping her up, "hang in there . . ." He pulled her onto his back and walked towards the exit of the chamber. He stumbled. Dizziness was filling the gaps as blood continued to leak from his wound. "I'll fix you . . ." mumbled Simon. He dropped. Simon squeezed Vel's hand. "You'll be alright . . . I'll fix this . . ."

The only thing that denied darkness was the Primal Heart, radiating like a beacon of life. It was his only chance. He had to get it to Vel.

"I'll . . . make . . . you feel . . . better . . ." groaned Simon, edging closer to the heart. Vel's hand was getting colder. Or was it him? He couldn't tell anymore. "It's going . . . to be . . . alright . . ."

Inches from the heart, Simon's arm failed. His chin hit the soil. The darkness was getting to him first. "No . . ." he croaked. "No . . ." He faded, but not before he saw a brighter light. A silhouette of a small child and lucent hair.

chapter twenty-five ~~~~
The Primal Heart

The light was warm, but it wasn't the heart. Why was it so bright? Where was he? Was he still in the cave? Or was he in heaven?

Simon blinked. He was within a bed of feelers, and they were carefully prodding him. Simon got up. The brilliantly sparkling gems, the flowers that were bigger than his head, the bed of water that partially submerged the room; he was in the chamber of Primals.

"Siiiiiiiiiiiiimmmmmmmmmmmmmmmoooooooooooonnnnnnnnnnnnn."

Ventus was on top of him. Simon gasped, "Ventus! Quick, Vel! She's about to —!"

"He's awake!" cried Ventus, topping Simon's voice easily. "He's awake! He's awake! He's awake!"

"Yes, thank you, Ventus."

Cybele was sitting next to him. Ignis was curled by her side, sleeping. Terram and Aqua were surfing just like they did the last time Simon saw them. Upon Ventus's call, they veered course and neared Simon. Everybody was here.

"So the boy finally wakes," said Ignis, opening his eyes. "Good."

Simon was confused. "What happened?" he said as he pushed himself up.

"Careful," said Cybele calmly. "You lost a lot of blood. We're mending you."

"But Vel!" yelled Simon. "Where's Vel? Is she alright?"

"Never listens," growled Ignis, getting on all fours. "Very well. You will be pleased to hear Velox Windly is out of immediate danger. We are still monitoring her condition, but for now her vitals look promising. She is in the remedial department, and we presume she will make a full recover within the week.

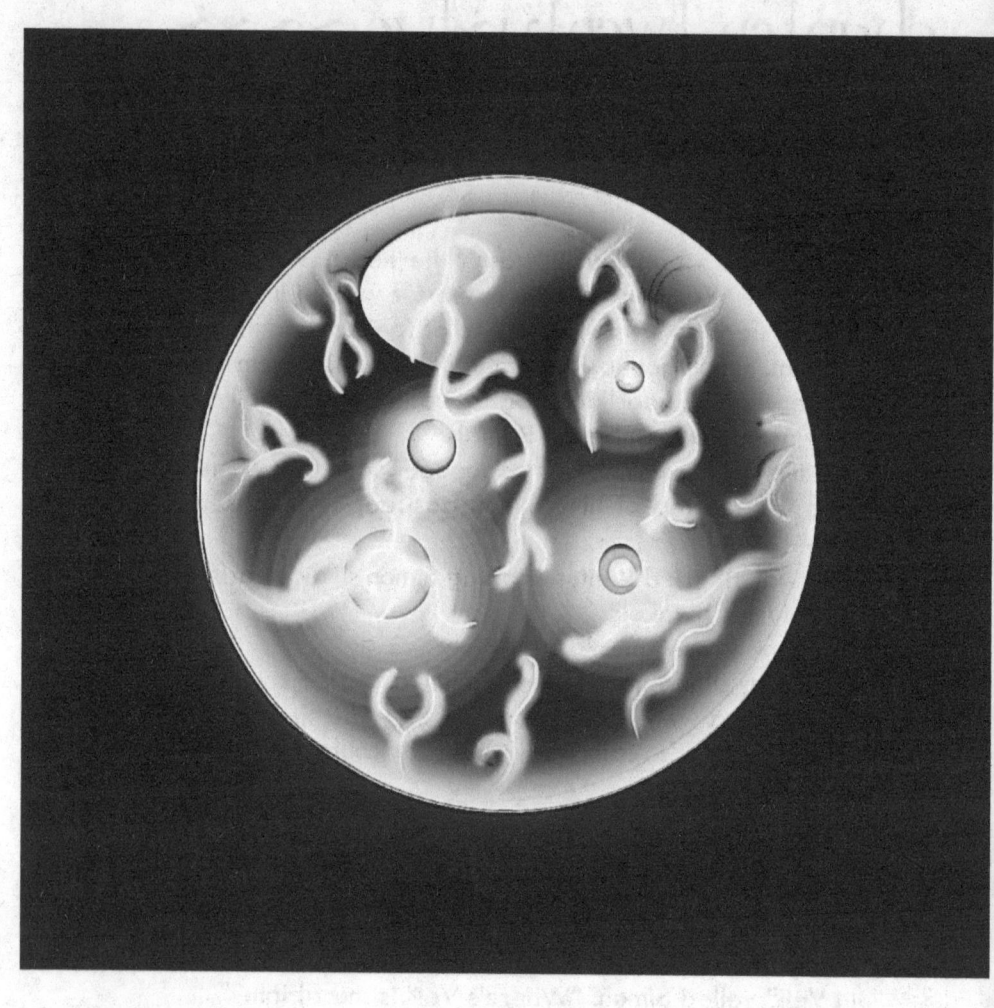

"And to answer other matters," Ignis continued as Simon opened his mouth. "Rachel Fairburn and Fortis Goldstone returned safely and did their utmost best to inform us. The wardens, who took no action before our arrival, were harshly dealt with, and Lady Cybele and us Governors managed to get to you in time before things were too late."

"Your sentry, Agilis . . . was unquestioned of any actions that contradicted his oath as a sentry. The circumstances were, by all means, rather unconventional to pass on discrimination, thus it only seemed wrong to pass judgment on actions that occurred in those periods.

"And that falls for *you* as well. You risked great danger to two other pupils, but since their voluntary efforts and act of valor were theirs by choice, there won't be any faults addressed.

"Conclusively, because of your and your companions' selfless acts, Eldwoods was able to prevent casualties." Ignis added dryly, "That is what has been publicly announced, but as for my *personal* opinion, you were treading dangerous territory, both politically and morally." Ignis showed his fangs. "You were an *idiot*, you hear?"

That was a lot to take in. Simon processed the account one by one. "So . . . " he said slowly, "everybody's fine, right?"

Cybele smiled, admiring the fact that Simon had no concerns of the political aspects whatsoever. "Yes. Your friends are in good health." She folded hands politely before her lap. "The Luminaries took some convincing, but the Head Scholars, especially Hildegard White and Frao, were very devoted in defending you. They even went far as to discriminate the Head Warden."

"At which they deserved," said Terram quietly, bristling. "They should've done better."

Cybele caressed Terram to peace. She then reverted her attention back to Simon. "That is the current state of events. Are you satisfied?"

Satisfied? Not really. Simon wasn't sure what he was feeling right now. Relief? Yeah, for the most part. But there was more he needed asking. "Uh," he began, finally coming across things that needed answering. "Where's the Primal Heart? Do you have it?"

Cybele nodded. "Yes, it is safe with us."

Simon remembered the details of how Lamia acquired it, and he asked cautiously, "Was it your parent's?"

Cybele inclined her head the second time. "Yes," she said, and she stroked her fingers. "My father's." She finished shortly.

Simon said quickly, "Sorry."

"Hardly a matter to apologize. Quite the contrary," said Cybele. "You risked your life to retrieve it, knowing you would be facing mortal peril. And above that, the gorgon was defeated, the heart was safe, and Velox Windly was spared of a cruel death. Answering your questions is the least I can do to express my gratitude."

"You got to me just in time," said Simon, shaking his head. "I didn't save Vel. You did."

"Modesties can be spared. If not for your friends, I would never have known where the chamber was." She closed her eyes. "I've never felt my heart stressed so much when I heard their confession. All I hoped was for your survival. Thank you for lasting as long as you did."

A pause.

"Anything else?"

"Yeah," said Simon. "How come nobody knew about that underground tunnel? This is your home, right?"

"Yes, it is our home. But mind you, the only ones that live to tell the tale of the old days are the Governors, Head Warden, Head Scholar Altum, and Head Scholar Venator. If they do not know, then it's only natural what we must do is speculate.

"Upon the creation of Elder Tree, there were no records of secret passages and chambers. *But*," she added, "we — as in everybody — know this place was mostly occupied by the Philosophers. It may be possible it was *they* who created the underground tunnels."

"For what?"

"For refuge, research, I can't tell. Head Scholar Frao's postulation, after careful examination, was that the chamber may have been used when creating the Rune of Belief."

"The Rune?"

"Yes. Eldwoods was built for the sake of the Philosophers' researches. It comes to no surprise."

Simon nodded. He moved on.

"Sometimes, in my sleep, I saw Lamia. And Grendel."

Cybele, in this particular subject, looked uncertain. "I heard the descriptions from Rachel Fairburn and Fortis Goldstone. Right now, we aren't certain what kind of magic you were performing. Clairvoyance have been practiced on occasion, but it never truly showed any potential. I'm sorry," said Cybele inclining her head, "I'm afraid you will have to wait for that answer."

"Right," said Simon. He had other questions, anyways. "Then what happened to the other gorgon? With Medusa?"

"She did not comply. Her interest was at peak, but in the end she felt no need to give her services to us. Our proposition to find a cure for her seemed to give little impression."

That was odd. Lamia was so eager to be cured. And yet, the other gorgon refused? "Why?" asked Simon. "Don't gorgons want to return back to their original form?"

"I can't be certain, but even if she did accept, she already knew the procedure would be a long, unpredictable one. Or," Cybele added thoughtfully, "she no longer sees the reason to go back. She seemed rather fond of her . . . *hair* when we departed."

Simon didn't quite get what she meant, but he took no mind of it.

"Lamia said that . . . Elds would live forever." Simon looked at his hands. He kind of feared what the answer to his next question would be "Does that mean that I'll, too?"

Cybele shook her head. "Elds have . . . a remarkable lifespan, and in most rare cases, there were even some who seemed to defy age. The ones that you see before you," Cybele indicated Ignis, Aqua, Ventus, and Terram, "are perfect examples, and I, too, have not felt age take its place for a long time. But the problem with the belief of eternal youth, Simon, is not from spells or rituals that must be repetitively done. It is *insight* that gives time. Some may refer to it as power, others may call it knowledge. As you would well know, Head Scholar Altum and Venator are not Elds, and yet they have lived millenniums, longer than I, in good health. It may not be *eternal youth*, but they are quite the example.

"That said, the gorgon, Lamia, has also demonstrated her strength. She may not have exercised her power for good purposes, but her knowledge and power prolonged her life. She did not notice that all these long years she *had* acquired what she dreamt of before."

"But, that doesn't mean I will, right?" said Simon.

"No," said Cybele gently. "This great trophy of timeless life that you can acquire comes with *choosing*. There were countless more who took no pleasure in prolonged life. The most notable wranglers that rejected this gift in these past years were the ones of Passion. They are strongly convinced that all fire must extinguish in the end, so that new life could sprout."

Simon sighed in relief. "Good," he muttered. "Good . . ."

Cybele looked astounded. "You feared immortality?"

"Well," said Simon slowly. "I mean, it would be great. But I . . . kind of want to grow old. With Rachel and Fortis, you know. I think it would be kind of sad to live really long . . . "

Cybele smiled warmly and nodded. "Such wisdom from a young age. You surprise me too often, Simon." She asked, "Anything else?"

There was one more he wished to know.

" . . . Was Grendel loved?" asked Simon quietly. "Or . . . did gorgons have any love?"

Cybele looked at Simon very deeply. "You ask a question I cannot answer." She turned to Terram. "Perhaps another may, though."

Terram crawled into Simon's lap.

"Your affection for the poor child is a charitable trait." Terram looked up at Simon. "The gorgons were once very beautiful, as you would already know. It was true that the gorgons loved. They loved dearly. Perhaps obsessively and violently, but still loved. The curse which they brought upon themselves must have left an irreversible fissure." Terram shook her head rather sadly. "I don't believe Grendel received the rightful love he deserved. Perhaps during those last moments, Lamia realized her fault." She smiled with great effort. "But, you put him to ease. It was mercy what you gave him."

Simon wished to believe that.

"Does . . . it . . . bring back . . . memories . . . young one . . . ?" asked Aqua.

Simon didn't say. He would rather not talk about it.

"Well," said Cybele, getting to her feet. "You will be happy to return to your unit. Oh, and," Cybele added with a warm smile, "might I add the pupils are quite thrilled to hear your endeavor, but promise me you won't become . . . pompous."

Pompous? Why would he feel pompous? He just almost killed himself. "Why?"

Ignis purred in disbelief. "You have *wrangled* a gorgon. It may not be the most conventional way, but that is how it is portrayed, now."

" . . . So?" asked Simon, not getting the full picture.

"*You defeated a gorgon*," repeated Ignis bluntly. "Whatever you may say, it does not change the fact that you succeeded in a mission no wrangler could possibly do alone. You have become a new champion of Eldwoods. Admirers will emerge."

Ignis was indisputably right about him emerging as a champion. The remaining days in Eldwoods were twittering, loud, and celebratory. Simon was visited by wranglers and pupils alike, wishing him the best and praising his bravery. Uro and Aro were absolutely going nuts. Uro was so desperate to present the head of Lamia, but since barbarism was out of the question in Eldwoods, he instead made a horrid, fake head made of paper, paint, and glue, and he stuck it on a stick and left in in front of Simon's door (Simon was quick to bring it inside and hide it under his bed). Aro, who showed similar taste with different tools, showed a clumsy painting of Simon riding a gorgon, a blade in one hand (Simon hid the painting, too). Jamey and Brendon came by with board games and cards, spending almost an entire week in his unit to listen to Simon's adventures. Of course, Simon tried not to elaborate.

Mary, who came with tears of joy and fear, dropped to her bottom at the sight of Simon and cried for several minutes.

"Mary, I'm fine," said Simon, picking her up.

"You s-saved Vel!" she wailed as she soaked Simon's cloak. "I-I was so — so worried that y-you die! A-and Vel t-t-toooooo!"

Simon comforted her for another half an hour.

Seeing Rachel and Forits was his most relieving moments. Fortis was walking straight. Rachel still had her arm wrapped in bandages, but it was no longer suspended in slings.

"I got back alright," said Fortis when Simon asked. "Agilis dropped me off at the remedial department. I told the wardens, but when Agilis came back with Rachel they chained him, and they tried to lock us away in our own remedial wards, but that's when Lady Cybele came."

"Mrs. White was furious," said Rachel, shuddering. "I never saw her scream like that. She really started *fighting* the wardens."

"*Mrs. White did?*" Simon spluttered. Of all the people, Mrs. White was not someone he expected to flip. "Yikes . . ."

But in truth, Simon was rather gleeful Mrs. White did what she did, because wardens were constantly knocking on his unit door. Their business was simple: *briefing.* Simon couldn't stand it. Especially when Head Warden stood looking daggers at him, Simon faked dizziness and exhaustion and told a very short version of his adventure.

On the following week, Vel returned on wrangling session. Simon was in the middle of doing some ridiculous maneuvers that Captain Shark was demonstrating before the seedlings. The tale of Simon wrangling a gorgon had elevated his interest to a new level.

"That's how you do it, lads," said the captain as Simon did an embarrassing evasive roll. "You have to wait to the last second, you hear me? Lad here got some impressive reflex to able to do it. A gorgon's mighty fast, I tell you. You need to — come here, Simon. Bend your knees, yes, be on your toes — and when I strike — yes, that's it, lad! Got to be nimble as a cat, lightning reflexes and — oh, hello, missy!" Captain Shark waved as Simon dodged another sweep, hating that he was doing this in front of everybody he knew in Eldwoods. "Vel here's equally praise worthy, you hear, lads? Nicked a Primal Heart out of a gorgon's hands — now that's some elite trick!"

Vel looked uneasy as the attention shifted towards her. Simon feared she might suffer the same fate as him.

"Come, missy! Let's see how fast you —"

"Captain Shark!" yelled Rachel. "Weren't we supposed to review how to spot kobaloi nests?"

"What?" said the captain. "Ah, yeah, you're right, Rachel! Right, moving on —"

Simon sat down between Rachel and Vel, brushing the grass off of his hair and shoulders. "Thanks," he muttered. "I really didn't want to continue."

"Oh, I was more concerned about Vel than you," said Rachel mildly, and she pushed Simon out of the way and swapped spots. "How are you, Vel?" she said kindly as she held Vel's hand.

Vel nodded. "Fine."

Simon shook his head as he settled next to Fortis. "*Girls.*" Vel looked over at Simon. Simon quickly said, "I meant — girls are so understanding, you know? You two just — just sticking together and hugging it out."

"Oh, Simon," grumbled Rachel, shaking her head.

Vel, on the other hand, made the tiniest smile.

It was their last day in Eldwoods. Summer wrangling season was upon them. As a group, Simon enjoyed spending time outdoors. It was a good way to forget about the dark, clammy, horrific tunnels. Uro and Aro were playing gorgon as Jamey and Brendon played Simon and Vel, doing those awkward and jocular moves Captain Shark taught them.

But not everyone was so happy.

Excusing themselves for a moment, Simon, Rachel, Fortis, Vel, and Mary went closer to the woods where the forest was more compact. Mary, who was sobbing again, held Chipper dearly.

"You have to take care of yourself, Chipper!" she squeaked, ignoring Chipper's annoyed kicks. "You have to live with your friends now, so be kind to them, okay?"

Simon had to admire the thinner profile. Chipper was now able to *run*. Run! That was just amazing. It was all thanks to Vel's final coaching. Chipper was really looking more like a wolpertinger, now.

"He'll be alright," said Fortis, kindly. "He's going where he's supposed to be."

Mary nodded, but tears continued to soak Chipper's coat. Simon helped the releasing process by tugging Chipper out of the death lock. When he let Chipper down, Chipper sniffed and stood on his hind legs. Just ten yards away, another wolpertinger was bounding, quite determined to keep airborne as long as possible. Chipper flicked his tail, and then went after it.

"Good bye, Chipper! Oh, good bye!" Mary called out as she dried her eyes.

"It's okay, Mary," said Vel dully. "He'll learn."

"Yes, Mary," said Rachel, stroking Mary's hair. "He's back home. He'll learn how to make a home, make friends, and even glide! He'll be alright."

Mary nodded, and the five of them headed back and sat on the grass. Uro was now attacking Aro, and the whole storyline was no longer making much sense.

"So," said Simon. "What're your plans for the summer?"

"I'm visiting my uncle in California," said Rachel excitedly. "He's a veterinarian, so I'll be working at the animal clinic."

"Might come up later August," said Fortis. "To Nocville. Asked if I can hang out with you."

"Do it," said Simon, feeling great that he could spend part of his dull summer vacation with Fortis. "Please, do it."

"And what about you, Vel?" asked Rachel. "Do you have any plans?"

Vel nodded. "Canada. Tes wants me to come over."

"Your brother?" asked Simon.

"I didn't know you had a brother," said Rachel, astonished.

"He's a rover," said Vel. "He's not around."

"Hey, look."

Out in the distance, Simon saw the great Explorer swim towards them. The ship was being prepared at the west side of the Elder Tree. Soon, the ship would be tied to the Explorer, and off they would be, back home . . .

"You know, after all that we went through, I might miss this place," said Simon.

"Then you're mental," said Fortis. "But so am I."

"We'll be back," said Rachel. "Summer goes fast, anyways."

"Yeah," said Simon getting up. "Yeah, it does."

chapter twenty-six ~~~~
The Rune Snatcher

The copper snake hissed as the children's presence moved away. It skidded to the deeper parts of the forest, hunting for any pray. But then it stalled. A stalky presence stood in its path. It lifted its body, preparing to strike. But a hand tightened around its throat, and the snake writhed. The snake knew it was no kid. It was much more intimidating. Much more mysterious.

"Snatching, snatching, little snake."

Lamia the snake spitted as it squirmed for freedom. Its head vanished behind jagged teeth.

"You don't know what came to wake."

The playful voice cackled as it tossed the remainder of Lamia into its mouth and munched. Swallowing, the creature peered at Simon from the brambles.

"Let's all light a birthday cake, cause Jack Snatcher came back to play!"

about the author ~~~~~~
Jeramiah Think

A mystery.

visit the author ~~~~~~~
Social & Other Media

Publisher:

www.donnaink.com

Social Media:

Facebook
http://www.facebook.com/authorjeramiahthink

LinkedIn
http://www.linkedin.com/in/donnaink

Twitter
http://www.twitter.com/authorjeramiahthink

WordPress:

http://www.wordpress.com/authorjeramiahthink

special offers

If you would like to get on Jeramiah Think's mailing list for future T-Shirt, poster, mugs and "other" merchandise offers write to: jeramiah.think@donnaink.com.

In 2015 – 2016, Jeremiah is featuring a suite of merchandise and perhaps a newsletter regarding fantasy fiction – you can visit his WordPress blog and join the followers he has there as well.

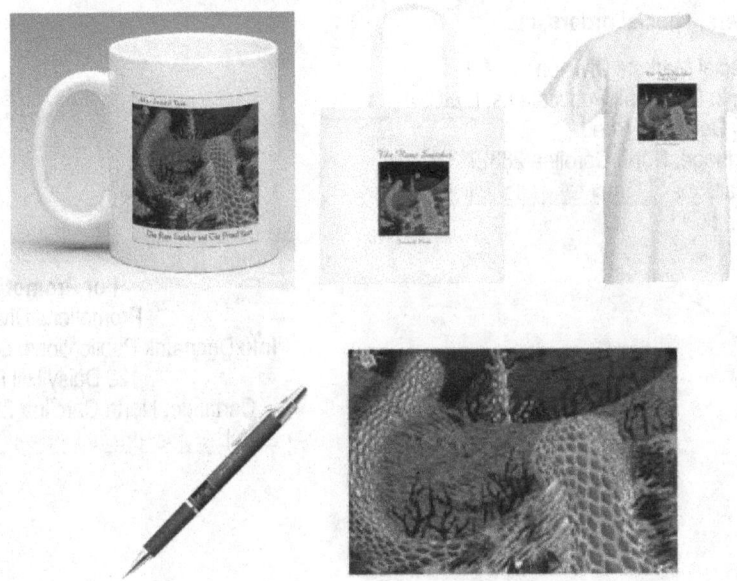

Publisher
www.donnaink.com

For bulk orders, special orders, etc.

Special Markets Division
dpInk: Donnalnk Publications, L.L.C.
129 Daisy Hill Road
Carthage, North Carolina 28327
Email: special_markets@donnaink.com

For Promotions:
Promotions Division
dpInk: Donnalnk Publications, L.L.C.
129 Daisy Hill Road
Carthage, North Carolina 28327
Email: promotions@donnaink.com

ZENCON ART OF
ZEN CONSULTANCY
PR & Marketing

www.ingramcontent.com/pod-product-compliance
Lightning Source LLC
Chambersburg PA
CBHW011352010726
47494CB00008B/2273